P9-DDJ-585

Erotic fantasies of him inundated her....

Electricity shot through Amanda: a bolt of lightning that jolted every nerve ending in her body.

In the half second she had to anticipate Michael's kiss, she expected harshness, an aggressive demand. Instead, a soft, subtle persuasion parted her lips and then made her tongue curve sensuously around his.

He held her now carefully, almost uncertainly. For a moment she stood there, arms down at her sides, reveling in a helplessness that wasn't really her, but belonged instead to the schoolgirl she had been.

"I want you," he rasped against the throat she had bared to him.

Years ago the young girl had daydreamed about Michael Quinn, not really knowing what she wanted. But now the woman knew.

ABOUT THE AUTHOR

Saranne Dawson is a human services administrator who lives deep in the woods of central Pennsylvania. Her hobbies include walking, sewing, gardening, reading mysteries—and spending time with her grandson, Zachary.

Books by Saranne Dawson

HARLEQUIN INTRIGUE

Don't miss any of our special offers. Write to us at the following address for information on our newest releases.

Harlequin Reader Service
U.S.: 3010 Walden Ave., P.O. Box 1325, Buffalo, NY 14269
Canadian: P.O. Box 609, Fort Erie, Ont. L2A 5X3

Lawman Lover
Saranne Dawson

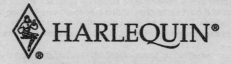

HARLEQUIN®

TORONTO • NEW YORK • LONDON
AMSTERDAM • PARIS • SYDNEY • HAMBURG
STOCKHOLM • ATHENS • TOKYO • MILAN • MADRID
PRAGUE • WARSAW • BUDAPEST • AUCKLAND

If you purchased this book without a cover you should be aware that this book is stolen property. It was reported as "unsold and destroyed" to the publisher, and neither the author nor the publisher has received any payment for this "stripped book."

ISBN 0-373-22503-2

LAWMAN LOVER

Copyright © 1999 by Saranne Hoover

All rights reserved. Except for use in any review, the reproduction or utilization of this work in whole or in part in any form by any electronic, mechanical or other means, now known or hereafter invented, including xerography, photocopying and recording, or in any information storage or retrieval system, is forbidden without the written permission of the publisher, Harlequin Enterprises Limited, 225 Duncan Mill Road, Don Mills, Ontario, Canada M3B 3K9.

All characters in this book have no existence outside the imagination of the author and have no relation whatsoever to anyone bearing the same name or names. They are not even distantly inspired by any individual known or unknown to the author, and all incidents are pure invention.

This edition published by arrangement with Harlequin Books S.A.

® and TM are trademarks of the publisher. Trademarks indicated with ® are registered in the United States Patent and Trademark Office, the Canadian Trade Marks Office and in other countries.

Printed in U.S.A.

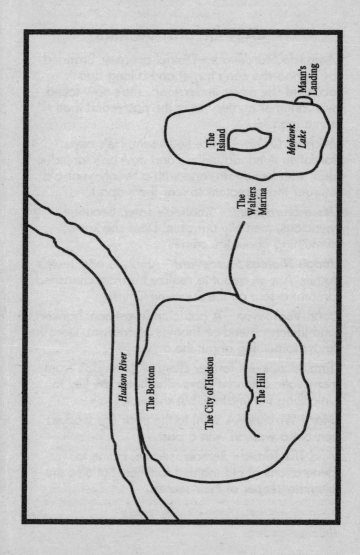

CAST OF CHARACTERS

Amanda Sturdevant—District attorney. Branded by a man she can't forget and a long-ago accident she never understood, she's now faced with another mystery from the past—and that same man.

Michael Quinn—Police lieutenant. He's never forgotten Amanda, either, and now he's forced to deal with her again, and with a twenty-year-old murder that threatens to tear them apart.

Jesse Sturdevant—Amanda's sister. Beautiful, vivacious, mentally unstable. Does she know something about the crime?

Judge Thomas Sturdevant—Amanda and Jesse's father. A man about to realize his most cherished dream: a seat on the Supreme Court.

John Verhoeven—A patrician investment banker and lifelong friend of Thomas Sturdevant. Does *he* know something about the mystery?

Tina Jacobs—A former client of Amanda's from her public defender days. She holds the key to unlocking the mystery, but she won't talk.

Mary Walters—A saint to the poor she worked for, but a woman with a past.

And *The Island*—Remote, serene. Home to generations of old-monied families. But also the ultimate keeper of their secrets.

Prologue

The expensive champagne turned to vinegar in Amanda's mouth. One minute, she was chatting with the mayor's wife, quietly savoring her own victory in the midst of the mayor's birthday celebration—and the next minute, the victory became hollow.

What was *he* doing here?

Politics, she told herself, answering her own question. Mayor Teddy was big on supporting the police, and Michael Quinn had received a lot of publicity recently when he broke up a major drug ring.

She watched Michael move easily through the crowd, grateful that at least he hadn't seen her yet. By all rights, *he* shouldn't want to see *her*, instead of the other way around.

Was there a Michael Quinn in every woman's girlhood? she wondered, suspecting that to be the case. Somewhere during that time when sexuality first surfaced with all its attendant blushes and giggles and daydreams made vague by inexperience, every girl surely developed a crush on the wrong boy. She knew she should count herself among the lucky ones whose longings had gone unfulfilled—but the memory lingered.

He seemed perfectly at ease, even in this high-powered crowd, flashing the smile that was all the more devastating for being so rare. He'd always been comfortable with himself. She was startled to realize suddenly that perhaps that had been part of her attraction to him then: that supreme self-confidence, even though his father had been serving a long sentence in Attica and his mother was rumored to be a prostitute and an alcoholic.

Amanda resolutely turned her back on Michael and resumed her conversation with the mayor's wife. With luck, he wouldn't even notice her among the noisy crowd of birthday celebrants.

IT WAS THAT SWINGING MANE of champagne gold hair that alerted Michael to her presence as she turned to the mayor's wife. He wasn't surprised to see Amanda here, of course; she'd grown up next door. Michael smiled as he lifted the glass of champagne to his lips.

Amanda Sturdevant had laid him out before God and the judge and twelve jurors—strung him up to dry—but still he smiled. She was perfect in court: cool, but not cold enough to turn off the jury; very competent, but not arrogant; finely balanced between femininity and too-cute-to-be-taken-seriously. She'd go far, he thought, though she'd have done that anyway, simply by virtue of being a Sturdevant. No doubt she planned to follow in her distinguished daddy's footsteps.

Michael could afford to smile at her victory. His own reputation was intact. Everyone on the squad knew that Wilson scumbag was guilty, and they would get him sooner or later. Michael had just tried to make it sooner—and Amanda Sturdevant had caught him at it.

He knew that she'd had a crush on him in high school, though he'd never done anything about it. First of all, she was three years younger than him—a big difference at that age—and second, she'd given no hint then of the beauty she would become. Between the braces and the glasses and the tall, skinny awkwardness, she'd had nothing to offer him then—except for the satisfaction that he could appeal even to a girl from the Hill.

But that was ten years ago, and somewhere in there, the

ugly duckling had been transformed into an elegant and beautiful swan. The braces had done their job, leaving her with a smile that had damn near melted his holster and the 9 mm automatic in it. And the glasses had vanished, as well, baring thick-lashed, green-flecked eyes that had thrown sparks of challenge at him.

And the body. Michael snagged a second glass of champagne as he peered through the crowd at a pair of long, slender legs exposed all the way to midthigh now—legs he'd only imagined while she was stringing him up in court. The crowd shifted a bit, and he stared appreciatively at the curves displayed to their best advantage in pale green silk.

Ten years ago, she could have been his. He wondered what time had done to his prospects.

"GOOD EVENING, COUNSELOR."

Amanda turned slowly—deliberately slowly—so that she could affix a polite smile to her face first. She knew that deep, slightly husky voice well. She heard it every time she relived her triumph in court.

"Good evening, Detective." Then, because she'd had two glasses of champagne and because she resented the little curls of heat that were spiraling through her, she added, "Or aren't you a detective any longer?"

He chuckled, a low sound that vibrated through her and made her even angrier. "Yes, I'm still a detective. We see things differently on the other side of the plaza."

He was referring to the fact that the county court building that housed the public defender's office stood opposite the police headquarters on the new plaza downtown that was the most visible sign of Port Henry's rebirth.

"I see," she said, returning his steady gaze measure for measure, though not without some difficulty. "Then I suppose I can look forward to many more victories."

"If that's what you want to call it," he said, shrugging his wide shoulders. His tan raw silk jacket was quite handsome and looked expensive. She'd heard somewhere that he moonlighted, something to do with computers.

"And what would *you* call it, Michael?" she challenged.

His deep-set Celtic eyes glittered with black fire. "What I *wouldn't* call it is justice. I'll be sure to let you know the next time the defendant beats up some poor old lady for her Social Security money."

She flushed and hated herself for it. "When that happens— *if* it happens—I'd suggest that you catch him fair and square, instead of talking the victim into remembering a face she never saw clearly."

He leaned closer to her, and she caught a whiff of some woodsy cologne she liked. "'Fair and square' isn't exactly the way of things down in the Bottom. But I wouldn't expect you to understand that."

"Justice is justice, Michael—no matter where you live." She refused to give him the satisfaction of drawing back, even though her legs were actually trembling a bit. His impact on her at close quarters was even greater than she'd feared.

He moved back a few steps and chuckled again. "You don't have a clue, do you? I thought your job would have opened your eyes a bit by now. What's it called, Amanda— noblesse oblige? Is that why you're dedicating yourself to the defense of scumbags?"

She wanted to smash her champagne glass into his handsome face and add a few more scars to the tiny one on his cheek. Instead, she merely smiled. "Is this your way of reasserting yourself, Michael—I beat you in court, so you feel the need to denigrate me?"

"'Denigrate.' I like that word. I guess it pays to hang around Yale graduates. Sort of a self-improvement vocabulary course."

She knew she should just walk away. But she didn't do it. Instead, she gave him a saccharine smile. "No doubt it's an improvement over the Marine Corps."

She saw the surprised look on his face and knew immediately that she'd committed a major error: the mistake of letting him know that she knew anything about him. He'd mentioned Yale, so she'd brought up the Marine Corps. A dangerous game of one-upmanship. Two people admitting that they hadn't completely ignored each other for ten years.

"As a matter of fact, it is. It's an improvement over the language at the station house, too." He tilted his dark head, studying her through those bedroom-at-midnight eyes. "When are you going to get tired of defending scum like Wilson and move on?"

"They deserve a competent defense," she replied, parroting the words spoken regularly by all public defenders.

He leaned toward her again. "What they deserve is to be tossed into the river wearing cement boots. It would cost a lot less, too."

"Does that include *you,* Michael? As I recall, you had a few run-ins with the law yourself."

This time, his chuckle turned into outright laughter. He was still too close to her, and she was mesmerized by the gleam in his eyes.

"You're right. Score one for you, Counselor. But I was just a kid, and I didn't break into the apartments of old ladies to steal money for drugs. All I did was take a few things from some stores."

"If Joseph Wilson is guilty, *you're* more to blame than *I* am for his getting away with it."

"Maybe so, but I'm still going to show up on your doorstep with photos the next time he beats up an eighty-year-old woman—just to share the blame a bit."

Amanda wondered if he meant it. The thought of having Michael show up on her doorstep didn't have quite the effect she assumed he'd intended. Or maybe it did. There were two conversations going on here.

Then suddenly, they seemed to have run out of talk, leaving far too much space for the other, subliminal conversation: raw, primitive, charged with a dark and dangerous heat.

She glanced over his shoulder; the crowd was thick and

noisy. It was time to go, time to back off from this flirtation with disaster. She thought about pushing her way through the throng to say good-night to her host and hostess, then decided they'd forgive her if she just slipped away.

"Is your coach about to turn into a pumpkin?" he asked dryly.

She smiled and nodded, then put out her hand. "Thank you for a pleasant evening, Detective," she said, mimicking his tone.

He held it just a shade too long. "Is your car next door? I didn't see it out front."

She nodded, trying not to feel the satisfaction of knowing that he must have been looking for her.

"I'll walk you over to it. You never know when Joey or one of his buddies might decide to come up here where the *real* money is."

Later, she would think about this moment and how she should have refused his offer. But she didn't. Instead, they walked across the stretch of lawn and trees that separated the mayor's home from her family home, the sounds of the party gradually fading away behind them. And in the silence, the imagined conversation grew ever louder, inundating her with fantasies far more erotic than those of the teenager she'd been remembering.

When they reached her car, which was parked in the circular driveway in front of the house, he asked her to drop him off at his car, saying that he'd been forced to park several blocks away because he'd arrived late. She couldn't refuse, of course. To do so would be a tacit admission that she was afraid to be alone with him.

"On the right, down there—the dark blue Cherokee," he said a few minutes later as she drove slowly along the dark street.

She stopped in the middle of the deserted street, and he reached for the door handle. It clicked open, and then he stopped and turned to her. He seemed to be about to say something, but before any words came out he was instead leaning across the seat and his mouth was on hers.

Electricity shot through her: a bolt of lightning that jolted every nerve ending in her body. In the half second she had to anticipate his kiss, she expected a harshness, an aggressive demand. But what happened instead was its opposite: a soft, subtle persuasion that parted her lips and then made her tongue curve sensuously around his.

It went on that way, filling one moment and then the next. Her hands continued to grip the wheel. His were braced against the seat. Only their lips were joined—and she knew it wasn't enough. The young girl had daydreamed, not really knowing what she wanted. But the woman knew.

He backed off a few inches, and his breath fanned against her lips, which bore his imprint. "I don't live far from you— at Windcrest. Follow me there."

His voice was as soft—and as persuasive—as his kiss. And when she looked back on this moment, Amanda would be honest enough to admit to herself that she couldn't have refused. It was too late.

HIS HOME WAS NEAT and sparsely furnished with obviously good pieces—somehow not what she would have expected. And that made her vaguely uneasy. But how could he be more of a stranger than he already was? Until tonight, the only words she'd ever spoken to him had been in court.

He took off his jacket and holster and slung them over the back of a leather chair, his movements casual and unhurried. The air-conditioning whispered softly, the only sound in a room filled with a silent tension.

Then he held out his arms to her. There was a touching vulnerability to his gesture, a willingness to be rejected. But there was also an unspoken promise—or threat. If she walked into his arms, she could not walk away. She went to him.

It started as before, his lips gentle against hers, his hands now holding her carefully, almost uncertainly. For a moment, she stood there passively, arms down at her sides, reveling in a helplessness that wasn't really her, but belonged instead to the schoolgirl.

Michael's warm, firm lips teased hers, then brushed against her cheek. His teeth pulled lightly at an earlobe before he began to forge a slow path down along the curve of her neck. She moaned softly, and the sound seemed to be coming from somewhere outside her as it mingled with his low growl. His hands slid down and drew her against him.

"God, how I want you," he rasped against the throat she had bared to him.

"Yes," she whispered, the word barely out before he scooped her up into his arms and carried her to his bedroom.

He set her down on the big bed, then switched on a low bedside lamp. In the soft light, his eyes were dark, bottomless pools of desire, dizzying depths into which she plunged willingly, with no thought of whether she could ever surface again.

He began to undress her slowly, kneeling at first to remove her shoes. But this thing between them, created by two bodies that were already heated to the flash point, was soon commanding them both. They fumbled with buttons and zippers and even laughed a bit at their clumsiness. And then they were naked on the bed, and his hard, hair-roughened body was tangled with hers.

His mouth was at her breast and his fingers were probing her moist warmth, and they were both beyond anything but pure sensation and an impossible greed. The thing had taken them over completely, ignoring their impulses to go slowly and savor every nuance.

Michael plunged into her, and she arched her body to meet his thrusts, and they let it take them and weld them together and carry them beyond themselves to a pulsing, pounding climax that they clung to as they clung to each other, shuddering and gasping.

SOMEWHERE IN THE NIGHT, they both awoke, moving up slowly from a deep, sated sleep. Uncertainty hovered briefly at the edges of her consciousness, then vanished beneath a new sensual onslaught. She was ripe and heavy with wanting again, and he was hard and taut with renewed hunger. But this time, they found the gentleness that had eluded them before.

Their bodies became an erotic playground, familiar only in its outlines, but not in the details. Her fingertips traced rock-hard muscles and bristly hair and the satiny skin of his throbbing shaft. And his hands and lips found every curve and hollow, every private place that had once been hers alone.

There were tiny hesitations as she tried to hold on to that privacy, those inhibitions of a lifetime. But Michael was relentless, the intrepid explorer, demanding that she yield it all up to him. And she did, giving her self away even as she demanded and received the same from him.

And later still, she awoke again, this time to see a pale light outlining the windows. The bedside lamp was still on, showing the disorderly heaps of clothing scattered about on the floor—mute testimony to the night's frenzy.

Images drifted slowly through her wakening mind: Michael's dark head moving slowly up between her legs, his big hands curved around her hips as he held her atop him, her blond hair drifting over his dark, curly chest hairs as she slid down his body, teasing him unmercifully by moving very slowly toward the object of her erotic journey.

She wanted him again and she smiled sleepily at the impossibility of it all. But the light at the window was growing steadily brighter, chasing away the dark passion of the night and bringing the harsh reality of the day.

She fought that reality for a time, but its grip only strengthened. So she got out of bed, moving slowly and carefully, not wanting to disturb him.

He opened his eyes as she was struggling with the back zipper of her dress. He sat up quickly, even though sleepiness still dulled his dark eyes. She averted her gaze from his nakedness as he pushed aside the bedcovers.

"You're *leaving?*" he asked in a voice still thick with sleep.

"Yes." She turned away, searching for her shoes, then finding them half under the bed. When she bent down to pick them up, he slid an arm around her and tumbled her back into the bed.

"What is this—guilt time?"

She pushed away from him and scrambled out of bed—away from the feel of him, the smell of him. "I have a busy day."

"It's Sunday." He sat up again and swung his legs over the side of the bed, then sat there staring at her as she balanced on one foot and then the other, putting on her shoes. She hated him for being so comfortable in his nakedness and his memories of the night.

"I know it's Sunday."

"What's going on here, Amanda?"

"Maybe *I* should be the one asking that question."

He ran a hand through his disheveled hair. "You really *are* feeling guilty. Why?"

"You won, Michael—okay? Let's just leave it at that."

He stared at her for a very long and uncomfortable moment, and she almost let herself believe that he was puzzled by her words. But then he nodded.

"Okay. It was a memorable victory, Counselor."

Chapter One

Diesel fumes fouled the air of the island as the bulldozer and the front-end loader drove off the barges, leaving deep tracks in the white sand that had been brought in long ago. It looked like an invasion—and to the island's owners, it was.

The island had no name. Two miles long and nearly a half mile wide at its center, it sat in the middle of Mohawk Lake, forcing the deep, clear waters to part around it. The island had been claimed by the first Dutch settlers in the Hudson River Valley, though it was more than a century before they decided to do something with it.

By the mid-1800s, the owners had become prosperous, and after establishing themselves in suitably grand mansions in nearby Port Henry, they began to build summer homes on the island. There were five families, linked by long histories and much intermarriage over the generations, and they all built large homes they called cottages, despite their size.

The families had long since set up the island as a private corporation. Through the past winter, there'd been meetings and letters and phone calls and faxes: the first dissension within the group—though, being the kind of people they were, it was a genteel sort of dissension. But in the end, they agreed to permit the construction of a new cottage by one of the families, whose numbers had increased more than the others, thanks to a politely frowned upon divorce and second marriage.

So the bulldozer began to rip up ancient trees and to dig into the dark, rich soil. None of the owners was present, though all knew that construction was about to begin. Most of them had come to terms with it by now.

But one of them sat in his richly paneled office and stared at the date and worried. He reminded himself that only a small portion of the island's 320 acres would be touched. The odds were certainly in his favor. But still, he wished desperately that his memory of that night were clearer, even though he'd spent the past twenty years trying to forget what he *did* remember.

At some point during those years, he'd managed to separate the man he was from the man he'd been that night. That man had been an aberration, fueled by fear and anger and too much Scotch. He had long since forgiven himself because that man wasn't really *him.*

"T.G.I.F.," AMANDA SIGHED as she reached for her glass of wine, took a sip and set it down again. She'd found some wonderful jumbo shrimp—the big, chewy kind—and was making a bowl of shrimp salad. She'd have some for dinner tonight, then take the rest out to the island with her tomorrow.

She was looking forward to spending the weekend out there—the first since last fall. And she'd have the place to herself, too. No one else was planning to go out this weekend.

Not that it was going to be a weekend of leisure—unfortunately. She grimaced as she thought about the bulging briefcase she'd brought home. It was exactly a month since Lewis Brogan, her boss and for many years the district attorney, had reluctantly announced his retirement due to ailing health. Amanda was now the acting D.A., and until a new assistant could be hired, she was doing two jobs.

And as if that weren't enough, there was a decision to be made. She was thinking about that as she finished preparing the shrimp salad, when the doorbell rang, startling her. She wasn't expecting anyone, and her condo complex of busy young professionals didn't generally extend to impromptu neighborliness. She barely knew any of them.

When she peered through the little security eye, all she saw was a magnified detective's shield. She had just made out the word Lieutenant when a very familiar voice came through the door.

"It's Michael, Amanda."

In the space of a second, nine years vanished and she remembered the threat he'd made that night, at Mayor Teddy's party. He'd said he was going to show up on her doorstep some night, with photos of her client's next victim. But nine years had passed. Surely...

She undid the locks with trembling fingers as the other images of that night flooded through her, images that by all rights should have faded long ago. Except that they hadn't, and she'd come to fear that they never would.

She opened the door, uncomfortably aware of her ratty T-shirt and faded jeans. Somehow, she managed to affix a polite smile to her face, together with a genuinely quizzical look.

"Sorry to bother you at home," he said, stepping into her foyer and filling entirely too much space. His gaze swept over her, and she felt even grungier—especially when she saw amusement glitter in those dark eyes.

Amanda had seen that look before—especially recently, as her new job and his brought them into fairly regular contact. But she realized, with a prickly awareness, that this was the first time they'd been alone together since that night.

"I need some information, and you came to mind."

"Information?" she asked, puzzled. "About what?" One of her staff was always on call if the police needed something.

"The island. Do you happen to have a beer? I'm thirsty."

She nodded, barely able to restrain a smile at the brashness that was so much a part of him. She started back to the kitchen, and he followed her. After taking a bottle of beer from the refrigerator, she was about to get out a mug, but he reached around her and took the bottle.

He pried off the top and took a long swallow. Then she saw him eyeing the shrimp salad. "Would you like some to go with your beer?" she inquired.

"That'd be great." He leaned forward to peer at it. "What are those dark specks in it?"

"Tarragon." She spooned some onto plates for each of them, then cut two wedges of cheddar. When she handed him his plate, he sniffed at it.

"Oh yeah, I've had this before. I like it."

They sat down at the small kitchen table, Amanda having decided that the occasion didn't warrant the dining room. Then she remembered the loaf of French bread and got up to get that. Michael was already busy demolishing his plate of shrimp salad. His manners weren't crude, but he ate with gusto—which, she thought, was pretty much the way he did everything. More memories shivered through her.

"Why are you interested in the island?" she asked as she got out a bread knife and started to slice the loaf. Was she really so foolish as to be hoping that he'd only used it as an excuse to come here? Yes, she decided, she probably was.

"We found a body out there this afternoon—or rather, the construction crew did. It was a skeleton, actually. The bulldozer dug it up."

She whirled around in astonishment. "A *body?*"

"Yeah. Would you mind putting down that knife? Knives make me nervous."

She put it down and sank into a chair. Michael got up and finished slicing the bread, then carried it to the table and calmly began to butter a slice.

"I know the construction's not at your family's place, but I couldn't get hold of any of the Verhoevens. So until I do, I thought I'd see what you might be able to tell me."

Amanda stared at him. "You're not putting me on, are you, Michael?" She continued to hope that this was a joke, a way of getting to see her alone.

"Cross my heart," he said—and did. "Is there any chance that someone from the Verhoeven family could have been buried out there?"

"Not that I know of. I never saw a marker. Besides, all the Verhoevens are buried up at the Old Dutch Cemetery. Their mausoleum is right next to my family's. I can't believe this. You said it was a skeleton?"

"Right, and I don't think there was a casket or a marker, though I guess a wooden casket could have rotted away."

He paused to wolf down some more shrimp salad, then got up to refill his plate. "The thing is that it's all a damn mess. The crime-scene squad has been there and they'll be back tomorrow, but I don't have much hopes of them finding anything. The bulldozer had torn the place all to hell and back before the skeleton was discovered. In fact, they still haven't found all of it."

Amanda grimaced, then began to eat her shrimp salad. Such grisly conversations had long since ceased to affect her appetite: they went with the job. "So you haven't any idea how long it's been there?"

"No. I've already contacted a forensics expert with the state police. There are tests they can run, and they'll probably come up with a pretty good guess—especially if we find some pieces of fabric, too."

"Well, as you probably know, the families have all been on the island for nearly 150 years. But I just can't see anyone burying a family member out there. And if there *was* a grave, there'd have been a marker—and I would have known about it."

"Then I have to consider the possibility that someone decided it would be a good place to dump a body."

She thought about that and nodded slowly. "I guess it would be—especially during the winter when no one's out there. There's a caretaker for the island, who goes out regularly during the winter to check on things, but that's all.

"You said that you hadn't been able to reach the Verhoevens. Did you try Lise?"

"Is that Jan's wife—the ones who are building the house?"

"No. Lise is Jan's sister. She lives in Manhattan. Let me see if I can reach her now."

Amanda got up and lifted the cordless handset from its base, then punched out Lise's number. Lise Verhoeven was one of her oldest and closest friends. She worked in the family's investment-banking firm on Wall Street. She answered on the third ring.

"Lise, it's Amanda. I have some rather strange news. The construction crew working on Jan and Stacey's cottage unearthed a body."

"A what?"

"A body—a skeleton. We don't know yet how long it's been there. The lieutenant in charge of the investigation hasn't been able to reach your parents or Jan and Stacey." She glanced at Michael, who gestured for her to give him the phone.

"He's here now and he wants to talk to you."

She handed the phone to Michael, then sank back into her chair as he began to talk to Lise. She was stunned—and she was beginning to feel something else, as well: *violated!* There was no other word to describe it. The island had always been a haven for her—a place where the world and all its problems couldn't intrude. That had become very important to her during her years as a public defender, and continued to be important after she'd switched sides and gone to work for the district attorney.

Anger began to bubble up inside her. How dare someone do such a thing, desecrate her beloved island!

Amanda was certainly far more aware than the average citizen of the horrors of contemporary life—but the *island?* It was nearly unthinkable! Strangely enough, there'd never even been any vandalism on it. And now this.

She pushed aside her personal thoughts and began to think professionally. Why would someone go to all the trouble to carry a body out there and bury it, when there was the lake itself, or the nearby Hudson—or the thousands of acres of wilderness close by? It didn't make any sense to her—unless there was some connection to the island itself.

But that made even less sense to her. She knew all the families well and was, in fact, distantly related to all of them. If there were any dark secrets, they would certainly be known to her. And as for the possibility that any of them could be a murderer...

Amanda was certainly not so naive as to believe that murder couldn't happen in any family, but she was quite certain that no such thing had ever occurred in these particular families.

She wondered how long the body had been there and how closely they would be able to pinpoint the time it had been buried. The arcane science of forensics was beyond her understanding, though she never failed to be impressed by the experts who testified in various cases she'd been involved with over the years.

Then Michael handed the phone back to her and said that Lise wanted to speak to her again.

"This is just *incredible,* Lise," she told her friend. "I feel...*violated.* Nothing has ever happened out there before."

"That's what I told Lieutenant Quinn. Is he the same Michael Quinn I remember from high school—that hunk who was a big jock?"

"Uh, yes," Amanda replied, feeling very uncomfortable with Michael's gaze on her.

"Somehow, I always thought he'd end up on the other side of the law, even though he was very nice to look at— not to mention fantasize about." Lise chuckled.

Amanda had to struggle to conceal her reaction from Michael. She couldn't recall one single time when Lise had ever indicated any interest in Michael. But then, neither had she. It appeared that he'd been a very private fantasy for them both.

"Are you sure that no ancestor of yours could have been

buried out there?" Amanda asked, eager to get the conversation back to safer territory.

"Of course I'm sure. They're all tucked away up there next to your family. Eccentricity just doesn't run in our families—well, maybe except for Jesse, that is, and she's only mildly eccentric. Mother and Father are going to flip out when they hear about this. And Jan and Stacey! After all they went through to get permission to build the cottage, they're going to think there's a curse hanging over the place."

Then Lise laughed. "Remember when we were kids and we used to complain because there wasn't a single ghost on the whole island?"

Amanda laughed. "I remember."

Michael got up and went to the bowl of shrimp salad again, arching his brows questioningly. She nodded. There went tomorrow's lunch. She sighed.

"I was planning to go out there tomorrow for the weekend."

"I wonder if it could be a Native American—if it's old enough, that is."

"I suppose that's possible," Amanda admitted. "But didn't they always bury their dead in big burial mounds? There were never any mounds on the island."

"Right. Well, it was a thought, anyway."

They hung up, and Amanda saw that Michael was watching her with those dark eyes that seemed to miss nothing but gave little away, either. Flat black obsidian. He was definitely in his cop mode—not that he was ever completely out of it.

Well, *almost* never, she amended silently, cursing the memories that could still be so vivid after all this time.

"Could I have another beer?" he asked.

She got up to get it for him, suddenly back to the realization that they were alone together for the first time since that night. She knew that he hadn't forgotten about it, even though he'd never mentioned it. It was there in his eyes; she was sure she wasn't imagining it. But she was equally certain that his memories weren't as vivid as hers.

"You're planning to go out there tomorrow?" he asked as she handed him the beer.

"I was. Now I don't know." She sat down again, annoyed suddenly that he seemed so at home here, so completely at ease. It was a quality he had that she'd noticed before.

"The island has always been a special place for me," she told him. "A safe place with so many happy memories. I'm still having trouble accepting that something like this could happen there."

"It can happen anywhere. You, of all people, should know that," he replied, though with surprising gentleness.

"I know it rationally, but not emotionally. Can you make any guess at all as to how old the body could be?"

He shook his head. "There are too many factors to consider. How deep it was buried, soil composition—things like that. The only other time I was involved in something like this was right after I got my shield. We found a body buried out at Piney Haven, when they were first developing it. It turned out to be a man who'd disappeared about thirty years earlier. He was identified by his dental records.

"Unfortunately, our chief suspect had dropped dead of a heart attack a few months before we found the body. I always wondered if the heart attack was a result of his knowing that the body was likely to be dug up.

"Anyway, it seemed to be in about the same condition as this one, but I'm not sure that means much."

"What about its size? Does that tell you anything?"

"It's fairly small—probably female. The forensics team should be able to establish that right away. And I think the cause of death might have been a blow to the back of the head. There's a pretty serious crack in the skull."

Amanda winced. The skeleton was beginning to seem all too real. "Well, I suppose there's nothing to do now but wait. I hope we find out who it was."

Michael frowned thoughtfully. "The more I think about it,

the less sense it makes for someone to go to all the trouble of carting a body out there to bury it—unless the island had some special significance to either the victim or the killer. Or unless it happened there,'' he added after a brief pause.

"That's impossible!"

"Murder happens even in the best of families," Michael said with a shrug.

A sudden anger surged through her. It seemed that all her emotions were raw and close to the surface when he was around. "Maybe you'd like to think that, but I know these people."

He held up both hands in a placating gesture. "Hey, don't go off on me. I was just stating the obvious. I understand that there was some resistance to the construction. It could be that someone was worried."

She fought down her anger. He was right, of course. They were just questions he had to ask. But she couldn't help thinking that he was enjoying the prospect of casting her family and the others as suspects.

"There *was* resistance. It's been nearly 150 years since anything was built out there, and we all like the island as it is—or was. I wasn't too happy about it myself, and I certainly didn't bury any bodies out there."

"So who *really* resisted the idea?"

"Stop it, Michael! When you find out how long the body's been there, *then* you have the right to ask those questions. For all we know now, it could have been buried long before any of us were born."

"Okay, you're right. It isn't as though I don't have enough on my plate at the moment."

She was rather surprised at his meekness; that wasn't like him at all. Of course, angry outbursts weren't like *her*, either. It seemed that both of them wore their emotions on their sleeves where the other was concerned.

They began to talk about another case, where an indictment had just been handed down in a case of attempted murder. Michael and his team had built a strong case, even if it was all circumstantial.

When they kept their conversation focused on business, there were times when she could almost forget the impact he had on her. But that never lasted long. There'd be brief pauses or quick glances or words spoken in innocence that echoed with double meanings.

And there were times, as well, when she could draw back and watch Michael Quinn with utter fascination, as though he were some sort of exotic species. He was so *different*. He was all hard edges and barely leashed aggressive masculinity, despite his expensive wardrobe and all the other accoutrements of his newfound wealth, the result of amazing success on the part of his small software firm.

"I understand that your software company is doing very well," she said into a brief silence, following her thoughts.

He grinned, a look of such boyish pleasure that it startled her. "Yeah, it is. I managed to hit a big new market with software to train police officers. I just hired someone to run it for me, and that was a real big step. It means I'm giving up day-to-day control. In case you haven't already noticed, I'm a control freak."

She laughed. However much she disliked some things about him, his occasional outbursts of self-deprecating honesty both amused and charmed her.

"Most cops are," she said. "Did you ever consider leaving the force to run it yourself?"

"Yeah, I thought about it, but not for long. I can't see myself as a businessman. And then, when the chief created the major-crimes unit and asked me to run it, I knew I couldn't leave."

They skimmed over several other topics, and then Michael abruptly shifted to the subject of her sister, Jesse, asking if she'd talked to her lately.

"About a week ago, I think. Why?" She felt a slight twinge of uneasiness, as she always did when her sister's name came up. Her sister regularly attempted to find Amanda a husband, and she often wondered why Jesse hadn't pushed her toward Michael.

"According to Steve, there's some trouble." Michael was a friend of Jesse's husband, Steve.

"That doesn't really surprise me. Jesse can be difficult, and Steve isn't exactly perfect himself."

"I like him. He's a damn good handball player and golfing partner."

Amanda laughed. "That sounds like a man. Believe it or not, Michael, there are more important things in a marriage than being good at sports."

"I didn't say there weren't, even though I'm not so sure what makes *you* such an expert. You dated Steve for a while, didn't you?"

She nodded. At the time, she hadn't known that Steve and Michael were friends. "It was never that serious. He's not my type."

As soon as the words left her mouth, she regretted them. But to her surprise, Michael didn't follow up with the obvious question. Instead, he turned the discussion back to Jesse and Steve.

"He says she's having an affair."

"She may well be. It wouldn't be the first time." Jesse was on her third marriage, and she hadn't been faithful to the other two, either.

Michael drained the last of his beer and tilted back in his chair. "I don't understand that kind of thinking. Hell, if you want to keep screwing around, why get married? Maybe it's because I've seen too many battered wives and too many bodies that resulted from someone forgetting that they were supposed to be married for better or for worse."

For the second time this night, Amanda found herself touched by something he'd said. It was very disconcerting. But as usual, she felt compelled to defend her sister.

"Some people seem to need the security of marriage, and I think Jesse is one of them. But that doesn't necessarily mean that she's any good at it."

"Steve also says that she's drinking again. He says she had a problem with alcohol before—and with coke, too."

Amanda felt a surge of anger with Steve for talking about Jesse's former addictions. But Michael's words also confirmed her own fears that her sister was drinking again.

Michael was watching her intently. "Don't worry, I'm not going to blab your family's secrets all over town. Drug addictions—like murder—can happen in the best of families."

Despite his words, she was angry—and getting angrier—even if she didn't exactly know why. "But it pleases you to know that little secret, doesn't it, Michael?" she asked coldly.

"Yeah, maybe it does. When you grow up with a father who's a two-bit criminal and a mother who's a part-time hooker, it can be sort of comforting to know that the big folks up on the Hill have their problems, too."

She could think of nothing to say to that and she didn't want to talk any more about secrets, lest he bring up their own little "secret."

"What I don't understand is how two sisters can be so different," he stated. "But maybe that's because I'm an only child."

"Just because you're raised in the same family doesn't necessarily mean that you're raised the same way," she said, thinking that they'd just exchanged one uncomfortable topic for another.

"So you're saying that your folks favored you over Jesse?"

"No, it was just the opposite—especially with my father."

"Huh? I would have thought that your father favored *you*, since you seem to be following in his footsteps. Or is that why you did it?"

"That was part of the reason—at least in the beginning. Now it isn't important anymore." She was uncomfortable talking about these things with Michael. It seemed too intimate, laughable as that sounded, given their history.

Michael studied her a moment longer, and once again, she

held her breath, waiting for him to raise *the topic*. But instead, he stood up and carried the remains of his dinner to the sink. "I'd better get going. I still have to make my rounds."

"What rounds?" she asked, both glad and not glad that he was leaving.

"Down in the Bottom. I talked the chief into letting me hang on to my string of informants down there. It took a long time to build them up, and I didn't want to let them go."

"You are definitely a control freak, Michael," she said with a laugh as she followed him to the door.

He opened the door, then paused, half-turning back to her. "But not always. I can think of a thing or two I've let go."

Then he vanished into the night, leaving behind the echo of his words to torment her.

THE STURDEVANT COTTAGE sat on the highest point of the island, at its south end. Though its view of the rest of the island was mostly obscured by the huge old trees that covered the land, the twelve-room "cottage" had a superb panorama of the lake and portions of the mainland on both sides.

Amanda spent most of the day on the big porch that wrapped around three sides of the old stone cottage. She would certainly have preferred to while away the gentle spring day reading a mystery novel, but instead, she spent it buried in her work. But at least the setting was more congenial than either her office or her condo. Birds called in the thicket, and the distant drone of boats on the lake was soothing.

Finally, late in the afternoon, she shoved the last of the papers into her bulging briefcase and got up from the old porch swing. Having completed the work she'd assigned to herself, she now felt free to give in to her curiosity.

When she'd arrived at the dock just before noon, a police boat was already there, together with a big barge loaded down with concrete blocks. She grimaced, thinking that if

Michael's cherry red cigarette boat had been there, as well, she might not have gotten any work done.

She knew what kind of boat he owned because she'd seen him a few times at the marina, generally with one of the women who seemed to pass through his life with great regularity.

For nearly nine years, they'd moved along the periphery of each other's lives. But now, with her appointment as acting D.A. and his promotion to head up the newly created major-crimes unit, that was changing.

Amanda thought that she was beginning to move beyond embarrassment over her obsession with him to a sort of amusement. They were so clearly unsuited to each other in every way that she was quite certain the obsession would fade with regular exposure to him.

Besides, there was her position—and his—to consider. A romance between a D.A. and a cop could be a problem— and it was further exacerbated by Michael's new position as head of a unit involved in high-profile crimes.

One very important part of her job was to decide if there was sufficient evidence to bring a case to trial—something that the police quite naturally always wanted. So if she were to become involved with Michael, her judgment could easily be called into question.

She walked down off the porch, calling for Angus, her mother's old cairn terrier. When he appeared, they both set off through the woods. Angus loved the island, having spent every one of his sixteen summers here. But since her mother's death years ago, her father had been coming less often to the island, so Amanda always picked up the little dog and brought him out with her.

She'd called her father last night in Washington, where he was, as he put it, "politicking." He was currently a judge on the court of appeals, and had his eye on the Supreme Court, where a vacancy was anticipated soon. He wasn't at his hotel, but he'd returned her call this morning, and had been as shocked as she was at the discovery of a body on the island.

She told him about Michael's suggestion that one of those who had opposed the new construction might have done so out of fear that the body would be discovered. But he'd pointed out, quite correctly, that if that had been the case, the murderer could simply have dug up the body before construction began. They'd all known since last fall that Jan and Stacey wanted to build on that particular spot.

Amanda decided that she wouldn't pass on that bit of wisdom to Michael. Let him interview her father. Judge Thomas Sturdevant would waste no time destroying Michael's theory. She rather wished that she could be present for that encounter.

She'd left a message for Jesse, both at home and at her sister's clothing store, but hadn't received a return call before she left for the island. Michael's revelation that Jesse was having an affair and was also drinking again continued to trouble her.

As she walked through the woods toward the construction site, her thoughts remained on her beautiful older sister. It seemed to Amanda that Jesse's life had always been a series of crises, between which were periods of relative calm such as the past few years.

She wondered who her sister's new lover could be. In the past, though married herself, Jesse had always taken single lovers, once making the absurd claim that she didn't want to be a "home wrecker." That was unfortunately typical of her sister's twisted logic.

Then she left off her thoughts as a break in the trees gave her a glimpse of the dock. The police boat was still there, but there was still no sign of Michael's boat. The disappointment she felt suggested that her obsession with him hadn't begun to fade, after all.

Through the trees, she could see part of the construction site: big, raw-looking mounds of dirt and some bright yellow excavating equipment. She wondered if the mystery of the body would ever be solved. It would probably depend on how long the body had been there. But she didn't doubt that Michael and his unit would do their best.

One of the qualities that made Michael Quinn such a good cop was his extraordinary tenacity. Lewis Brogan, her predecessor, had once said that Michael took every crime personally—that he gathered into himself all the rage, if not the anguish, of the victims or their families. And she'd already seen proof of that herself as he doggedly pursued a suspect, interviewing and reinterviewing until he'd gleaned every last shred of evidence and followed every lead, no matter how tenuous. He just didn't let go.

Then she recalled his parting remark last night. She still didn't know if *she* was the one he'd let go, but a brief glimmer in those dark Celtic eyes had suggested that's what he'd meant.

Her thoughts had just begun to veer toward that night nine years ago when they were blessedly stopped short by a full view of the construction site just ahead.

When she had arrived at the dock earlier in the day, Amanda hadn't really seen the site, which was largely hidden from view by trees. So now, her first reaction, upon seeing the piles of dirt and the uprooted trees, was anger over the desecration of her lovely island. She hadn't actually spoken out against the construction, but only because she was fond of Jan and Stacey. In truth, though, she *did* resent it, no matter how much care had been taken by the architect to design a cottage that would blend well with the existing structures.

There were half a dozen people milling about. She recognized all but one of them as being members of the crime-scene squad: the people whose unpleasant task it was to sort through all manner of debris, take photographs that sickened juries and carefully bag and label all possible evidence for later study.

Jerry Hoffman, the head of CSS, saw her and raised a gloved hand in greeting. Amanda liked him. He had a dry sense of humor and was an excellent witness in court, with his quiet but competent manner and his ability to explain even the most arcane matters simply and clearly.

"I guess you already know about this," he said as he came over to her.

She nodded. "Michael told me last night."

He waved an arm at the mess around them. "In my nightmares, I've imagined a crime scene with a bulldozer, but this is the first time I've actually had to deal with one. The only good thing is that the construction workers had enough sense to stop as soon as they found the body."

"Have you found anything else besides the skeleton?" she asked, recalling what Michael had said about the importance of finding fabric or other items.

"Yeah. We've bagged some stuff that looks like fabric and we found one of her shoes."

"'Her'?" You're sure, then, that it's a woman?"

"Ninety-nine percent sure. Young, I'd say—probably somewhere in her teens. And the probable cause of death is a skull fracture. Looks like someone clobbered her from behind."

Amanda winced. "Do you have any idea how long ago it happened?"

Jerry gestured to the one man she didn't know. "That's John Saunders, the new state-police forensics expert. At this point, he's guessing about twenty years—somewhere in there. But it's too soon to be sure.

"Actually, right now, the best basis for guessing is the shoe we found—assuming, of course, that it's hers. Annie says that style was popular about twenty years ago." Annie Phelps was one of Jerry's crew.

Amanda suppressed a shudder. Twenty years. She'd been hoping that it would be much longer than that—that it had all happened long before her own lifetime. But now it appeared that sometime during her childhood, when she'd wandered this lovely place in total innocence, someone had killed another girl and then dumped her body here in an unmarked grave.

Twenty years. Her gaze went automatically to the water-ski jump out in the middle of the lake, and a pain she'd thought long buried jolted through her. It wasn't the same ramp, of course. The accident had destroyed that one, and there'd been one other before the present jump.

It would be strange, she thought, if the murder had happened exactly twenty years ago. She hadn't come out to the island at all after the accident—not even after she'd recovered from her injuries, because it had taken much longer for her to recover from her grief.

Then, just as she was about to turn back to Jerry, she caught sight of a red cigarette boat knifing through the water, swinging in a wide arc to avoid a wet-suited skier. Her nerve endings skittered with awareness of Michael, and a flock of butterflies suddenly took up residence in her stomach. So much for getting over her obsession.

"Here comes Michael now," Jerry said unnecessarily. "I figured he'd show up sooner or later. And he's going to want answers yesterday."

Amanda managed a laugh. "One could say that he's just a bit impatient."

"That and a few other things—including that he's a damn fine cop. If anyone can find justice for that poor kid, he can."

Jerry removed his baseball cap, then reset it on his graying head as he watched Michael's boat streak toward the dock. "The way I figure it, the killer probably brought her body over by boat to the dock, then just carried her up here and buried her." He waved an arm around them.

"If you look at the lay of the land, coming up here made the most sense—especially if you're carrying or dragging a body. The slope is steeper everywhere else.

"Still, why come here at all? Seems like there are plenty of other places a lot easier to get to—including the lake itself. He could have just weighted her down and dropped her in."

"Maybe it was winter and the lake was frozen," Amanda

suggested, her eyes following Michael as he nosed up to the dock, then leaped out with the ease of a born athlete. "Most winters, the lake is frozen solid."

"Yeah, but then he'd have had to bring her out in a snow-mobile—and they're damn noisy."

"In all likelihood, even if there was anyone around to hear it, they wouldn't have paid any attention. There'd have been no one at all on the island, and the lake is always overrun with snowmobiles when it's frozen," she commented as Michael approached them.

"Probable cause of death a skull fracture. Most likely a teenage female. Possibly about twenty years ago. Does that answer your questions, Quinn?" Jerry said by way of greeting Michael as he jogged up the slope.

Michael laughed. Amanda barely noticed Jerry's dry humor as Michael's eyes met hers briefly, then swiveled back to the CSS chief. The boat ride had ruffled his thick black hair. A pair of worn and faded jeans hugged his trim waist and muscled thighs. Beneath his dark blue windbreaker, he wore a polo shirt the same color as his boat. She could see a few dark chest hairs curling out of the open neck and was tormented by a vision of her own golden hair spilling over them. How could nine years seem like just last night.

"I don't know, Jer," Michael said, grinning. "Sounds like a lot of *probable*s, *most likely*s and *possible*s there. Could be a record—even for you."

Amanda had tuned out the men's good-natured banter. She was lost in her memories of that night: a night when she'd done things and felt things that seemed impossible. When Michael's gaze once more fell upon her briefly, she screamed silently, *No! My body belongs to* me!

And yet, she knew that for that one night, it hadn't.

Michael and Jerry moved off to talk with the state-police forensics expert. She started to follow them, then stopped. This was police business—not the D.A.'s business yet. Lewis Brogan, her predecessor, had often irritated the police by meddling in their investigations, and Amanda was determined not to make that same mistake. She had no intention of making what could already be a prickly relationship any worse, even if she did have a personal interest in this investigation.

She started to turn to go back to the cottage, but stopped as her gaze fell once again on the ski jump. Twenty years. Almost exactly twenty years. Early spring, just like now. Tears sprang to her eyes, and she turned away from the lake. And as always when she thought about that night, they were tears both of grief and of frustration.

Chapter Two

The phone began to ring just as Amanda reached the cottage. Since there was no answering machine, she hurried to the phone, assuming that it would be Jesse returning her call. By now, her sister probably knew about the discovery of the body, since it had been in the morning paper and on the local radio news.

"I just heard about the body," Jesse said without preamble. "How long has it been there? Do they know anything yet?"

Amanda thought her sister's voice sounded a bit strange: the result of a hangover, perhaps? She couldn't tell. So she told Jesse what they knew thus far. "And they're guessing that it's been there about twenty years, though they won't know for sure until some tests are run." She explained about the shoe that had been found.

When she had finished, Jesse was quiet for so long that Amanda finally asked if she was still there.

"I'm here. I was just thinking."

"About what?" Amanda asked in surprise. "Don't tell me that you know something about it?"

"No, of course not. But if it was twenty years ago, then it was around the time of the accident with Trish and you."

"Yes, I thought about that, too, even though there's obviously no connection."

"Is Michael handling the case?"

"Yes. He's here now—at the site, I mean."

"Will they be able to figure out exactly when it happened?"

"I'm not sure. Probably they can pin it down to within a few years, anyway. And by the way, Michael's already suggesting that one of *us* could have been the killer."

Jesse laughed, but it didn't sound quite natural to Amanda. She began to wonder if her sister might be drinking at the moment. Strangely enough, she couldn't always tell that easily.

"That sounds like Michael," Jesse said, laughing again.

Maybe it was the way she said his name, or maybe it was that laugh. Amanda would never know. But suddenly it struck her that *Michael* could be her sister's new lover! Or had that thought been lingering there at the back of her mind ever since last night, when Michael had brought up the subject—perhaps probing to see if she knew anything?

She felt sick, but she knew she had to consider that possibility. It would certainly explain why Jesse, who was forever trying to fix her up with any single man she ran across, had never once suggested Michael.

No, she told herself as Jesse went on about the unpleasantness of having such a thing happen on the island—despite the fact that she herself rarely came out here.

Surely Michael wouldn't do such a thing. Jesse's husband, Steve, was his friend. And yet she knew that it had happened before. Jesse had had an affair with the *brother* of one former husband. And anyway, what made her think that Michael would resist her sister's charms, when no other men could? Jesse was beautiful and she had a sexy wildness to her. And she was also relentless when she wanted something or someone.

"Does Father know yet?" Jesse asked.

"Yes." She told her what their father had said.

Then suddenly there was a loud rapping at the front door, followed by Michael's voice calling her name. She said goodbye to Jesse quickly and hurried to the door.

"Am I interrupting something?" Michael asked when she opened the door. "I thought you were here alone."

"I am. I was talking to Jesse. Come in."

"She doesn't know anything, does she?" he asked, though seemingly without much interest. Could that be because he'd already talked to her last night? She shook her head.

She thought about last night, when he'd left abruptly, saying that he had to see his informants. And she thought, too, about the fact that Jesse hadn't been home when she'd called her right after Michael left.

Stop it! she ordered herself. *If anyone came to you with "evidence" like that, you'd laugh them right out of your office.*

She saw Michael's gaze take in the large living room to the left and the dining room to the right, and she knew exactly what was going through his mind. She'd seen that look before on the faces of first-time visitors. But Michael, not surprisingly, was the first to give voice to that surprise.

"This isn't what I expected."

Amanda smiled. "We're not exactly into luxury out here. *Serviceable* is the word."

Most visitors expected a rustic version of the luxury they had seen in her family home. But instead, the cottage was furnished with sturdy, simple things not very different from most summer homes. The bare wood floors were covered in spots with bright, washable rag rugs, and the walls were filled not with art, but with photos of family summers from the past.

"The Sturdevant version of slumming it," Michael said as he studied one of the photographs, which she noted was one that showed her at her gawkiest, next to her gorgeous sister.

"Something like that," she replied. That Michael resented her family's wealth she took as a given. Certainly that was behind his suggestion that someone from one of the families could be the murderer.

He continued to peer at the photo, and she was sure that it must be Jesse who had captured his attention. Both of them

were wearing swimsuits. She looked like the proverbial bean-
pole, while Jesse looked like a budding starlet. He tapped the
photo and turned back to her.

"That brings to mind the old story about the ugly duckling
that turned into a swan."

She was confused, given her thoughts at the moment, and
her face must have shown that.

"Okay, so you weren't really an ugly duckling," he said
with a grin.

"I prefer 'late bloomer,'" she replied dryly, wondering if
it really could have been her picture that he was interested
in. More likely, Michael had just inherited a touch of the
blarney.

"Would you like some lemonade?" she asked. "I'm afraid
that's all I have to offer. We're not stocked up for the summer yet."

He accepted her offer and they were soon seated in the big
old Adirondack chairs on the porch. He gestured to her open,
well-stuffed briefcase. "Working on weekends?"

She nodded. "There's a lot to catch up on. Until we hire
a new assistant D.A., I've been doing both my old job and
my new one."

"Are you going to run in the next election?"

"Yes. I'll be making my announcement on Wednesday."

"Rumor has it that Neal Hadden wants the job," he ob-
served neutrally.

She wondered if he knew about her past relationship with
Neal. Probably he did. She nodded. "I've heard that, too. He
could be a tough opponent."

"He's a tough guy—or *thinks* he is, anyway."

"You don't like him?"

Michael shrugged. "He likes to grandstand, but so did
Brogan."

"And me? Do you think I grandstand?" She hated herself
for asking the question, for seeming to care what he thought
of her. But she *did* care—very much.

"No, you don't—at least not that I'm aware of. And you're as tough as you *can* be."

"What does *that* mean?" she asked, bristling.

Michael smiled, letting her know that he'd heard her slightly querulous tone. "Women have to walk a fine line, whether it's in the police department or the D.A.'s office. They can't be *too* tough, but they have to be tough enough. So far, you seem to have found that balance."

"Thank you," she replied, trying to ignore that warm glow inside. His shrewd observation didn't really surprise her, though. On several occasions recently, when he'd been in her office to discuss cases, she'd discovered that Michael was a keen observer of nearly everything.

"And you have my vote, too."

"I appreciate that."

"Of course, you could be getting it just because I think I can push you around easier than I could Neal Hadden."

"You haven't so far," she reminded him.

"No, but I'll keep trying—just so you know."

He grinned at her, and silver lights danced in his dark eyes as the silence between them grew heavy and deep. Amanda knew that she was good at reading people—very good, in fact. But she could not read Michael Quinn most of the time. What was she to him? A challenge? Merely an old conquest? The clueless sister of his current lover? A source of amusement because he knew she was still attracted to him?

She got up quickly, using the excuse that she had to look for the dog. He'd wandered off on his own before she'd reached the construction site.

"We ran into each other in the woods," Michael said. "He was headed in the other direction."

"He's probably looking for Misty, the Blauveldts' dog," she replied, turning back to him, relieved that she'd succeeded in changing the conversation.

"I came here mainly to let you know that I'm going to camp out on the island tonight."

"You are? Why?" And she thought, *This island isn't big enough for us to share. I should go home.*

"The news about the discovery of the body just might bring out the killer—assuming he's still alive and in the area."

"Do you really think so?" she asked doubtfully. She'd heard that old saw about criminals returning to the scene of the crime, but she'd never seen any evidence of it.

He shrugged. "I'll admit that it's a real long shot. But I told the media that we'll be back tomorrow, since we haven't finished searching the area, and that we're hoping to find something that would help to identify her. If the killer is still around, that could make him nervous enough to want to search himself. Besides, I'm not exactly overwhelmed with evidence at the moment.

"Anyway, it's a nice weekend and I don't have any plans. I'll set up camp somewhere near the Verhoevens' place. They have a good view of both the dock and the area where the body was found."

"That won't be necessary. I can let you into their cottage. I'm sure they won't mind."

"You have a key?"

She nodded. "We all have keys to all the cottages. But what about the boats? If the killer does come, he'll know someone's on the island."

"Right. That's the other thing I wanted to talk to you about. How about if you take your launch back to the marina and I'll follow you? Then we can go have some dinner over at Mann's Landing and I'll get someone there to bring us both back."

His tone was casual, but his eyes gleamed with challenge. And in the brief silence, Amanda became nearly certain that his decision to stay on the island was only a ruse.

"I owe you dinner anyway," he went on, "since you fed me last night."

He got up and stretched his lean, hard body. She averted her gaze. "I wish there was a spot where I could see all of the island, in case someone does come and lands someplace other than the dock."

Maybe she was wrong. Maybe he really did believe the killer might come. With that thought, she doused the fire that had been building up inside her.

"There *is* a place," she told him. "I haven't been up there in years, but I think it's still in good shape. Come on."

She led him off into the woods at one side of the house, foolishly eager to show him this special place from her childhood. There was a delicious sort of danger, and a poignancy, as well, to taking him there. It had been her place for daydreaming, and she knew that some of those daydreams must have included fantasies about an older boy who was far beyond her reach and not of her world.

She stopped at the crest of the hill several hundred yards from the cottage, and pointed. "Up there."

"This is great!" he said enthusiastically as he stared up at the old tree house. "How long has it been there?"

"This particular one has been here about twenty-five years. My father had it built for us, after we tried to climb the old one he'd had as a boy. Jesse fell and broke her ankle when a step gave way.

"And it's a perfect spot to see the whole island," she told him. "It's nearly invisible from the water. You have to know where to look."

Michael was already testing the wooden steps nailed into the thick trunk of a huge old oak. "They seem okay," he said as he started to climb.

"I'm sure it's safe. Father had some work done on it last summer when the DeGroot grandchildren discovered it and wanted to play up there."

"Perfect," Michael pronounced as he reached the big square platform at the top, which rested on a thick limb and was surrounded by a railing.

"There's a full moon tonight, too, so even if a boat approached without lights, I should be able to see them." He surveyed the scene with satisfaction, then turned to her. "Did you spend a lot of time up here?"

She nodded, caught in the uniqueness of the moment, of his presence here. "I used to pretend I was a princess in a tower, the ruler of the whole island."

Michael chuckled. "And did your prince ever come?"

"I wasn't really looking for a prince. I wanted the place to myself." But she wasn't sure that had been the case; it could be revisionist history.

And a voice whispered to her, *he* has *come, after all. But there's no happily ever after.*

"WHY ARE WE GOING to Mann's Landing?" she asked, shouting over the roar of his boat at full throttle. They were streaking across the nearly deserted lake after dropping her launch at the marina.

"Because if anyone's watching the island, they'd be most likely to come from the other side. The marina at Mann's Landing is a lot smaller. I'll have us dropped off on that side of the island, too, so we can't be seen from Walters' Marina."

That made sense, she realized, thinking that maybe he *was* taking seriously the possibility that the killer could show up, after all. Most of the boats on the lake were berthed at Walters' Marina or launched from there because it was just off the road from Port Henry. Mann's Landing was home mostly to small fishing boats belonging to people who lived in the rural area on that side of the lake.

"Besides," Michael shouted, "if the killer decides to pay a visit, he'll want to be on the water as brief a time as possible, and it's a nearly straight shot from Walters' to the dock at the island. Also, he'd be able to see from the marina if there are any boats tied up at the island's dock."

She nodded, doing her best to seem relaxed. Ever since the accident, she'd been afraid of boats like this one—especially when they were being piloted at top speed.

But Michael was clearly enjoying himself as he stood up

in the boat to see over the elevated bow. The wind swept back his thick black hair, and his square chin jutted out defiantly. He was smiling, and she wondered if he'd dreamed as a boy of one day owning a boat like this—and a Porsche to go with it.

It struck her then just how much she wanted to understand him and the forces that had shaped him. He was an enigma to her. Years ago, she'd heard the stories about his family, but she was still somewhat shaken by his casual reference to them last night. It was as though they'd grown up in different universes, when in fact they'd lived within a few miles of each other.

Mann's Landing came into view as they streaked past the tip of the island: a ramshackle collection of low buildings that all needed a coat of paint. A motley assortment of boats, ranging from a few large cabin cruisers to rowboats and paddleboats, was tied up at the dock.

Michael throttled back, and the bow settled into the water for the first time during their crossing. He nosed into an empty slip beside a paddleboat, where a family was just disembarking. A boy of about ten or so stared with undisguised envy at Michael's boat.

Amanda had just caught sight of a faded sign on one of the buildings that said Restaurant, when Michael started off toward the more visible sign that said Office. She followed him, thinking about the dinner she'd planned: cold lobster curry from her favorite gourmet deli.

An obese man looked up as the bell announced their entrance into the small office. The place looked as though it hadn't been cleaned in this century, and it reeked of fish and cigar smoke—a nearly lethal combination.

"Hey, Michael! Thought I saw a red streak out there." As he greeted Michael, his small, pale eyes appraised her.

"Amanda, this is Butch Miller. Butch, Amanda Sturdevant. After dinner, we're going to need a ride over to the island. I'm leaving my boat here."

"Sure, no problem. I hear you found a body out there."

"Yeah. We'll talk once I'm more certain about how long it's been there, but it's looking like maybe twenty years or so. You might want to give some thought to that, and ask around a bit. We'll see you in about an hour—and you can top off my tank when you get around to it."

"You've never been over here, have you?" Michael asked as they walked toward the restaurant.

"No." She was tempted to lie, because she knew he was goading her.

He leaned close to her as they reached the restaurant. "The food's not as bad as you're thinking."

She would have liked to protest that she hadn't been thinking any such thing, but since she was, she said nothing. And as they walked into the restaurant, she did her best not to wince at the country music blaring from too many speakers.

But a short time later, she discovered that he was right. They'd both ordered the Catch of the Day, which was striped bass, and if the ambience and the presentation left quite a bit to be desired, at least the fish was fresh and well prepared.

Michael was greeted familiarly by several of the other customers, and she commented that he must come here regularly. That she didn't was equally obvious from the curious glances sent her way.

He nodded. "Except for Butch, no one over here knows I'm a cop. That's what I like about it."

She smiled. "They might not *know* it, but I'll bet they've *guessed*. You have *cop* written all over you, Michael Quinn."

"Damn. And here I thought maybe I looked like a dentist or something."

"A *dentist?*" She laughed. "Where did you come up with that?"

"I didn't see much of a dentist when I was a kid, which is why I'm seeing far too much of them now. But when I did see one, I was really impressed with all the equipment and the power they had, standing over you with drills and everything. So at one point, I decided I wanted to be a dentist."

"The dental profession has obviously suffered a great loss," she remarked dryly.

"It took me some time to find my true calling," he went on. "Needless to say, when my father was around, I didn't hear much good about cops."

"Are your parents still alive?" she asked.

"My mother is. Dad died a few years ago. Mom's gotten into religion in her old age. There's nothing like an ex-hooker who's gotten religion. But at least I finally got her out of the Bottom. She's living at Harmony Hills, that retirement community out on Valley Drive."

Amanda could think of nothing to say. It seemed to her that they must *still* be inhabiting different universes. How did one reach a point where he could matter-of-factly refer to his mother as an ex-hooker?

"What did you mean when you told Butch that you would talk to him after you know more about the body?" she asked, deciding it was best to get the conversation back to a neutral place.

"Butch has been running the marina all his life—and I mean that literally. His father was a drunk who more or less handed it over to him as soon as he was old enough to pump gas and make change. If Jerry's right about the time, Butch could be a help."

"You mean if the killer came from over here?"

"Don't underestimate Butch. There's nobody who knows more about both sides of the lake than he does. He could probably tell you the last time your family had a party on the island—and maybe even what was served for dinner."

"Then he already knew who I am, even before you introduced us?"

"Sure. He told me once that you and Jesse were the best-looking of the whole lot of them on the island." Michael grinned at her. "He also said that you're the only one he's ever seen sunbathe topless out there. He's probably right. I never saw anyone else, either."

"What?" She stared at him, too shocked to even think of

fighting the heat that rose into her face. "But that's impossible! No one can see…"

"Oh yes, they can—if they know where to look and have a good pair of field glasses. Don't worry. I'm sure he didn't tell anyone else. He was kind of embarrassed about it, actually."

"But *you* certainly weren't!" she accused angrily, the words out before she could stop them.

"Why should I be? I have a very good memory."

So there it was: the unspoken had finally been spoken, after all these years of silence.

"I wondered when you'd bring that up," she stated coldly.

"I thought I worked it into the conversation pretty well," he said, still grinning. "Don't I get some credit for subtlety?"

"Michael," she began, not at all sure what she intended to say, even though she'd imagined this discussion many times.

"I know. You'd had too much champagne, and you've never behaved that way before or since."

"No. That isn't true—about the champagne, I mean. It was a long time ago, Michael, and I think we'd both better forget about it."

"Maybe we should, but we haven't," he said in a low voice. Then he paused, dropping his gaze to his plate for a moment. "I guess this would be a good time for me to say that you were wrong about why it happened. But I think you might have been half-right, at least."

He looked up at her only as he finished his statement, and Amanda saw regret in his eyes. Or was she only imagining it? Over the years, she'd veered back and forth from believing that it had happened only because she'd beaten him in court, to believing that it had been something truly unique for them both.

"I don't want to talk about it, Michael."

"Okay. But remember—I didn't say that you were *completely* right."

They finished their dinner in an uneasy silence—or at least

it was uneasy for her. Every time she caught him staring at her, he retreated behind his impassive cop's gaze, so she had no idea what he might be thinking. If she could have looked at it objectively, she might have credited him for his honesty, but she couldn't look objectively at anything connected to Michael Quinn.

He persuaded her to join him for a piece of the house specialty for dessert: a tart lemon pie that was truly the best she'd ever had. And over that, he told her that he'd spent part of the day at headquarters after Jerry had told him it was looking like twenty years or so.

"I decided to get a jump on things by looking through the missing-persons reports for that time period."

"Did you find anything interesting?" she asked, eager once again to keep their conversation focused on safe topics.

"Maybe. There were three reports of teenage girls who went missing during that time, and no record that any of them were ever found. But that doesn't mean much. From what I could tell, the record keeping was pretty sloppy back then. I'll get someone to check them out.

"Records that old aren't on the computer and they were just kept chronologically, so there was a lot to go through, and in the process, I came across the report on your accident. I hadn't known about it. I was in the Marines then." He leaned back in his chair, studying her. "Tell me about it."

Amanda felt herself go cold inside, and almost told him that she couldn't talk about it. But how could she explain what had to be an overreaction? Twenty years was a long time—more than enough time to put some emotional distance between the girl she'd been then and the woman she was now.

"I'm sure it's all in the police reports," she said, temporizing.

"Not all of it. For example, what the hell were you doing out there at night in the first place? You were only thirteen."

"Nearly fourteen—and Trish was sixteen. It was just a

crazy thing we decided to do, that's all. You don't have to have a reason when you're that age.

"Trish's brother had just gotten a cigarette boat and she was angry with him because he'd taken her new sports car without her permission. So she decided that she'd take his boat. It was the first warm night that spring."

"One of the things that struck me," Michael said, "was how someone who was familiar with the lake could have rammed into the ski jump. And the best guess was that you were probably going full throttle at the time."

"The lights might not have been on on the jump," she said defensively.

"But still," he persisted, "she must have known where it was."

"Why are you so curious about this, Michael?"

He shrugged. "I'm just nosy, that's all. The report said that you didn't remember anything, that you had shock-induced amnesia."

She nodded curtly, wishing he'd drop the subject before her emotions got the better of her.

"But doesn't that generally go away after a short time?"

"It didn't in my case. The doctors and the psychologist said that the physical trauma probably contributed to it, as well. They're really not sure what happens to the brain when the body's temperature is lowered like that. I was in the water for over an hour and the temperature was just under fifty degrees at the time. In fact, they were concerned about possible brain damage for a while."

"You're damn lucky to be alive," Michael said quietly. "It's a miracle that you didn't die like your cousin."

"Yes, it is." She looked away from him as she felt the tears begin to well up.

Then she jumped as his hand covered hers. He removed it quickly. "Sorry. I didn't mean to upset you. Sometimes I just let my nosiness carry me too far."

She smiled at him, touched by the sincerity of his regret. "It was so long ago. I should be able to handle it better than

I am. I suppose it's because I've never been able to remember anything. At the time, the psychologist told my parents it was better if I didn't remember, but I think she was wrong."

She'd intended to let it go at that, but Michael's gentle concern seemed to be urging her on. "You see, everyone thought that Trish was guilty of recklessness. But she wasn't that way. I *do* remember the first part of it, when we left the dock. And I know she was being careful with Rob's boat."

She stopped and sighed. "Losing her was terrible enough, but I've always felt so guilty that I couldn't remember why it happened."

"You wanted to exonerate her," Michael said, nodding.

"Exactly. But I never could."

"I think you probably gave the answer yourself a little while ago, when you said that kids don't need a reason. What's making it tough for you now is that you're looking at it through adult eyes."

"Maybe so, but even then, I wanted to find a reason. Jesse told me that maybe I could be hypnotized into remembering, but when I asked my parents about that, they refused to have it done.

"Then, years later, I went to a psychologist who used hypnosis and tried it, but nothing was there."

"IT'S A PERFECT PLACE for a stakeout—plus I get to realize a lifelong dream," Michael said as he studied the island through his field glasses. Dusk was just turning to night, and the waters of the lake were silver in the waning light.

"What lifelong dream?" she asked.

"Sleeping in a tree house," he replied, lowering the glasses and turning to her. "I would have built one myself when I was a kid, except that there weren't any trees around.

"Then one spring, the city decided to beautify our neighborhood, and they planted all these little trees. I must have been about eight or nine, and I had a pretty vague idea of how long it takes for a tree to grow. I figured that in a couple of years, I'd be able to build my tree house.

"If you should ever happen to stop at that Mobil station at Tenth and Hudson, check out their mechanic. He's still wearing a scar I gave him when I caught him ripping out the tree in front of our building."

She laughed, but Michael thought it was an unnatural sort of laugh. What the hell was he supposed to do: pretend that he'd grown up the way she had?

"Well, enjoy your night up here, then," she said as she started back down the steps. "I'll see you for breakfast."

Michael leaned on the railing and watched as she climbed down and then disappeared into the woods, trailed by the little dog that had been barking nervously ever since she'd abandoned it to climb up to the tree house.

"This is not exactly what you had in mind for tonight, fella," he muttered to himself as he picked up the glasses again and scanned the lake.

He didn't really believe that the killer would show up, but he'd seen his opportunity and had taken it. Amanda was going to be out here, and he had a reason to be here, so...

But he'd messed up again. Why could he never seem to get it right where she was concerned? Was somebody trying to tell him something?

Everything had seemed okay until he'd tried to apologize for that night. Okay, so it hadn't been much of an apology, but he'd been honest. He'd thought she would appreciate that.

Michael wasn't inclined to introspection, but he'd given that night a lot of thought. Sure, part of it was that he'd wanted some sort of victory after the hosing he'd taken from her in court. But that wasn't *all* of it—not by a long shot. And he'd thought she would understand that.

He wondered suddenly if he'd been misjudging her. She had all that poise and polish that came with old money, and he'd just assumed that self-confidence came with it. But maybe he was wrong.

He thought about her statement that her father had favored

Jesse. Michael was an only child, so he didn't really understand sibling rivalry.

But now, as he thought about the gawky kid she'd been and the beauty her sister had always been, he began to see that some of that kid might still be there inside her.

"Damn!" he swore softly. He'd probably *really* blown it now.

In all the years since that night, their paths had crossed from time to time in professional circles but that was all. And yet, every time he *did* see her, he had this sense of something left unfinished, something of the past and maybe of the future, but not the present.

Now they'd be working together regularly, and he was worried that if he tried to start anything between them, she'd see it as an attempt on his part to ingratiate himself with the D.A.

Michael knew that a cop and a D.A. weren't exactly a match made in heaven, and he also knew that it posed more problems for her than for him. The most he'd get would be some ribbing. But she'd find everyone second-guessing any decisions she made regarding his cases, which would also be her most important cases.

He peered out at the lake, watching the rising moon stipple the dark water with silver. And he thought about a night he couldn't seem to forget—and a woman he knew he still wanted.

AMANDA TOSSED AND TURNED. The bed was too big—and too empty. And when she finally fell asleep, it was to find herself in a dark dream of speeding across the lake, shivering in a cold wind, the roar of the boat at full throttle assaulting her ears. Trish was shouting something, but Amanda's teeth were chattering from the cold and she couldn't respond.

Then suddenly, she saw the blinking lights of the ski jump just ahead. She screamed, but the wind snatched the sound and flung it into the darkness. The roar of the boat grew even louder then was lost beneath the world-shattering explosion!

She sat up with a cry as the sound of the explosion died away. Although the room wasn't cold, she wrapped her arms around herself and shivered with the memory of the cold wind.

It's only a dream, she reminded herself. A dream and not a memory. She'd had it many times before—especially in the months following the accident. And when she'd told the psychologist who'd hypnotized her about it, he'd explained that it was just her subconscious, trying to fill in the missing details. Under hypnosis, she'd recalled no such thing.

Then she jumped and cried out as another explosion shook the cottage. Thunder! Of course. She could remember having that dream before during nighttime thunderstorms.

Lightning flashed at the window and in its brief glare, she could see the wet curtains fluttering and she belatedly became aware of the rain. She got up to close the window and was reaching for the sash when she suddenly remembered that Michael was out there in the tree house.

No, surely he'd come into the house by now. Or had he? Had she locked the door? She couldn't remember. She might have; locking the doors at night was an automatic thing.

The thunder crashed again and the wind-driven rain pelted the window. Not bothering with a robe, she ran from her bedroom, down the long hallway and down the stairs, wondering what he must have thought if he'd come to seek shelter only to find the door locked.

And it *was* locked. She saw that as she reached for the knob. She'd even put on the security chain. Had it been some subconscious attempt to lock him out of her life? Given the direction of her thoughts when she'd left him in the tree house, that was quite likely.

She opened the door just as a brilliant flash of lightning illuminated the big porch. He was wrapped in his sleeping bag on the old porch swing that was rocking gently in the wind.

She started across the porch to wake him and apologize, then stopped when she was only halfway there. He appeared to be sleeping soundly, and the rain wasn't reaching him. That old adage about letting sleeping dogs lie came to mind.

So instead, she stood there, shivering in the coolness as she watched him: watched and remembered. Strong hands caressing her every curve, trailing fire across her body, driving an already powerful need beyond endurance.

And her own hands twitched with the memory of the feel of him, all hard and bristly beneath her fingertips, his own body writhing with a fire that was consuming him, too.

She took another step—and stopped again, now remembering that he might be her sister's lover. She was aware of the dichotomy: she didn't believe it, but she *needed* to believe it.

Finally, she turned and walked back into the house, this time leaving the door unlocked, even though she knew he wasn't likely to check it again.

Chapter Three

"Lieutenant Quinn is waiting in your office."

Amanda nodded, then signed the court documents handed to her by her secretary. Her hand trembled slightly, but very fortunately, her secretary's attention had shifted to the ringing telephone.

Then she straightened up and actually took a few steps toward her old office before she caught her mistake. Not wanting her secretary, who was an incurable office gossip, to see how frazzled she was, she continued on to the rest room in the far corner of the office suite.

She stared at herself in the mirror over the sink, lifting her chin defiantly and meeting the hazel eyes of her reflection. She'd recently begun to wear glasses again instead of contacts and decided that it had been a good move. The metal frames gave her an air of cool professionalism.

The woman who stared back at her was exactly what Amanda wanted her to be—on the outside, at least. But inside? She clenched a fist. Would it be easier if she saw him every day? In fact, she hadn't seen him since that morning, nearly two weeks ago, at the cottage, when she'd apologized too profusely for having locked him out during the storm. He'd shrugged it off, but she'd seen the knowledge in his eyes: an understanding of the unintended symbolism.

She unclenched her fist and raised her hand to stare at it.

No more tremors. She tucked a stray lock of her golden hair behind her ear and left the rest room.

This time, she walked purposefully to the door in the opposite corner of the suite, where a brass plate said District Attorney. The door was slightly ajar, and she pushed it open soundlessly. Michael Quinn stood with his back to her, his hands braced against the windowsill as he stared down into the plaza. She saw that there were actually a few streaks of silver in his black hair, and wondered how it was that she hadn't noticed that before.

Why is it still there? she asked herself as that treacherous heat stole through her. *I'm not even sure that I like him, let alone...* But *like* had had nothing to do with it—not then, and apparently not now.

She didn't think he'd heard her enter, but now he turned his head slightly. "Come over here a minute."

She walked over to join him at the window, but only after a tiny hesitation as her memory replayed another order, issued nearly nine years ago. I don't live far from you—at Windcrest. Follow me there.

The row of windows wrapped around the corner of the building. She stayed as far away from him as possible, but still she felt his maleness reaching out to her, demanding a response. That sense of aggressive masculinity was one of the things she didn't like about him, though when she was being honest, she admitted that the problem was hers, not his. It was her reaction—not his action.

She looked out the window. The plaza was nearly empty on a day when the chill winds of March had suddenly returned after a prolonged spell of spring tease.

"See those two by the fountain?" Michael asked without turning to her.

"Yes." They were the only two stationary figures in the plaza. Everyone else was scurrying, their bodies angled against the wind.

"The one in the blue windbreaker is your old friend Joseph Wilson. The other one must be a prospective customer."

At first, she didn't recognize the name, since she was trying to run it through her mental file of recent cases. And then, when she suddenly *did* remember, she made a small sound, surprised at her own stupidity. Given her thoughts of a few moments ago, how could she have forgotten that name?

Michael turned to her. "You remember him, don't you? By the time I finally nailed the little bastard, you had already switched sides and a half dozen or so old ladies had lost their cat-food money."

Despite his words, there was no rancor in his voice, but in that half second before she turned back to the window, she saw the dark gleam in his eyes. He was daring her *not* to remember.

She studied the distant figure. Was it Joseph Wilson? She couldn't be sure. His face had long since faded from her memory, even if what had followed her gaining his acquittal certainly hadn't.

"So what are you doing up here?" she asked, issuing a challenge of her own. "If it's a drug deal, why don't you go down and arrest him?"

"Because not even Wilson would be dumb enough to be carrying the stuff with him now. He got out a couple of weeks ago—his second hitch—and he's just trolling for customers at the moment." Then he shrugged and spread his arms.

"But hey, at least he isn't mugging little old ladies anymore. He's become an entrepreneur. For all I know, he's even paying taxes."

She turned away and walked to her desk. His gesture had reminded her of that moment when he'd held out his arms to her. The difference was that he no longer looked vulnerable. She sat down, and he took one of the chairs facing her desk. A wide expanse of teak loomed between them, making her invulnerable, too—or so she wanted to think.

"I assume you're here about the Hanlon case," she said, glancing at the report she'd read earlier.

"Yes, ma'am. Have you read the investigative report?"

She nodded. "You don't have enough to get an indictment."

"He's guilty. He got tired of Mom's whining and the late-night phone calls and he blew her away, then set it up to look like a burglary."

"Maybe it *was* a burglary. Have you considered that?"

"Been there. Done that. It's him."

"Michael, the man's a respected businessman—with no criminal record."

"So? If he was some poor slob from down in the Bottom, you'd be telling me to haul his butt in here yesterday."

"No, I wouldn't!" she said, smacking her desktop with the flat of her hand—a gesture that surprised her, but failed to shock him. It was yet another thing that she disliked about him: his insistence that she was an elitist.

"You don't have the evidence!" She gestured angrily to the reports. "Look what you've got—two people who say that he was at his wit's end over what to do about her, and an eighty-four-year-old neighbor who *thinks* she saw him at her apartment that evening. According to his statement, he was there just about every evening—except the night she was murdered.

"Even his lack of an alibi for the time works on his behalf. If he'd really planned to kill her, he would surely have come up with something."

"He didn't plan it. He just got there and decided he couldn't take it anymore."

She was leaning forward. He did the same. They stared at each other across the desk, eyes dueling. Then something different flickered in his dark eyes, and she drew back. After a moment, he did, too, and a half smile tugged briefly at the corners of his wide mouth.

He shrugged, drawing her attention to his broad shoulders and his expensively tailored suit. She recalled that she'd heard just the other day that he was building a big house somewhere in the North Hills, the address of choice for the newly affluent.

"Okay," he said amiably. "I thought it was worth a shot, anyway."

"Was this a test, Michael?"

"Not really. I'd have tried it with Brogan, too—and probably with the same result." Then, in one of those moments that never failed to deflect her anger and touch her, he added, "It's pretty damn frustrating sometimes, you know? I *know* he's guilty. It's written all over him."

She found herself smiling. "So you force me to play the bad guy."

"Yeah," he replied, chuckling. "You do a good job of it, too. Hadden is already trying to put out the word that you're not tough enough for the job, by the way."

"That doesn't surprise me."

Michael tilted his head to one side and studied her. "It seems as though he's trying to turn this into a personal thing. I guess he didn't much like being dumped."

"That was over a year ago."

"That's not so long. Some of us have memories even longer than that."

"Is there anything else we need to discuss, Michael?"

"Yeah, there is." He waited just long enough for her to think he was about to bring up again the memory he'd obviously referred to, then went on.

"I just got back the forensics report on the body from the island. They're figuring twenty years—give or take a year or so. And they've definitely pegged it as being early spring— March or April. Female, probably seventeen or eighteen, Caucasian. And most likely poor. The tests indicated some degree of malnourishment during childhood and a definite lack of good dental care."

"But how do they know it was early spring if they can't even be sure what year it was?"

"Believe it or not, some violets were found with the body, and some seeds were embedded in the scraps of fabric we found. They're very sure about that."

Twenty years ago in the early spring. She stiffened, knowing what was coming even before he spoke.

"I reread that report on your accident. It happened at that time of year. And the one thing that keeps bothering me is that anonymous phone call to the police."

She shrugged. "Just someone who didn't want to get involved. That's not uncommon." In truth, she'd never given it much thought.

"It might not be uncommon now, but this was twenty years ago. And why didn't he try to save you?"

"You're assuming he or *she* had a boat."

"Why else would he have been out there at night at that time of the year?"

She had no answer for that, though she wished fervently that she did. She had begun to suspect just where this was all leading.

"You told me that your cousin wasn't reckless, and the caretaker swore that the lights were working on the ski jump. What if the accident happened because the two of you were running away from someone—like a killer?"

Amanda felt her stomach knot up. She discovered to her dismay that a small part of her actually wanted to believe it because it would exonerate Trish. But the rest of her wanted to lash out at him for raising the question.

"You're grasping at straws, Michael."

"No, I'm just taking a hard look at the pitiful evidence I have. One dead girl—or rather, two dead girls if you count your cousin—one accident that no one thinks should have happened and one anonymous caller who might have saved you both, but didn't."

"You're right—it *is* pitiful evidence." But she knew that she wouldn't be able to get it out of her mind, thanks to him.

"What about the missing-persons reports?" she asked, recalling that he'd mentioned before that there'd been several.

"We've tracked down two of them, and they're alive and kicking. So far, we haven't located the third, but we have reason to think she's still alive, too."

"Then wouldn't that suggest that the dead woman probably wasn't from around here?"

"It might—or she might have been the type whose disappearance didn't matter."

THE PHONE RANG just as Amanda was about to leave for the party at Jesse's. She hesitated, thinking that she should let the machine take the call, then hurried into her home office and snatched up the receiver, her thoughts on the party and whether or not Michael would be there.

Silence followed her "Hello," but she could hear sounds and knew someone was there. So she repeated her greeting impatiently.

"Is this Amanda?" a woman's voice asked. "Amanda Sturdevant?"

"Yes. Can I help you?" The voice sounded vaguely familiar, but she couldn't place it. She was hoping that this wasn't the wife or mother of someone in trouble. She'd had a few such calls before and had considered switching to an unlisted number.

There was another silence, and Amanda could hear some kids in the background. She became increasingly certain that it *was* one of those calls. She was about to repeat her question when the woman spoke again in a small voice with a pronounced lisp.

"It's about the body—the one on the island? I think I know who she is…was."

"In that case, you should be calling the police," Amanda said, taking care to keep her tone pleasant as she tried to think where she'd heard that voice before. "Lieutenant Quinn is the man you should speak to."

"I know, but it's just that…" The woman hesitated again.

"I'm sure Lieutenant Quinn would be happy to hear from you," Amanda told her when it appeared that the woman wasn't going to finish her sentence. In the background, the kids grew even noisier, obviously squabbling over something.

Then the line abruptly went dead. Amanda dropped the receiver into its cradle, frowning. Why had the woman called her in the first place? Was it really someone she knew?

AT LEAST A DOZEN CARS were parked at Jesse's house by the time Amanda arrived, but Michael's Porsche wasn't among them. She had half convinced herself that if he didn't come, that would be further proof that he was her sister's new lover. She knew Jesse and she knew that if Michael *were* her lover, her sister wouldn't be able to hide it. In fact, she probably wouldn't even try.

Jesse came up to greet her as Amanda entered the house. She looked sexier than ever in a very short red silk dress that set off her dark hair and her creamy skin. Thankfully, she also looked sober, though Amanda always found it difficult to be sure about that.

"Have you met Paul Varney yet?" Jesse asked.

"No, I don't think so. Who is he?"

"A hunk. He's new in town—a management consultant with his own company. Come along and let me introduce you."

Amanda reluctantly let herself be led into the crowd. "Is Michael Quinn coming?"

Jesse nodded. "He said he'd be late." Then she stopped abruptly and stared at Amanda. "Don't tell me you're interested in *him?*"

"No," Amanda said quickly, not sure what to make of Jesse's obvious surprise. "It's just that I need to tell him something and I didn't try to contact him earlier because I thought he'd be here."

MICHAEL DIDN'T ARRIVE for nearly an hour, though it seemed much longer than that to her as she tried to politely brush off Jesse's latest find for her.

She knew she couldn't really blame Jesse for thinking that Paul Varney might appeal to her, but he didn't. He was attractive and intelligent and pleasant enough—except there was nothing there. And just what it was that was missing from him became abundantly clear to her when she caught sight of Michael as he greeted Jesse's husband, Steve.

She felt...*incandescent.* There was no other way to describe what happened to her when his gaze met hers. Paul Varney's voice became nothing more than a low drone in the background as every one of her gazillion nerve endings began to quiver with anticipation. It was embarrassing. It was scary. And it was exciting.

Then Jesse materialized out of the crowd and slipped her arm through Steve's as she, too, greeted Michael. Amanda watched them, seeking confirmation of her suspicions while hoping for a denial. She got neither.

"Excuse me," she told her companion, totally oblivious as to whether or not she was cutting him off in midsentence since she hadn't heard a word he'd said after Michael's arrival. "There's someone I need to see."

Michael had already started in her direction, and they met halfway across the large, crowded living room. His mouth curved in a wry grin.

"Short, blond and handsome over there doesn't look too happy," he said as he nodded toward Paul Varney.

"He probably isn't. He's Jesse's latest find for me."

He shook his head. "Is it just me, or is there something weird about a woman who can't seem to settle down to one man trying to find someone for her sister?"

She laughed. "It isn't just you. I've thought about that, too."

Michael frowned. "I wonder why she hasn't tried to push *us* together. Or has she, and I just don't know about it?"

"She hasn't. Maybe even Jesse can see just how unsuitable we are." She kept her tone light, but her mind was churning. Was he being honest—or merely clever?

She told him that she needed to speak to him privately, and they made their way through the crowd to the rear of the house, where there was a small TV room. Amanda was wishing that Michael were anything but a detective. She knew how devious he could be, how good he was at playing mind games. But was he doing that now with her?

Why don't you just ask him flat out? she wondered. *Is it because maybe you really don't want to know?* Jesse made a convenient shield between them.

"I had a strange phone call tonight," she said as he closed the door behind them. "It was just before I left to come here. I would have called you, but I guessed that you'd be here."

"What was the call about?" he asked, his voice shifting effortlessly to cop mode.

"It was a woman. She didn't identify herself and she was very hesitant. She said she was calling about the body on the island, and that she thought she knew who it was.

"I told her that she needed to speak to the police and gave her your name. Then she said, 'I know, but…' and stopped. And then she hung up.

"To be honest, there were some kids screaming in the background and that might be why she hung up, but it just felt…strange. I even thought that her voice sounded familiar, but I can't place it."

Michael nodded toward the phone. "Why don't you check your machine? If she had to hang up because of the kids, she might have called back."

"You're right. I hadn't thought of that." Amanda picked up the phone, punched out her number and then added the code when her recording came on. "Nothing," she told him as she replaced the receiver. "Or at least if she did call back, she didn't leave a message. What I don't understand is why she called *me* in the first place, instead of calling the police."

"Maybe you're right and it was someone who knows you."

"Yes, but in that case, why not identify herself? And why was she so hesitant? Besides, it couldn't be someone who knows me all that well or I would have recognized her voice. She had one of those little-girl voices—and a definite lisp, as well."

She sighed. "I suppose I should have encouraged her more, but she really should have been talking to *you*, not to *me*."

"Well, I guess we'll just have to see if she calls me. But if she should call you again, don't worry so much about stepping on my toes. I'll be glad for any help I can get at this point. We finally tracked down the last of the missing girls from that time, so I'm fresh out of possibilities."

"I understand that you spoke with my father," she said. He'd called her about it earlier. Though he hadn't come right out and said it, Amanda knew that he'd been angry that Michael could even suspect any of the families in this.

Michael grimaced. "I don't envy you, growing up with a father like that. But he *did* make one good point that I should have thought of myself. Given the time lapse between when you all agreed to allow the new place to be built and the beginning of the actual construction, if the killer was someone in one of the families, he'd have had plenty of opportunity to move the body."

Amanda nodded, not at all surprised to hear Michael admit to his mistakes. It was part and parcel of that incredible self-confidence he had that she alternately envied and hated.

"So now you've crossed us all off your list of possible suspects?" she asked with a smile.

"I guess so, but I still can't help thinking that there must be some connection between the body and the island. There are just too many other places she could have been buried—places that wouldn't have required a boat."

He was right. She knew that, but didn't want to admit it. "You know, we've never had any vandalism out there, but that doesn't necessarily mean that there haven't been any intruders. With only the one dock, it's easy enough for anyone from the mainland to see if someone's there. And given the girl's age, I wonder if it could have been some kids sneaking out there to party—and then something happened."

"Yeah, that's possible. I thought about that, too. The thing is, though, that they would most likely have left something behind. I talked to the caretaker. Mr. Thompson said he's been working for the families for nearly thirty years, and he's never seen any evidence of kids partying out there.''

He was silent for a moment, then held up a hand placatingly. ''Look, I know you don't want to talk about the accident again—or about any possible connection it could have to the murder. But think about this.

''If there *is* a connection, you could be in danger. The killer might start to worry that you could remember something. He left you both there for dead—except that you didn't die, which must have come as a shock to him. Then, when he found out that you didn't remember anything, he'd have begun to feel safe again—until the body was discovered.''

''Michael…''

''No! Hear me out! All I'm saying is that I think you should be careful—until I get him. Maybe I'm wrong. In fact, I hope I'm wrong. But in the meantime, I don't want to be worrying about you.''

Amanda was startled by the vehemence in his tone. Their eyes clashed as a silence grew between them, becoming heavier with each passing second.

''You don't have to worry about me,'' she said finally, tearing her gaze away from his. ''I can take care of myself— and there's nothing to worry about anyway.''

''You're wrong about that,'' he said in a softer voice.

It was that sudden change in his tone that told her they were talking at cross-purposes. She'd meant that there was nothing to worry about because there was no connection between her accident and the murder—but she knew that wasn't what *he* meant.

''We should get back to the party,'' she said, getting up and starting toward the door.

Michael had remained standing and now he put out a hand to grasp her arm lightly. She stopped as the heat from him and that powerful male presence coursed through her.

''I have something to say—and this time, you're going to listen. Sit down.''

She sat, not because she was obeying his order, but because she could sense that he was about as reluctant to speak as she was to listen. Whatever he was going to say, she was sure she couldn't want to hear it, but she was equally certain that she *should* hear it. Maybe then it could end.

"You're actually going to listen to me?" he asked, clearly surprised.

"I'm listening."

He ran a hand through his dark hair, confirming the nervousness she'd sensed beneath his order. She thought that if she weren't so nervous herself, she might actually be enjoying this.

"Okay, so here goes. This is how I see it. Part of it *did* have to do with what happened in court. And it wasn't just that you embarrassed me. It was also because I knew you were *enjoying* it."

She started to protest, but he put out a hand to stop her. "You said you'd listen—so listen. Maybe I *did* want to get back at you, but not that way. In fact, it makes me wonder just what kind of man you think I am, if you believe that.

"The simple truth is that I wanted you. I wanted you then—and I still do." He looked away from her, shaking his head slowly.

"You mess with my head, Amanda. I always felt like you were…unfinished business." He stopped abruptly, then ran his hand through his hair again. "Am I making any sense?"

"Maybe. Michael, are you having an affair with Jesse?"

His shocked expression gave her her answer even before he spoke. "What? Are you serious? Did *she* tell you that?"

"No. I just thought…"

"First of all, Steve's a good friend of mine. And second, the truth is that I find her kind of pathetic. She came on to me a couple of times, and then, when she didn't get the result she wanted, she apparently decided to look elsewhere."

Michael came over and leaned close to her, bracing his hands against the arms of the chair. Amanda drew back, but it wasn't nearly far enough. She'd never seen him this angry before, but he clearly was now.

"Dammit, I can't believe you'd think that of me! Or does this all have to do with what happened between *us?* You think that I go after every attractive woman who crosses my path? And why did you enjoy making a fool of me that day in court, then come to my bed that night? What's going on here, Amanda?"

She forced herself to meet his fiery gaze. "I had a big crush on you in high school, but you never even knew I existed. Maybe that day in court was my way of getting even. You're right—I *did* enjoy it."

"And?"

"And what?"

"And why did you come to my bed that night?"

"Because I wanted to." She knew now—too late—that she should never have let this discussion begin. Somehow, she'd managed to forget about his annoying persistence.

"You mess with my head, too, Michael."

"Even though you think I'm a scumbag who's having an affair with your sister?"

"I didn't really believe it."

"But she made a good shield to use against me—just in case you got the urge again."

"Maybe."

"Well, that shield's gone. So what happens now? Do we try our best to ignore each other until one of us can't take it anymore and shows up on the other's doorstep some night?"

"That won't happen," she said as he backed away. But she was far less certain than she sounded—and she knew he knew that.

WHEN THE PHONE RANG, Amanda had a sudden premonition about who it would be. It was much later than her previous call, and three days had passed—but somehow she knew.

"It's me again," said the soft, lisping voice. "I didn't

mean to hang up, but the kids were fighting. They're in bed now.''

''That's okay. I understand. You said that you thought you might know who the dead girl was.'' Amanda hadn't called the police in the interim. Michael had called her office and left a message just this afternoon.

''I'm…not sure, but it *could* be her. I mean, she always said that she was going to get out of here—go down to the city, you know. That's what everyone thought she did, but I think she would have told me. Said goodbye, you know.''

Where had she heard that voice before? It was driving her crazy, but she was reluctant to ask any questions at all, lest the woman hang up again. So she said nothing.

''Will they abe able to identify her, do you think?''

''No, I don't think so—not unless someone helps.''

''I told her that she was going to get herself in trouble, you know. But she always said that she was careful, that she didn't just go with *anyone*.''

Was she saying that the girl had been a prostitute? It sounded that way to Amanda, but she didn't want to ask, in case she was wrong.

''See, there was this woman we both knew, and she had this business, you know? She took the calls and then sent them out. She wanted me to do it, too, but I *couldn't*.''

Then she was silent for a long time as Amanda held her breath, wanting desperately to ask questions but fearing that anything she said would cause her to hang up again.

''I think maybe it would be best if they never find out who it is. I mean, it was partly her own fault, anyway.''

Amanda just couldn't take it any longer. ''But if she was your friend, don't you want to see her killer caught?''

''Yeah, I do, but… The thing is, you were real good to us. That's why I…''

Amanda was holding her breath again, and this time, she managed to curb her tongue. But a moment later, the woman hung up again.

She sank into a chair, then grabbed a pen and some paper

and began to write, not stopping until she had written down everything she could remember. It wasn't easy, given the disjointed nature of the conversation—or monologue, really.

When she had finished, she reviewed everything. There seemed to be no doubt that the girl she was talking about had been a prostitute. But why was the caller afraid to go to the police? Could it be that she feared the woman she'd mentioned, the one who "took the calls and then sent them out"?

The woman was obviously a madam, but it didn't seem likely that she'd still be in that business after twenty years. But that didn't mean that she wasn't still around and perhaps capable of causing trouble for the caller. Maybe she'd gotten respectable and wouldn't want her name dragged into a scandal.

Amanda looked at her notes and her gaze stopped at the last few lines. The caller had confirmed that she did in fact know her—but how?

She sat there for a long time, thinking about it. Finally, she decided that it was most likely that the caller knew her from her days as a public defender. She'd had far more contact with families then. Since she came to the D.A.'s office, contacts with families of both victims and sometimes defendants were handled mostly by the victim-witness advocate.

She had to find out who the caller was and why she was so afraid. But she'd handled literally hundreds of cases as a public defender. Maybe thousands, now that she thought about it.

She reached for the phone to call Michael, then pulled her hand back again. It was late, and she thought about his statement that one of them would show up on the other's doorstep some night.

It could wait until tomorrow. Maybe she'd have a sudden burst of inspiration before then and remember where she'd heard that voice.

Chapter Four

"So you think she was involved in one of your P.D. cases?" Michael asked as he finished reading the "transcript" of her call.

Amanda nodded. "I'm assuming she isn't the one who was in trouble, but rather that it was someone close to her—father, brother, boyfriend, son. Well, I guess it couldn't have been a son. She doesn't sound old enough to have a kid in trouble."

Michael shrugged. "I think we can safely say that she's about the same age as the victim—and she'd be thirty-seven or thirty-eight by now. So, yeah, she *could* have a kid old enough to have gotten into trouble—even four or five years ago."

Her disbelieving and then shocked expression amused him. Michael didn't doubt that she tried hard to understand the people she dealt with—both here and at her previous job as a public defender—but it just didn't always work. In her world, women didn't have babies at fifteen or even at twenty.

"Yes, you're right," she said finally. "But remember, I heard kids' voices at the time of the first call—and they were young."

"There was a family in my building when I was growing up who had a total of twelve kids. The first batch was taken from them for neglect and abuse, so they just had a second litter. The age range went from one to twenty-three, as I recall.''

She stared at him, but Michael couldn't really be sure what she was thinking. He never was, when he was talking about his past. Maybe that was why he kept doing it.

"Michael, how…?"

She stopped abruptly and shifted her gaze briefly away from his. He had no idea what she intended to ask, but when she spoke again, her tone was all business.

"I spoke to Jeff Green this morning." Green was the chief public defender. "I really had no idea how many cases I might have handled when I was working there. His best guesstimate is at least a thousand, perhaps as many as fifteen hundred. And there's no way to sort them out by computer. They can sort for client names and for type of crime and a few other things, but not for the attorney who handled them."

"So the only way for you to find her would be to go through all their records to find your cases, and then check them all and see if any bells ring."

She nodded. "Or I can hope that she'll call again. Maybe she will."

He got up and walked over to the windows. Michael was always restless, she'd noticed, but never more so than when he was sitting across that big desk from her.

"Well, she's given us *something,* anyway. Apparently no one reported the victim missing because everybody thought she'd gone down to the city. And she was apparently a hooker—a *teenage* hooker. I think Sam Hadley, who heads up vice now, was already on the force twenty years ago, and working in vice even then. I'll talk to him."

"You won't have to wait long. I have an appointment with him in just a few minutes. He has a case he wants to discuss."

Michael nodded. "What do you make of those last statements of hers?" He returned to the desk and picked up the typed transcript, then quoted from it.

"'The thing is, you were real good to us. That's why I...'"

"I'm not sure I know what you mean. As I said, she obviously believes I did her, or them, some favor."

"Right. But what about what she started to say after that?"

Amanda frowned. "I assume she meant to say, 'That's why I called you, instead of the police.'"

Michael wasn't so sure. If it was the reason she gave, then why did the woman hang up again? Something didn't feel right to him, but before he could pursue it, Amanda's secretary rang to say that Lieutenant Hadley had arrived.

"HUMPH! Twenty years ago, huh?" Lieutenant Hadley shook his gray head. "Sometimes I can't remember what happened last week—and you're asking me about twenty years ago?"

"Yeah, right," Michael said with a grin. "I've heard your stories, Hadley. Either you're making them all up, or your memory's just fine."

"Could be a bit of both," Hadley responded with a twinkle in his eyes. "Okay, let's see. There *was* something going on back then that could be what you're looking for. The only trouble is that I don't think you're going to find any records, because to the best of my recollection, no arrests were ever made."

"So tell us what you remember," Michael urged.

"I was new to vice then, but some of the older guys had gotten word somewhere that there was a teenage-hooker ring operating through a woman in Parkside."

"Parkside?" Amanda echoed in shock. "But that's always been a middle-class neighborhood."

"Yeah, I know," Hadley said. "But the story was that this woman was catering to a middle-class clientele, with the girls and with coke. Remember, in the midseventies, coke was big with the upwardly mobile. Or maybe you *don't* remember, since you were just a kid then."

"You're sure there were no arrests, either for prostitution or for drugs?" Michael asked.

"Pretty sure. I can remember one of the guys saying that it wasn't likely because of the type of clientele she had. The department wasn't exactly squeaky-clean back then, you know."

He shrugged. "There's a couple of retired guys I can check with, and I'll have our clerk go back through the records. But I'm not sure we'll come up with anything."

"IS THERE ANYTHING new on the skeleton from the island?" Lise Verhoeven asked after she set aside her menu.

"Not really," Amanda answered. Lise already knew about the two phone calls she'd received. "We thought we might turn up something from old vice-squad records, but it didn't pan out. And the retired detectives Lieutenant Hadley contacted didn't remember any more than he did about that teenage-prostitution and drug ring."

They ordered dinner, then continued to sip wine. Lise had come up from the city for the weekend because there was a party scheduled for her grandmother's eightieth birthday.

"Father is really upset about it," Lise said, shaking her head. "I never knew him to be so...territorial about the island."

"Well, it *did* happen practically in his front yard," Amanda argued, thinking that she would probably be more upset than she already was if they'd unearthed a skeleton in her own yard.

The truth was that the case was beginning to fade a bit for her. The anonymous caller had never phoned back. Michael didn't appear to be getting anywhere in his investigation. And when she'd gone out to the island for the day last weekend, construction had resumed on the new cottage.

In addition to that, she had several important cases on her hands, one of her assistants had just handed in his resignation and she had a campaign to plan.

In short, twenty-year-old skeletons just weren't high on her list of priorities right now, and she was sure the same could be said for Michael, though she knew him too well to believe that he'd given up.

Lise started to say something, then stopped and stared at something behind Amanda. A moment later, she was shaking her head and rolling her eyes.

"I guess I should be very grateful that I'm not living here any longer," she said with a smile.

"What do you mean?" Amanda asked, casting a quick glance behind her, but not turning all the way around.

"Two words—Michael Quinn. He just came in with some woman. I can't believe how well I remembered him—and how little he's changed, except that he dresses a lot better."

Michael with a woman? Now she *had* to turn around, even if she was being a masochist. Fortunately, Michael had his head turned toward their server and didn't see her staring.

She only got a quick look at the woman with him, but Amanda was nevertheless surprised. Not only did the woman appear to be older than Michael, but she was also very plain—bordering on ugly, in fact. Definitely not the sort she'd seen him with in the past.

"I never told you that I had a thing for him, did I?" Lise asked, still smiling. "Of course, nothing ever happened."

"I did, too," Amanda admitted. "Probably every girl in school had a crush on him."

"What's he like?"

Amanda sighed. "That's a lot harder to answer than you might think. In some ways, he's just what you probably expect him to be—brash, aggressive, too…male. But he's also very bright and…well, sometimes, there's a gentler side to him."

Lise had cocked her head to one side, frowning. "Uh-oh. You haven't gotten over that crush, have you?"

"Maybe not," Amanda admitted. "But I'm not going to do anything about it, either."

Lise was too old and too close a friend not to recognize that end-of-discussion tone, so they talked of other things over dinner: Lise's recent promotion, which would entail considerable travel, Amanda's reluctant campaign for district attorney and, of course, Jesse. Lise had always been caught between them, since she was exactly midway between them in age. Jesse resented Lise's closeness to Amanda, but Amanda welcomed Lise's friendship with Jesse, which she privately called "sharing the burden."

"So you still don't know what's going on with her, either?" Lise asked, after describing her last phone call from Jesse.

"No. She's been calling me nearly every day, but all she wants to talk about is her business and the body from the island." Amanda sighed.

"That's always been her pattern with me. She calls constantly when she's in trouble, but she finds something else to talk about. And no matter how carefully I try to bring up the real problem, she just gets defensive and hangs up."

"Mmm. She *does* seem to be obsessing about the body. She's brought it up with me, too." Lise paused, frowning thoughtfully. "Is it possible that she could know something about it?"

Amanda gave her a startled look. "How? What do you mean? She was away at school when it happened—if the forensics people are right, that is."

"No, she wasn't—remember? If it happened around the time of the accident, she was home. She had mono and missed that semester."

"Oh." Amanda realized immediately that Lise was right. "But even if she was home, how could she know anything?"

"Look, we both know she was sneaking out at night to party, even though she was supposed to be resting. That's why it took her so long to recover. And she didn't always hang around with the best people, either. That's when she started to use drugs.

Lise shrugged. "I'll admit that it's pure speculation on my part. I never heard anything about her and her friends partying on the island, but she was definitely hanging around with a bad crowd that spring.''

"I don't think they were going to the island, though. Mr. Thompson said he'd never found evidence of kids partying out there. He told Michael that, too.''

"So maybe Jesse was just being very careful.''

Amanda doubted that, but she couldn't quite dismiss the possibility that Jesse might know *something*. She certainly wasn't going to tell Michael about it, but perhaps she'd better find a way to talk to Jesse.

As luck would have it, Michael and his date were leaving the restaurant at the same time as Amanda and Lise. Amanda could not avoid acknowledging his presence, which then prompted introductions. It turned out that Michael's date was the person he'd recently hired to run his software company: an old classmate and a former neighbor.

When he explained who she was, Amanda saw the wicked gleam in Michael's dark eyes, and knew that she hadn't managed to be as casual about his presence there as she'd thought. And just for good measure, he managed to throw in a comment about the woman's husband and children.

It was one of those times when Amanda could all too easily imagine herself becoming violent where Michael was concerned. She knew he was taunting her, letting her know that he knew she'd been jealous.

She wanted only to escape, but Lise seemed all too willing to stand there and chat with Michael and his date, so it was a long five minutes before the group broke up.

"Would you care to revise your earlier statement that there's nothing going on between you two?'' Lise said as soon as they were in Amanda's car.

"I don't know what you mean,'' Amanda said, though of course she did. Maybe their colleagues didn't notice the tension between them, but Amanda wasn't surprised that Lise had picked up on it.

Lise laughed. "Okay, I won't pry. I'll just sit here and envy you.''

AMANDA DROPPED LISE OFF at her grandmother's house, then drove home feeling guilty. They'd always been so close, and yet she couldn't seem to bring herself to talk to Lise about Michael. Maybe, she thought with a sigh, it was because she just didn't know what to say. When Michael had said that she "messed with his head" and she had replied in kind, she, at least, had spoken the truth.

And perhaps Michael had, as well. She didn't know. Certainly he seemed to be able to handle it better than she was. And despite that threat he'd made, he hadn't shown up on her doorstep yet.

He had parked in a visitors' space, and she was so lost in her thoughts that she failed to notice the Porsche until she got out of her car and he called her name. She turned, her breath catching in her throat.

He walked over to her, then stood there, his hands jammed into his pockets, watching her but saying nothing. The silence went on too long, and she felt compelled to end it.

"Would you like to come in?" she asked, then immediately began to worry that he'd read more into the invitation than she'd intended. Or at least more than she'd consciously intended. Desire was already whispering through her, drowning out everything else in the process.

He followed her inside, and she offered him a drink. He asked for coffee instead, saying that he still had to make his rounds in the Bottom.

She glanced at him, wondering if that remark had been made to reassure her. But he was wearing his bland cop face, so she couldn't be sure, which was generally the case where he was concerned.

They talked of inconsequential things while the coffee brewed, strings of words punctuated with heavy silences that were driving her crazy but seemed not to bother him.

When the coffee was ready, she suggested they sit in the living room, which seemed to her to be far less intimate than the kitchen. He seated himself on one end of the sofa, but instead of taking the other end, she sat down in a chair, putting more space between them. A smile tugged at his wide mouth, but he said nothing.

"Michael, the silent treatment probably works well on your suspects, but it annoys me. Why are you here?"

He let the silence go on for another long moment, during which she forced herself to meet his gaze. She knew that he wouldn't suddenly jump up from the sofa and sweep her into his arms and carry her upstairs, but it still *felt* like he might do that.

"I finally got around to going over to talk to Butch today," he said after a time.

It took Amanda a moment to realize he was referring to the man who ran the marina at Mann's Landing on the far side of the lake. Michael had said that Butch knew everything there was to know about the lake and its visitors.

"He said he's been doing a lot of thinking and he seems to recall that John Verhoeven—Lise's father—was spending some time out there then, during the winter and spring, when no one else was there. But he wasn't really sure about the years, just that it was around that time."

Amanda frowned in thought, having some difficulty switching gears. She was also aware of a certain disappointment, even though she'd just been swearing to herself that nothing was going to happen.

After thinking about it for a few minutes, she realized that Lise's parents had split up the winter following her accident. So if the forensics people were right, their marriage might well have been in trouble at that time.

Then she recalled, with a sudden chill, Lise's mentioning that her father seemed almost obsessed with the body.

She told Michael the first part of it, suggesting that he might well have gone out there to escape for a time from a marriage going bad. She did not mention his interest in the investigation.

"What do you know of their problems?" Michael asked. "Is it possible that he could have gotten involved with someone and was taking her out there?"

Amanda shook her head quickly. "I suppose he might have found someone else, though I never heard anything like that. But he'd never have gotten involved with…" she hesitated, about to say *a prostitute*, but fearful of sounding elitist.

"A hooker?" Michael shook his head and chuckled. "Sometimes you amaze me. Who do you think are the customers? The poor can't afford to pay for sex, Amanda. Maybe you should ride along with me down to Maple Street and see all the Beemers and Mercs and Lexuses. They don't all belong to drug dealers."

"You don't know John Verhoeven," Amanda said, ignoring his taunt. "He's about as likely to do something like that as *my* father is. As far as his marriage goes, all I can remember is what I overheard my parents saying. Sara, Lise's mother, was always…fragile. Emotionally, I mean. Even as a child, I knew there was something not quite right about her.

"Lise never blamed her father for the breakup. She said that he'd tried for years to get her mother some help, but she always refused. After they split up, Lise's grandmother stepped in and her mother was sent away to a private psychiatric facility for a year. It was obviously what she needed. When she came back, she was much better."

"That sounds to me like a damn good reason why he might have been looking for some emotional support elsewhere," Michael said.

"I suppose that's possible, but I'm sure it wouldn't have been a teenage prostitute."

"I'm going to have to talk to him—in person this time. I know he lives in the city, but is he up here for the party Lise mentioned?"

"Yes. He's staying at the family home—Lise's grandmother's place."

Michael finished his coffee and stood up. "Look, I'm trying to take it easy on these people. But this *is* a murder investigation, and like it or not, they're going to have to answer questions."

She stood, as well. "I know that—and I want you to find out who killed that girl. But I know you're wrong to be looking at the families on the island."

She followed him to the door, where he stopped. "If it weren't for *you*, I'd be looking at them a hell of a lot harder, you know."

She heard his words, but what really struck her was his tone: the softness and gentleness that was so at odds with his normal voice.

She could think of nothing to say to that, and her gaze slid away from his. They were standing close together: *too* close. She felt—or imagined that she felt—the heat of him reaching out to her.

Then it was his hand reaching out to cup her chin and draw her face up to his. She made a small sound, and her lips parted to blend with his in a kiss that was all she remembered: soft, persuasive, filled with a subtle promise.

He was the one who withdrew, leaving her lost in a world of sensations that drained away very slowly as he reached for the doorknob. Her hands went back to grasp the edge of a table in the foyer. For a moment, neither of them moved, and Amanda had the crazy thought that each of them was clinging to something to avoid being swept into a maelstrom created by their own passions.

"It's still there," he said in a husky tone. "Someday, we're both going to have to face up to that."

And then he was gone, once again leaving the echo of his words to torment her.

"TALK ABOUT looking for needles in haystacks." Jeff Green shook his graying head. His longish ponytail shifted about.

Amanda pushed back from the computer keyboard and took off her glasses. "I know. And the worst part of all is that I could easily see the name and it won't mean anything. Already, I'm finding that I don't remember a lot of them, unless they've been repeats or particularly serious crimes."

"Well, I'm calling it a day—or night, actually. Just turn off the lights and lock up when you leave."

"I will—and thanks, Jeff, for letting me work on this."

He chuckled. "You owe me one—and you know I'll be there someday to collect."

She heard the outer door close, and then she was alone in the public defender's warren of offices, thinking about her foolishness in being here in the first place.

It hadn't taken her long to realize how many of her former clients she'd forgotten, despite the fact that she'd been a conscientious defender of their rights.

She was at the keyboard for hours, until her eyes began to glaze over and she realized that she wasn't likely to recognize her own name, let alone the name of a defendant with a lisping relative.

The cases were all there, but the system wouldn't permit her to select only her own cases—or even just cases that had come in during her time in the office. Instead, they were alphabetized by last name, with nothing more than a summary of charges and the disposition of the case. In three hours, she'd gotten through the *A*s and partway through the *B*s. It was hopeless.

It also made her aware of the inequities in a supposedly fair judicial system. In the D.A.'s office, their retrieval system was far more sophisticated, allowing for retrieval by date or by type of crime—or by prosecutor. The pay was much better and the caseloads were lighter, too. She decided that if she won the election, she was going to join with Jeff to demand more funding for the public defender, which would probably cause heart attacks among her law-and-order political colleagues.

She left the office and drove home, her mind still on the evening's work. Given her job and the necessity to plan her campaign, it could be a month or more before she'd be able to get through all of her old P.D. cases.

It was a waste of time, and she knew she was foolish to

be pursuing it. But after beginning to recede from her mind, that twenty-year-old murder was back to haunt her.

First of all, there was that enigmatic phone call—or rather, Michael's reaction to it when she'd given him her notes. She knew that something about that last line was troubling him. She'd seen it in his expression just before her secretary announced Sam Hadley's arrival. But when he'd said nothing more, she hadn't raised the issue again.

What she *had* done was reread the transcript—and then she'd seen what the problem was. The caller had said, "The thing is, you were real good to us. That's why I..."

Amanda had assumed that what the caller had meant was that she'd chosen to call Amanda rather than the police because she knew her and was grateful to her. But after several rereadings, another meaning was suggesting itself to her: one that sent a chill through her even as she thought about it now. And it was that second meaning, she was sure, that had troubled Michael.

What if the caller's *real* meaning was that she had contacted Amanda rather than the police because what she knew could cause problems for Amanda?

Still, it would have been easy for Amanda to dismiss that possibility if it weren't for several other factors. First of all, there was Jesse's continued interest in the case, now looming larger because Lise had reminded her that Jesse was home then and running around with a wild crowd.

And now there was Michael's suspicion that John Verhoeven, Lise's father, knew something. Michael had interviewed him this past weekend, while he was up from the city for his mother's party. John had readily admitted to having spent time out at the island that winter and spring, but he'd insisted that he'd always gone alone and that he'd never seen anyone else out there.

Michael had told her afterward that his antennae were twitching, that he was pretty sure John had been lying about *something*. Under normal circumstances, Amanda would be inclined to trust his instincts, which were already legendary around police headquarters. But this time, she wasn't so sure. Despite his protestations to the contrary, Amanda suspected that Michael would be delighted to nail someone in one of the families for the murder.

For her own part, Amanda conceded privately that John *could* be lying. Given his marital troubles at the time, it was certainly possible that he'd taken someone out there. But that someone could not have been a teenager—and certainly not a teenage hooker. Maybe Michael thought her naive, and maybe he was even right about that some of the time, but not about this. If John Verhoeven was lying, it was out of embarrassment or to protect the identity of his female companion.

She was nearly home when it suddenly occurred to her that perhaps there was a way for her to find out if she was right about John Verhoeven. John and her father were best friends, and had been all their lives. If John had been having an affair prior to his divorce, her father would likely have known about it.

She picked up her car phone and called her father, then turned around and drove up to the Hill. She let herself in with her own key and then went to the large, handsome study her father kept at one rear corner of the huge house.

Judge Thomas Sturdevant looked up over the rims of his glasses as she walked in, then slid some papers into a folder and stuffed them into the briefcase next to his leather chair. Amanda sat down on the cordovan leather sofa that faced his desk, and he leaned back in his chair.

"I believe I could use a cognac about now," he said. "Will you have some?"

She got up. "I'll get it and I'll have some sherry myself."

She walked over to the wall and pressed a button that opened a mahogany panel, behind which there was a small bar setup. Then she poured him some cognac and poured herself a small glass of sherry, thinking about how much she loved this house and how much Jesse loved it, too, and how that certainly posed some serious problems for the future.

Her father knew that, as well, and his will left the house to them jointly. As he'd put it, they'd have to "sort it out" themselves. Fortunately, that day didn't seem likely to arrive soon.

When she had given him his cognac and then seated herself again, he asked her about her campaign plans, and she was forced to confess that beyond naming a manager and a treasurer, she hadn't yet done anything.

"I hate campaigning," she said with a grimace.

"So do I, but it's necessary. I'd managed to forget just how much I hate it until recently."

She smiled sympathetically, knowing he was referring to his necessarily quiet but still intense campaigning for the Supreme Court. She asked what he thought his chances were.

"I think they're quite good, actually. One candidate has already taken himself out of the running, and another may be out as a result of some financial questions. I've been told—just today, as a matter of fact—that I'm the leading candidate if the vacancy occurs."

"Father, that's *wonderful!*" Amanda exclaimed.

He smiled. "Let's not get too excited. For all I know, the same person who told me that might be telling several others the same thing. But it *did* come from the White House—off the record, of course."

They talked some more about campaigning, and Amanda could not help feeling both proud and happy with her father's encouragement and praise—something she'd certainly seen little of during her childhood, when it seemed that all his attention had been focused on Jesse.

Finally, she got around to asking her question, after telling him about Michael's interview with John Verhoeven.

"Michael's very good, Father. I know he's brash and aggressive, but he's already practically a legend. So if he says that John wasn't telling him the truth, I have to consider the possibility that he could be right."

"It seems more likely to me that it's wishful thinking on Lieutenant Quinn's part. He'd like to pin that poor girl's death on one of us because he hates us. Class envy can be a powerful thing."

"I agree, and Michael himself has all but admitted that. But I still think it's possible that John could be lying, though not for the reason Michael believes."

She went on to tell him her theory, but her father was already shaking his head even before she finished.

"You're wrong, Amanda. There were no other women in John's life until after his divorce. In fact, it was nearly a year after that before he met Melinda. He *was* going out to the island that winter and spring, but he went alone. I offered to go with him once, but he said he wanted to be alone, so I respected that."

He grimaced. "Quinn may have convinced himself that John is lying, but he isn't. Don't forget, Quinn interviewed me, as well, and his prejudices were very obvious."

Amanda thought about telling him about the phone calls, but decided against it. She did however, mention Jesse's interest in the case. But her father quickly dismissed that.

"You know how she is, Mandy. She's always had this tendency to become obsessive at times. How could she possibly know anything relevant to the murder?"

Amanda told him Lise's theory: that Jesse might have gone out there with some of her wild friends.

"I suppose that's possible," he admitted. "But I seriously doubt it. Mr. Thompson never found any evidence that kids were going out there."

"ARE YOU READY to order yet?" the young server asked with what Amanda thought was a trace of impatience.

She glanced at her watch again, then at the small crowd around the bar, obviously waiting for tables. "Yes. I'm afraid I've been stood up."

As soon as she had given him her order, Amanda took her cellular phone out of her purse and hit the automatic redial. After four rings, Jesse's voice came on, asking her to leave a message. Since she'd already done that, Amanda hung up, then punched out her own number, followed by the code that allowed her to pick up messages. There were none. She hadn't really expected any, since Jesse also had the number for her cellular phone.

Her sister was now nearly an hour late for their dinner date, and while this wasn't unusual, Jesse had at least called to make her excuses in the past. Amanda unfortunately thought she knew, not where Jesse was, but what she was doing, which was drinking.

Guilt washed over her as she wondered if her insistence that they meet and talk had precipitated a bout of drinking. But then she remembered the family-counseling sessions they'd gone through when Jesse was struggling to overcome her addiction. Alcoholics and other addicts were always very good at pushing the blame for their behavior onto other people—and family members in particular were all too willing to blame themselves.

Amanda had set an early dinner date, in part because that would give Jesse less time to start drinking after she closed her shop, and in part because she had intended to go from the restaurant to the P.D.'s office to continue her search of her old cases.

She had foolishly hoped to accomplish two things: to talk to Jesse about her drinking and urge her to get back into therapy, and to find out if in fact Jesse *did* know anything about the body found on the island. But in thinking about it now, she realized that it wasn't likely she could have accomplished either thing, let alone both of them.

Her dinner came quickly and she ate just as quickly, all the while trying to decide what to do when she left here. It would be difficult, perhaps impossible, to focus on those records while she was worried about Jesse's whereabouts. But she had no idea where her sister might have gone, either. Steve, her husband, might have been able to guess, but he was out of town and she had no way of reaching him.

After refusing dessert and requesting her check, Amanda decided to check Jesse's home one more time. But there was still no answer, except for the machine. So she left the restaurant, still uncertain about what to do. Should she simply drive around, checking out the parking lots of all the upscale drinking spots?

She sighed, knowing from past experience that Jesse could be *anywhere*—even down in the Bottom, if she got drunk enough first. There was a recklessness to Jesse even when she was sober, and it got even worse when she'd been drinking.

Briefly, she thought about Michael. The truth was that she didn't want to have to go into a bar alone—especially since she knew Jesse would probably make a scene. Without letting herself think too much about the possible consequences of enlisting his assistance, she picked up her car phone and called him at home. He wasn't there, and she didn't bother leaving a message. For all she knew, she might even run into him down there contacting his informants.

Before setting off to the Bottom, Amanda decided to try her home machine one more time. Jesse knew that number by heart, so if she called drunk, she would be more likely to use it than the mobile number.

She waited impatiently through her own message, then suddenly heard her sister's voice. "Mandy, I need help. I want to get out of here and I shouldn't be driving. I'm out at Lakeview."

Amanda replaced the phone and pulled out of the parking lot. Jesse's voice had sounded normal, except for a certain edge of impatience, which Amanda had heard before when she'd been drinking. But that meant little, she knew from past experience. Jesse could be falling-down drunk and still sound normal.

She knew where the Lakeview was, and she also knew that it was only marginally better than the bars down in the Bottom. It was an old roadhouse that catered to heavy drinkers. There'd been several shootings there in the recent past.

She thought about calling Michael again, but decided against it. Somehow, involving him in this seemed wrong, even though he knew about Jesse's drinking. She didn't want to become dependent on Michael for *anything*. It was too risky.

A half hour later, she pulled into the crowded parking lot at the Lakeview. Even with her windows closed, she could hear the blare of music, and before she could get out of her car, two men came staggering out. Fortunately, they staggered off in the opposite direction.

She was halfway across the lot, praying that Jesse wouldn't create a scene since she'd actually called for help, when she suddenly spotted a familiar car: Michael's Porsche. What was he doing here? Had Jesse called him when she couldn't reach her?

Amanda hated herself for feeling relieved. She didn't want to rely on Michael, but she was very glad he was here. Was there anything about her relationship with him that wasn't conflicted? she wondered as she pushed open the door.

Chapter Five

Heads turned as Amanda stepped into the packed bar, and only then did it occur to her that she should have gone home to change first. She was still dressed in her work clothes: a conservative gray suit. Her picture had been in the newspaper recently, accompanying the announcement of her candidacy.

Trying to ignore the blaring music and the stares, she scanned the crowd, but didn't see either Jesse or Michael. There were booths toward the back, and she couldn't see into them. As she stood there hesitantly, she felt a rush of hatred toward her sister for dragging her into this.

Then, just as she was about to plunge into the noisy, drunken crowd, she saw them emerge from a hallway that probably led to the rest rooms. Michael had his arm around Jesse's waist, attempting to steer her past the edge of the dance floor. Jesse wore her I'm-totally-wasted-but-trying-to-act-sober face. Michael's face was unreadable. She hated her sister even more for having brought Michael into this.

It seemed to take forever for them to reach her, and when they did, Jesse gave her a surprised look, then asked what she was doing here.

"You left a message on my machine," Amanda told her, though she doubted that Jesse remembered that. "We had a dinner date," she added for good measure.

"Oh." Jesse tried to look apologetic, but it didn't quite

work. Then she snuggled against Michael. "Well, I don't need your help now. Michael's here."

THE EXPRESSION on Amanda's face made Michael wish that he were anywhere but here. She even refused to meet his eyes as they left the bar. Would she have preferred that he stay out of it—leave Jesse to an uncertain fate?

As soon as they were outside, Jesse pulled away from him and started to stagger toward his car. Amanda caught up with her and took her arm none too gently. He wondered who she was madder at: her drunken sister or him?

"Let me go!" Jesse cried, trying to extricate herself from Amanda's grip and nearly falling down in the process. "I want to go with Michael! I don't want to talk to you!"

"I'll take her home," Michael said as he began to steer Jesse toward his car.

Amanda followed them silently, and as soon as she had gotten Jesse into the car, he turned to her. "She called me and I figured I'd better come get her before she got herself into trouble. Why don't you follow us? I'm going to need your help when we get her home."

She still wouldn't meet his eyes, but she nodded and stalked off across the lot. He waited until he saw that she was safely in her car, then slid into the Porsche. She followed him out of the lot.

"She doesn't understand," Jesse whined as they drove back toward town.

"What doesn't she understand?" Michael asked, mostly to humor her. Conversations with drunks weren't high on his list of favorite pastimes.

"I won't tell her," Jesse said insistently. "I've never told *anyone!*"

Michael glanced over at her briefly. Tears were running down her cheeks, ruining her makeup. For some reason, he thought about that photo he'd seen at their cottage on the island. Jesse was still beautiful, he supposed, but he wondered if she knew that her ugly-duckling little sister had long since surpassed her. In his opinion, anyway, but then, he wasn't exactly objective where Amanda was concerned.

He glanced into the rearview mirror, wondering if he was going to pay the price for this, instead of Jesse. Probably. She knew damn well that he'd had no choice but to come get Jesse, but that wouldn't make any difference.

"I didn't believe it, you know," Jesse said, still sobbing. "I still can't believe he did it."

"Did what?" Michael asked, curious now, even though he didn't expect a rational answer.

"Nothing!" Jesse said suddenly, with a surprising vehemence. "Don't start grilling me, Michael!"

"Why would I be grilling you, Jess?"

"You're a cop, that's why. But I'm not going to help you."

She folded her arms across her chest like a petulant child and didn't say another word the rest of the way. Michael wondered what she was talking about, but after a few minutes decided that whatever it was, it probably made perfect sense to her—and no sense at all to anyone else.

By the time he pulled into her driveway, Jesse was asleep and snoring loudly. Amanda pulled in behind him and came up to him as he was trying to get the semiconscious Jesse out of the car. Together, they half carried and half dragged her to the front door, where Amanda dug through Jesse's purse and found her keys.

Jesse came to briefly when Amanda turned on a light. She blinked at her surroundings, then called out for Steve. Amanda told her that he was out of town, and she stared balefully at her sister.

"I won't tell you! I know that's what you want!"

Michael saw Amanda frown at her, then glance quickly at him—almost, he thought, as though she feared what her sister might be about to say.

"Come on, Jesse. Let's get you to bed," Amanda said briskly, taking Jesse's arm and starting toward the stairs.

In the end, he had to carry Jesse up the stairs. She was

snoring again by the time he dropped her on the bed, and he left it to Amanda to get her undressed and covered.

As he waited downstairs, Michael kept thinking about that quick, nervous glance Amanda had given him. What was she worried about? Michael doubted there was anything Jesse could have said that he didn't already know. Steve had been more or less crying on his shoulder for the past couple of weeks. Hell, he probably knew more about their problems than Amanda herself did.

AMANDA CLOSED the bedroom door, then leaned against it for a moment to compose herself. It was too much to hope for that Michael might have gone. He would be waiting for her downstairs.

She went into the bathroom to gain a few moments' time. Given Jesse's condition, it was impossible to be sure what she'd meant by that remark about not telling her. But it was also impossible for Amanda not to fear that Jesse did indeed know something about the murder on the island. And if so, she might very well have guessed that Amanda had intended to ask her about it.

But what if she'd said something to Michael on the way home? She knew Michael well enough to know that *anything* could make him suspicious. Cops were like that. Well, if she did, she'd just have to dismiss it as drunken rambling.

Amanda stared at her reflection in the mirror. Was she really prepared to thwart a murder investigation to protect her sister? She might not have to answer that yet, but she knew it could come to that.

She went downstairs to find Michael pacing restlessly around the living room. "I'm sorry you had to get involved in this, Michael," she told him, then explained that she'd planned to meet Jesse for dinner and that Jesse had subsequently left a message for her on her machine at home, saying where she was and asking Amanda to come get her.

"She must have decided to call me when she couldn't reach you," Michael said. "You're not angry with me for going to get her, are you? I didn't want to let her stay in a dive like that."

Amanda shook her head, touched by his concern that she would be angry with him. Which she was, of course, even though she had no right to be.

"What was she talking about?" Michael asked. "What didn't she want to tell you? She said something like that on the way home."

Amanda shrugged. "Who knows? The only thing I intended to talk to her about was her drinking."

Michael was silent for a moment. She had to force herself to meet his gaze. It was so difficult to lie to him.

"She said, 'I don't believe it. I still can't believe he did it.' Then, when I asked her what she was talking about, she told me to stop grilling her, and that she wasn't going to help me."

"I have no idea what she was talking about—and neither will she, when she sobers up."

Once again, he was silent as his dark eyes bored into her, and once again, Amanda met his gaze with difficulty. But if he didn't believe her, he apparently had decided not to say so. Instead, he suggested that they'd better go back and get Jesse's car.

"Leaving a Beemer out there is like dangling candy in front of a kid. It won't last the night."

Amanda hadn't thought of that, but she realized he was right. So she followed him out to his car. Michael was silent for a few minutes, but she could almost feel him brooding. Then he asked her how old Jesse was when her trouble with drugs and alcohol began.

Amanda sighed, grateful for the change of subject. "The first I knew about it was when I was fourteen—and she was nineteen. But it might well have started before that. We weren't all that close and we each had our own friends.

"I found out about it the summer after her freshman year in college, but Lise Verhoeven says that Jesse was sneaking out of the house that spring, when she was home with a case of mono.''

Then, when she heard her words, she realized that she hadn't gotten away from the subject, after all. But would Michael make the connection between that spring and the murder?

''Hmm,'' he said thoughtfully. ''That would have been the spring you had the accident—right?''

''Yes.''

''Where was she sneaking out to?''

''I don't know. I wasn't paying much attention to her—or to anything, then.''

''I keep running that conversation through my head—about how she wasn't going to help me. Is it possible that she was going out to the island herself—and she knows something?''

Amanda tried to ignore the cold, hard lump that was forming in her stomach. ''I doubt that. Jesse never liked the island all that much—or at least not since we were little.''

''Still, it wouldn't hurt to ask her when she sobers up.''

''Leave her alone, Michael! She has enough to deal with right now, and I'm sure she doesn't know anything. If she did, she would have told me.''

''But she said she wasn't going to tell you.''

''You're really determined to involve my family in this, aren't you?'' she demanded coldly.

''I'm determined to solve the murder,'' he replied calmly. ''And my gut's telling me that both John Verhoeven and now Jesse might know something.''

''I talked to my father about John. They've always been best friends. He said that John always went out there alone. He wanted to get away to think. And Father also said that John wasn't having an affair with anyone.''

''With all due respect, Amanda, your father wouldn't admit it even if he *did* know something.''

''How dare you say that? He's a *judge,* for heaven's sake! He wouldn't lie to protect anyone!''

Michael turned to her briefly. "And you're a district attorney and you wouldn't lie, either."

"And you're a cop with a vendetta against my family—and the others. It isn't our fault that you grew up the way you did, Michael."

Neither of them said any more, but the air was filled with a tension that she knew he felt as strongly as she did. When he pulled into the parking lot of the Lakeview, she reached for the door quickly, but he grasped her arm and turned her to face him.

"You know what's *really* going on here, don't you? This isn't about the murder. It's about *us.*"

She started to protest, then stopped. He was wrong, but not completely wrong. "It's late, Michael, and I'm tired. Believe it or not, it's...hard for me to see Jesse like that."

His hand slid down her arm and covered her hand instead. "I know that. Look, could we try to spend some time together without our jobs getting in the way? I was thinking about dinner on Saturday."

It was his voice that did it—even more than the dark eyes that seemed to be devouring her. His voice now was like his kisses: soft and persuasive. But still she protested.

"It's not a good idea for us to be seen together, Michael. You know that."

"Then we'll go somewhere else for dinner."

She was wondering why she'd said it the way she had. What she *should* have said was that it wasn't a good idea for them to date, period. But she was already nodding her agreement as she thought it.

AMANDA PULLED UP to the closed double-garage doors and glanced at the dashboard clock. She had exactly one hour to try to get the truth out of Jesse before she had to meet with her campaign committee. That meant she might have to push her sister harder than she'd prefer, but she couldn't afford to have Michael get to Jesse before she did.

That Michael intended to follow up on Jesse's drunken

ravings of last night, Amanda didn't doubt at all. But she didn't think he could have gotten to her yet. She'd called Jesse's shop, and her assistant said that Jesse had been there all day, but had left early, saying she had a headache. Amanda certainly didn't doubt that.

Besides, she knew that Michael had been in court most of the day, testifying in a case she'd allowed to be pleaded down from first- to second-degree murder—to his noisily voiced disgust.

She got out of the car and peered through the windows in the garage door. Jesse's car was in there. She breathed a sigh of relief. At least that meant she hadn't decided to go out drinking again.

She rang the doorbell, and was about to reach for it again when Jesse answered with a big smile on her face that faded the moment she saw Amanda there. Whom had she been expecting: her lover? Or perhaps Michael?

Jesse's expression had turned sullen, but she stood back to let Amanda in. "All right, so I'm sorry about last night. If you've come to lecture me, you can leave now. I already called Dr. Hollings. I'll be seeing her tomorrow."

Dr. Lynne Hollings was the long-suffering psychologist who had pulled Jesse through her other crises. Amanda considered it a good sign that Jesse had called the psychologist on her own.

"Michael called me this morning," Jesse went on, talking over her shoulder as she walked back the hallway toward the big country kitchen. "For a man who doesn't have any children, he can certainly do a good imitation of a father."

"What do you mean?" Amanda asked.

"He's a nag, that's what. 'Jesse, you've got to get hold of yourself....Jesse, if you don't get some help, I'm not going to get you out of trouble again. You'll end up in jail.'"

"'Jail'?" Amanda echoed, not certain what she meant.

Jesse turned to her. "So he *didn't* tell you. He said that he hadn't, but I didn't believe him." She shrugged.

"I bought some coke at the Lakeview last night. Michael found it in my purse and got rid of it."

Amanda was stunned—and her expression must have shown that, although Jesse misinterpreted the reason for her shock.

"I didn't use it. I don't know why I bought it. In fact, I didn't even remember buying it until Michael told me he'd found it." She hesitated, and when she spoke again, her voice had changed. "That's why I called Dr. Hollings. I don't want to go through that again."

Amanda reached out to take her sister's hand. "I'm glad, Jesse—glad that you're going to get some help."

Jesse pulled her hand away. "There's just too much going on right now."

"You mean with Steve?"

"Steve—and other things."

"What other things?"

Jesse stared at her for a moment, then turned away and picked up the teakettle to fill it. "Nothing."

"Jess, you said some things last night—to Michael and to me. Something about not wanting to tell me and about not believing someone had done something." Amanda hesitated, then plunged into it. "Were you talking about the murder on the island? Do you know something about it?"

Jesse's back was to her as she put the kettle on the stove, so Amanda couldn't see her face. But she saw Jesse's shoulders hunch briefly, almost as though she were absorbing a blow. However, when Jesse turned to face her, her expression gave nothing away.

"How would I know anything about that?"

"I don't know, but I thought that might be what you meant. Were you going out there that spring?"

"No. I don't know anything about that body. Anyway, you said that they couldn't be sure it was *that* spring."

"That's true, but Michael seems to think it was. He's even suggested that my accident could be tied into the murder somehow."

Jesse's reaction was not what Amanda had expected. She saw no shock in her sister's eyes, but rather a wariness, quickly covered as she turned to get some tea bags from the cupboard.

"What makes him think that?"

"Oh, you know Michael. He suffers from terminal suspiciousness. That's part of what makes him such a good cop, but it's also annoying. He seems to think that Trish might have been running away from the killer, and that's why we crashed."

"That sounds pretty far-fetched," Jesse replied, now turning back to her.

"I agree, but I just wanted to warn you that he's probably going to be asking you some questions."

"Let him ask. There's nothing I can tell him."

THREE HOURS LATER, following her meeting with the campaign committee, Amanda's thoughts turned back to her conversation with Jesse. She was still shocked at Michael's action. What he'd done had to have been against all his instincts as a cop. But had he gotten rid of the drugs because of his friendship with Steve—or because of *her?* Part of her wanted to ask him, but another part didn't want to know.

And then there was Jesse's denial that she knew anything about the murder. Amanda wished that she had Michael's built-in lie detector. She just wasn't sure whether or not Jesse knew anything. It felt to her as though Jesse had been telling the truth when she said that she'd never gone out to the island that spring, but she wasn't so sure about the rest of the conversation.

"HEY, MICHAEL! Long time, no see. You'd think we weren't working in the same department."

"Yeah, it *has* been a long time, Carla. You're lookin' good."

"Save the blarney, Michael. I'm a married lady now."

The barmaid arrived with Michael's beer, and he asked Carla if she wanted another one. She shook her head, and the barmaid vanished. Michael studied his old friend and former neighbor. Carla *did* look good. Marriage—and maybe age—had softened her. She almost didn't look like a cop anymore.

"So how do you like the community-relations thing?" he asked.

"I like it a lot. I feel like I'm really in my element, you know? Every time I go down to the Bottom to the youth center, I see myself all over the place, and it makes me work that much harder."

Michael chuckled. "Did you ever think we'd both end up becoming cops?"

Carla laughed, too. "Not me, but I always kind of thought you would."

"Yeah?" Michael was intrigued.

Carla nodded. "I know you got into some trouble, but you must have broken up more trouble than you got into."

Michael frowned, thinking. "Maybe you're right. I guess I'd forgotten about that."

They reminisced for a while before Michael finally got down to business. "Carla, I need some information about Jesse Sturdevant. You were in her class, weren't you?"

"In a manner of speaking," Carla replied dryly, bringing a smile to Michael's face at his unintentional double entendre.

"I know that Jesse got into some trouble at some point—drugs, running with a bad crowd. Can you tell me anything about that?"

"Not directly. I wasn't part of either of her scenes, but I knew some of the kids she was hanging around with."

"Do you know if they ever went out to the island to party?"

Carla frowned. "I don't think so. If they had, I'm sure I would have heard about it somewhere. Why? Does this have something to do with that body you found out there?"

Michael nodded. "Did you ever hear anything about a ring of teenage hookers back then?"

"Yeah, I remember hearing rumors, but that was all. I never knew who they were. You're not saying that Jesse—"

"No, I don't think Jesse could have been mixed up with that, but there's some indication that the body we found might have been one of them. Can you point me to anyone who might know?"

Carla shook her head. "I lost touch with most of my classmates long ago—or at least with the ones who might know something. But let me think about it. Maybe I can come up with someone."

She frowned. "It sounds like you've got what they call a delicate situation there, Michael, what with Jesse's sister being the D.A."

"Tell me about it."

"I like Amanda—a lot better than I ever liked Jesse. I don't really remember her all that well from school, but we've served on a couple of panels together since she became acting D.A. She's a lot more down-to-earth than she looks."

Michael smiled. "Sometimes."

"DOWN TO EARTH" WAS NOT exactly the way Michael would have described the woman who sat across from him at the small, candlelit table. She'd piled her hair up, with a few wisps curling around her face. And the power suits had given way to a softly patterned silk dress that brought out the green in her eyes.

Still, it felt weird to be out on a date with Amanda, even though he was glad he'd suggested it—and still kind of surprised that she'd accepted.

He guessed that they *had* gotten off on the wrong foot, even though he couldn't bring himself to regret that night. And he wondered if it were possible for them to start over—or even to change direction now.

He'd brought her to an elegant old inn an hour and a half's drive from Port Henry, and in addition to making dinner reservations, he'd also reserved a room upstairs—just in case. But he was already pretty sure he wouldn't be needing that. She was trying hard to be easy with him, but it wasn't working.

"Okay," he said after their entrées had appeared. "What's bothering you? I haven't seen anyone I know."

Amanda didn't bother to hide a smile. *This* was the Michael she knew—not the man who'd been making polite conversation for the past couple of hours. Not that he was bad at that; in fact, she was surprised at the breadth and depth of his knowledge on a couple of subjects that proved he had interests beyond being a cop. But it had all felt false to her.

"It isn't that," she said. "I haven't seen anyone, either." She hesitated, then decided to tell him what was on her mind.

"Jesse told me that you found the coke she'd bought at the Lakeview—and that you got rid of it."

He nodded. "I suppose I should have guessed that's what it was. Look, that place is always filled with narcs, and I don't know who all of them are. She could even have made her buy from one of them, for all I knew. She swore to me that she hadn't been using again, and I believe her."

"Still, it must have been difficult for you to do something like that, and I want to thank you for it."

"You're welcome. Did she go to see her shrink like she told me she was going to?"

"Yes. I talked to her briefly today, and she said that she'd kept her appointment."

"But you still don't like my getting involved with your family, do you?" he asked, studying her closely.

"I'm...not comfortable with it, but in this case, I appreciate it. When I got Jesse's message that evening, I even thought about calling you for help."

"But you didn't."

"No."

"Didn't it occur to you that you shouldn't be in a place like that any more than she should?"

"Yes, I thought about that."

"Amanda, what is it that I'm not hearing here?"

"I don't know. I really don't. There aren't any easy answers where you're concerned, Michael."

He nodded. "You're right about that."

Amanda wanted nothing more than to escape from this dinner date from hell. Why had she ever agreed to it? Furthermore, it was now clear to her that Michael felt exactly as she did.

Well, she reflected, *perhaps one good thing has come from this. Maybe now we both know that anything beyond a professional relationship is impossible for us.*

But then, as they waited beneath the porte cochere for Michael's car to be brought around, a couple arrived and hurried past them as the valet took luggage from the trunk of their car. Amanda had all but forgotten that the place really was an inn, and that the rooms were supposed to be lavishly romantic.

She allowed herself to drift for a moment in a sea of fantasies before Michael's car arrived and the fantasies were dashed against the hard rocks of reality. It could never work for them. She knew that—and so did he.

HEADS SWIVELED in her direction as Amanda made her way through the truck stop toward her brother-in-law, who had managed to get a booth in the rear. They had agreed to meet here for lunch because it wasn't likely that they would be recognized. The restaurant served almost exclusively as a rest stop for long-distance truckers from the nearby interstate.

Steve, ever the southern gentleman, rose as she approached the booth, but his smile of greeting was tinged with sadness and she thought he looked tired. Briefly, she wondered what it was about him that had kept her from making the commitment he'd so clearly wanted when they'd dated nearly four years ago. Whatever it was, she had dithered until he'd lost interest and then turned to Jesse.

Was it Michael? she wondered, even though he'd been nothing more than a peripheral figure in her life then—and a memory. Had she unconsciously been making comparisons and finding Steve lacking? She hadn't considered that possibility at the time, but now…

The waitress appeared, and Amanda barely skimmed the menu before ordering. Steve ordered, as well, and after the waitress had departed, they both sat there uncomfortably, neither of them quite willing to initiate the discussion even though they both knew why they were here.

"Do you know what I realized while I was sitting here thinking about her?" Steve said, finally breaking the silence. "I know it's going to sound crazy, but I just realized that ever since I've known her, she's started to drink again at this time of year."

Amanda just stared at him as a chill slithered through her.

"I'm sure about it," Steve went on, "because of other things that were happening at that time. Last spring, for example, I was in the midst of expanding the business. And the spring before was when my partner decided to leave."

"Perhaps it was because you were preoccupied and not giving Jesse the attention she needs," Amanda suggested, trying not to sound desperate.

"I suppose that's possible, but I don't think so. Even when I've been really busy, I've always been careful to keep my work and my personal life separate. Besides, she started to drink before those things happened. I just meant that that's how I knew about the time of year."

"I hadn't known about those other times," Amanda confessed. "In fact, I thought she hadn't had a drink in years—since before she met you."

Steve shook his head. "It didn't get bad before and it didn't last very long."

Amanda was silent for a moment. She hadn't known quite how to approach this, but in light of what Steve was saying, the matter was clearly becoming more urgent.

"There could be a reason why she gets upset at this time of year, and if I'm right, it would explain why it's worse this time. I think she knows something about that murder that happened on the island.''

Steve's blue eyes widened. ''What? Are you sure?''

''I'm not sure about *anything,* Steve. But it's possible.''

She went on to tell him about Jesse's drunken remarks to her and to Michael, then told him, as well, about Jesse's behavior at the time of her accident, which might or might not have been the very spring that the murder had occurred.

When she had finished, Steve frowned. ''That's a real stretch, Amanda.''

''I know, but it would explain why she seems to have problems at this time of year—and why it's so bad this year. Steve, she's seemed almost obsessed with that murder, and she's never been interested in such things before.

''Besides, I thought of something else, too. After the accident, when I was still recovering and feeling so frustrated that I couldn't remember anything, Jesse kept suggesting that I should be hypnotized, even though the psychologist didn't think it was a good idea. In fact, she kept at it to the point where I went myself years later to a hypnotherapist. But there were no memories to be recovered.

''I thought at the time that she was just trying to help me and to help clear Trish's name, but now I can't help wondering if she had another reason.''

''You can't think *she* had anything to do with it?'' Steve asked incredulously.

''Her personally? No, of course not. But as I told you, she was running with a wild crowd that spring, and someone she knew might have said something.''

Then she went on to tell him about the phone calls she'd received and the possibility that the dead girl might have been a teenage prostitute, part of a ring that existed at that time.

''What I'm thinking is that Jesse might have heard something—some scraps of information that bothered her at the time, but that she might not have understood until the body was found.''

"But if you're right, then that doesn't explain why she gets like this every year," Steve protested. "She would have had to be more directly involved than that."

"You're right," Amanda admitted. "I hadn't thought about that because I didn't know until you told me that this was happening every year."

"What does Michael think?" Steve asked.

"He suspects that Jesse knows something, but he has to be kept out of this, Steve—at least until I've got it sorted out. I know he's your friend, but first, last and always, Michael's a cop—and a very persistent one. Besides, he'd like nothing better than to pin this on one of the families from the island."

"Why?" Steve frowned.

"Because he resents who we are, and he always has. I can't really blame him, given his own background, but the truth is that he just isn't very objective in this case."

"Neither are you," Steve said, though not unkindly. "And I think you might be overreacting, Amanda. Maybe Michael *did* feel that way when he was a kid, and maybe even a trace of that remains, but it wouldn't affect his judgment."

"Even if you're right, we have to keep him away from Jesse until I can figure out some way of finding out what she knows. Don't you see, Steve? If Jesse *does* know something, she doesn't want to talk about it. And if Michael pressures her, it will only make her worse."

Steve frowned for a moment, then nodded. "Okay, I see what you mean. I'll talk to him and see if I can get him to back off. But maybe Jesse really needs to talk about it. Maybe that's the only way she can get over whatever it is."

"You could be right," Amanda acknowledged. "But I know her well enough to know that the only way I'm going to be able to get her to talk is to confront her with irrefutable evidence that she *was* somehow involved. Then she'll talk because she'll have no choice."

"And you're going to try to get this evidence on your own?"

"I hope so."

AMANDA FOUND IT among the *J*s: *J* for Jacobs. She'd been ready to give up her study of the old records in the public defender's office. Even after reading the records of cases she'd handled, she still hadn't been able to recall more than a tiny fraction of them because there were so many and their stories were so depressingly familiar and most of them, in any event, were guilty as charged.

But when the name David Jacobs appeared on the screen, she had an immediate, startlingly clear recollection of him, and she wondered how she could have forgotten, even after nearly ten years.

He wasn't one of her very first clients, but his case had been assigned to her just at a time when she was beginning to despair of ever being able to defend someone who was actually innocent. And perhaps she was still smarting over Michael Quinn's tauntings on the Joseph Wilson case.

She had believed David when he'd told her that he wasn't responsible for sexually assaulting a twelve-year-old cousin. He was eighteen and clearly shaken by the charge, and he had come to see her with his mother and sister in tow.

The police clearly believed the victim, and at that time, the DNA evidence that would have cleared him hadn't been available. It was his family, more than the silent, terrified David, who had convinced her that the likely rapist was a seventeen-year-old known to them: a distant relative, as she recalled now.

Working with the family, Amanda had managed to come up with enough evidence against the other boy to get David cleared, and ultimately, the victim had admitted that she'd lied about the identity of her assailant because he'd threatened to kill her. It was he who had suggested she point the finger at David because of some dispute between them.

As she sat there in the quiet office, Amanda could clearly

remember the family's gratitude—and especially the gratitude of David's sister, Tina, who'd been in her early twenties
at the time and working as a waitress somewhere.

Tina Jacobs had been the mainstay of the family through
it all. David was a basket case, trying to survive in the county
prison because they couldn't raise bail. And the mother was
a pale, fragile woman badly beaten down by life.

But Tina was bright and bold and determined to save her
brother. Amanda remembered her clearly. She was tiny, with
a tangle of badly bleached curls and too much makeup and
a wardrobe that ran to very short skirts and very tight tops.
And she had a lisp that gave her little-girl voice an even
younger sound.

Amanda studied the record, but found no information
about Tina. At the time, she must have known where she
worked and where she lived, but that hadn't been relevant to
the case record.

How very strange that Tina should come back into her life,
she thought, recalling how the young woman had said over
and over how she wished she could do something for
Amanda. And she recalled, too, how she had actually liked
Tina. She'd admired her grit and determination and protec-
tiveness toward her younger brother.

She found a telephone directory, but there was no listing
for a Tina Jacobs. She hadn't really expected one. Obviously,
she'd married at some point. But there was no listing for
David or for their mother, either, although there were eight
Jacobses in the book.

She studied the addresses and was able to eliminate three
of them. It was too late to be making phone calls now, but
she jotted down the names and numbers of the remaining
five, then left the office, elated at the prospect of finally getting somewhere.

That elation faded quickly, though. She might be getting
somewhere, all right, but what exactly lay at the end of that
road? She had a sudden vision of herself hurtling through
darkness, and toward certain disaster.

Chapter Six

The address Amanda sought was a seven-story brick building, an ugly, squat-looking structure with no adornments except for the address etched into a concrete square over the sagging double doors. To the left of the entrance was a litter-strewn lot, where weeds grew up from the cracks in the pavement. A half-dozen old cars, at least two of them clearly incapable of movement, were parked haphazardly.

She drove slowly past the building, scanning the street for a parking space. A block farther along, she found a space in front of a small neighborhood convenience store. She parked, then reached over to grab her briefcase as she got out of the car.

She had struck out with the Jacobses listed in the directory. Either none of them were related to the family she sought, or they weren't about to admit it. So she had decided that her only hope of finding Tina Jacobs lay in talking with her former neighbors and hopefully finding one who remembered the family.

She entered the building and studied the old mailboxes, only a few of which had names on them. She had hoped to find a super, but none was identified through the mailboxes. She did, however, notice a door back behind the stairs, just past the elevator, and when she approached it, she could just make out the word Superintendent in the grime and graffiti. She pressed the doorbell and waited, then pressed it again when she got no response. It seemed to her that she could hear the noise of a TV beyond the door, but she couldn't be sure. It might be coming from elsewhere in the building.

Then, after pounding a few times with her fist and still getting no response, she returned to the lobby. The Jacobs family had lived on the fourth floor, so it seemed logical to start there.

Amanda began to climb the stairs. Michael grew up in a place like this, she thought—or perhaps an even worse place. How did he emerge from this unscathed? Well, the answer to that was that he *hadn't* emerged unscathed. If he had, she wouldn't be here because she would be able to trust him.

Or would she? Even if she didn't suspect Michael of wanting to pin the murder on one of the families on the Hill, she didn't think she would have told him she'd learned who her anonymous caller was. So what did that say about *her?* Wasn't she as much a victim of her own upbringing as he was? It wasn't a pleasant thought.

She reached the fourth floor and found 4D, the former address of Tina Jacobs's mother and brother. The bell didn't work, so she pounded on the door. Faint sounds reached her ears, but again, she couldn't be sure where they were coming from. Someone was listening to a rock station and someone was watching TV and somewhere a child was crying.

When she got no response to her second series of knocks, she moved to the apartment next door and pressed a bell that did work. By now, she was beginning to expect no response, so she was startled when the door opened a crack and someone peered out over a thick security chain.

"Hello," she said to the face she could barely see. "I'm trying to find someone who can help me locate the Jacobs family. They lived here in 4D some years ago."

The door slammed shut, then reopened as the safety chain was removed. A moon-faced woman of indeterminate age studied her in silence for a moment, her gaze traveling slowly over Amanda as though she were some alien creature who'd just stepped out of a flying saucer.

"Don't know them," the woman said. "How long ago'd they live here?"

"I'm not sure, but I know they were living here ten years ago."

"Try 4A. She's the only one I know who might have been living here then. But you'll have to pound hard and yell. She's hard of hearing."

Amanda barely managed to thank the woman before the door slammed shut again. She hurried down the hall to 4A and rang the bell, then began to pound on the door. After a few moments, it opened and there were *two* security chains in front of the wizened face that peered out at her.

Amanda repeated her statement, this time in a much louder voice. The door slammed shut, then opened after the chains were removed.

"You don't have to shout, young lady. I can hear you just fine."

Amanda blushed. "I'm sorry, but your neighbor said you had difficulty hearing."

The woman's expressive, dark eyes shifted briefly down the hall. "I just tell her that so she won't bother me. Come in, come in."

Amanda stepped in to what might have been another time. An ancient, faded Oriental rug covered most of the floor. A big, Chippendale-style sofa with faded cushions shared the small space with two equally faded wing-back chairs, their arms and backs covered with lacy antimacassars. Amanda actually surprised herself by remembering what they were called: one of those useless bits of trivia that had somehow stuck in her mind.

"Would you like a cup of tea, dear?" the woman asked, clearly eager to play hostess.

When Amanda said she would, the woman disappeared and Amanda could hear her clattering about in the kitchen. She glanced at her watch. She didn't want to stay too long, or it would be dark by the time she left. But despite her remark about not wanting to be bothered by her neighbor,

Amanda suspected that the woman was in no hurry to see her leave.

She returned with an elaborate and highly polished silver tea set and two china cups. Amanda was beginning to understand why she had two security chains on her door.

Her name was Estelle Johnson, and as it turned out, she'd lived in this apartment for nearly thirteen years. Her friends in the building were all gone now, but she planned to stay "until they drag me out feet first," as she put it.

She remembered the Jacobs family, and even remembered the false accusation against Amanda's former client, whom she described as a nice boy who would never have done such a thing. She remembered Tina, too, and said she was really a sweet girl beneath all that makeup and those flashy clothes.

Unfortunately, however, she had no idea where they might be now. She thought it had been at least eight years since they moved out and she recalled that Amanda's former client had gone into the military after graduation and that his mother had moved out of Port Henry—to somewhere in Pennsylvania, where she had a sister.

"It's really Tina that I'm trying to find," Amanda told her. "I have reason to think she's still here in Port Henry and I need her help with something. Can you think of anyone who might know where she is now?"

The woman frowned in thought. "No. I know she had a lot of friends, some of them nice and some not so nice. And she worked as a waitress somewhere. I remember seeing her in her uniform."

"Could you describe the uniform?" Amanda asked in desperation, thinking that if Tina worked for one of the national chains, she might be able to identify it from the uniform.

"Let's see. It wasn't exactly a uniform. Black pants and a white T-shirt with the name on it." She paused, and then her eyes brightened. "*Now* I remember. It was a Mexican place. She used to bring me those things, like Mexican sandwiches, you know?"

"Tacos," Amanda said, and the woman nodded.

Amanda thought she knew the restaurant. It wasn't a chain and she wasn't sure if it was still in business. It was in the heart of the Bottom. She'd gone there once to see a client, perhaps six or seven years ago—not long before she left the public defender's office.

Amanda spent another half hour at the woman's apartment, and when she reached the street, it was dusk. The street was deserted—except, that is, for a man sitting on the hood of her car.

Or was that her car? In the dim light, she couldn't be sure. She started in that direction, her hand fumbling through her purse for the can of Mace she always carried. She slid it out and then put it into the pocket of her jacket as she continued to walk toward her car, now certain that he was in fact sitting on it.

Then the doors to one of the apartment buildings burst open and two young men came running down the steps just as a car pulled up at the curb. They stopped when they saw her and she hurried past, ignoring their comments. But when she reached the corner, she glanced back and saw that there were now four of them following her.

Cold terror slithered along her spine. She was only a short distance from her car now, and the man who'd been sitting on it stood up, facing her. Behind her, the young men continued their taunts. Then, suddenly, one of them swore.

"See who that is? C'mon, let's get out of here."

Amanda turned around and saw the youths moving off onto a side street. Then she turned back and saw the reason for their sudden flight.

She was so happy to see him, but it was a very short-lived happiness. How was she going to explain her presence here?

"I was about to call in some reinforcements and start a door-to-door," Michael said, now leaning against her car door with his arms folded across his chest.

She said nothing as her mind spun, trying to find an explanation. Then, when it produced none, she went on the offensive.

"What are you doing here, Michael?"

"Waiting for you, obviously. I already called in to make sure that you hadn't reported your car stolen."

"I was just visiting someone." She winced, knowing how lame that sounded—not to mention unbelievable.

"Where's your car?" she asked, since she didn't see the Porsche anywhere around.

"I'm driving that," he replied, nodding toward a nondescript vehicle parked illegally in front of a fire hydrant. "Unlike you, I have enough sense not to bring my car down here."

"Unlike you, I don't have access to city vehicles," she replied, mimicking his dry tone.

"That's because you're not a detective. Still, that doesn't seem to have stopped you from playing one."

"I don't know what you're talking about," she said, digging her keys out of her pocketbook. Unfortunately, the cylinder of Mace fell out in the process and rolled against his shoe.

He reached down to pick it up, then dropped it into her purse. "That wouldn't have done you much good against all of them."

She heaved an exaggerated sigh. "Thank you, Michael, for being so fearsome that they ran away as soon as they saw you."

"You're welcome. Let's go get some dinner while you tell me what you found out."

"I don't have anything to tell you."

"Okay, we'll have dinner and I'll tell *you* what you're doing."

"I'm going home."

"Fine. I'll pick up some pizza and meet you there."

"I don't recall having invited you."

"A minor oversight on your part. See you in a half hour or so. You don't want anchovies, do you?"

She unlocked her car and got in, ignoring him until he

went to his car. He followed her for a few blocks, then turned off, but she knew he'd be a man of his word.

What story could she come up with that would satisfy him? It wasn't that she couldn't concoct *something*. The problem was that she doubted she could make it believable to *him*.

Furthermore, he was well within his rights to insist that she be honest with him. Otherwise, he could accuse her of impeding a murder investigation.

She wondered if he knew which building she'd visited. Perhaps not. It was probably too dark for him to have been able to see that distance clearly. Besides, it was a rather large building and surely he wouldn't go door-to-door in it, looking for whoever had talked to her. Or would he?

She had exchanged phone numbers with Estelle Johnson, and as soon as she got home, she called the woman.

"Mrs. Johnson, this is Amanda Sturdevant. I have a big favor to ask of you. It's possible that a man might be asking you if you spoke to me. He's a police lieutenant named Michael Quinn.

"I'd really appreciate it if you wouldn't tell him we talked. I realize that's asking a lot, but it's for a very good reason."

"Of course, dear. Mum's the word."

Amanda thanked her profusely and hung up feeling very guilty. It was one thing for her to lie to Michael, but quite another to be asking someone else to lie to a police officer. Had she stepped over the edge?

She tried to tell herself that she hadn't—at least not yet. After all, she wasn't really concealing information relevant to a crime. Michael already knew everything Tina Jacobs had told her during those calls. The only thing Amanda was hiding was her name.

But she still cringed inwardly, knowing she was splitting some very fine legal hairs. Armed with Tina's name, Michael was in a far better position to find her than she herself was.

The simple truth was that she *wanted* to trust Michael. She wanted him to help her get to the bottom of this. Or did she? Wasn't what she *really* wanted was for it all to go away? Or failing that, for the truth to be far away from her and her family and the Verhoevens?

The doorbell rang. She hurried downstairs and opened it. Michael strode past her toward the kitchen, trailing pizza fumes. She noted that they obviously preferred the same place.

Neither of them said anything as she got out plates and napkins and a beer for him and soda for her. When she stole a quick glance at him, he was wearing his inscrutable cop face. They sat down across from each other at the small kitchen table. He'd gotten everything but anchovies, which was what she liked, too.

"Did I give you enough time to come up with something you think I'll believe?" he asked in a pleasant conversational tone as he picked up a slice.

"If I recall correctly, *you* were going to tell *me* what I was doing down there."

"Well, in that case, let's start with what you *weren't* doing. You weren't visiting a sick friend or relative."

She said nothing, curious now about how close he could come to the truth, and still hoping for some last-minute inspiration that would sidetrack him.

"So, with that possibility eliminated, I considered the likelihood that you've taken on a second job selling Avon. But since the neighborhood you were in seems an unlikely place for that, I think I can eliminate that, too.

"That leaves one of two possibilities. Either your anonymous caller called again and identified herself, and you were visiting her, or you finally figured out who she is and you're trying to find her. My money, for what it's worth, is on the last."

"Why?"

"Elementary, my dear Watson. I happen to know that you've been spending some time going through the records at the P.D. office."

"How did you know that?" she asked, astonished.

"I *didn't* know—until now, that is. I was just guessing.

happened to be out in the plaza the other evening when I saw you drive into the garage. My office window faces the courthouse, and when I went back to it, I saw that there were no lights in your office, but there *was* a light on in the P.D.'s office."

"That's pretty thin evidence," she challenged. "I could have been in the law library. It doesn't have any windows facing the plaza. And I know from experience that people often work late in the P.D.'s office."

"True, but you just confirmed it. If I were you, I'd rethink any criminal career you might be planning. So who is she?"

"I'm not going to tell you—yet."

He arched a dark brow. "Do you know what 'obstruction of justice' means, Counselor?"

"I've heard the term somewhere. I haven't found her yet, so there's nothing to tell you."

"Maybe you should find a dictionary and look up the word *detective*. Finding people is what detectives do."

"She won't talk to you, Michael, but she might talk to *me*. Remember that I tried to get her to call you, but she didn't."

"Okay, then give me her name. I'll find her and you can talk to her first."

"No. First, I'll try to find her, and if I can't, then I'll tell you and you can try."

Michael was silent as he polished off his second slice of pizza. His dark eyes studied her thoughtfully. "You really believe that either Jesse or John Verhoeven is involved in this, don't you?"

"No, but *you* believe that."

"If I do, it's only because I'm following the same trail that you're following." He held up a hand and counted his points on his fingers.

"Number one, the body is discovered on the island in the Verhoevens' front yard. Number two, an anonymous caller— or a *formerly* anonymous caller—hints that she knows something about said body and she wants to tell *you*, not the police. Number three, Jesse also hints that she knows something, then clams up. And number four, it just so happens that John Verhoeven was known to be making regular trips to the island around the time of the murder, and his marriage was in trouble, making him a good candidate for an affair.

"Then there are all the other, extraneous things that might or might not mean anything—a ring of teenage prostitutes that could have included the dead girl, Jesse's drug problems around that time, your accident at the same time…. You think it's all connected, don't you?" he asked, his eyes flat, black obsidian as he gazed impassively at her. "If you didn't, you wouldn't be sneaking around, playing detective."

She said nothing as she got up to pour herself some more soda and get him another beer. But she knew it was only a temporary reprieve. His tone indicated that he intended to demand an answer.

She seated herself again and met his gaze. "I don't know if it's connected, but I do *not* believe that John Verhoeven—or anyone else in the families—was responsible for that girl's death."

"It's possible that it was accidental, you know," Michael said.

She frowned. "But you've already declared it to have been murder."

"Technically, that isn't true. I'm carrying it at the moment as a 'suspicious death,' because the medical examiner says that the blow to the back of the head, which was almost certainly the cause of death, could have happened in a fall or something like that.

"But she certainly didn't bury herself, so at the very least, we've got failure to report a death and a few other charges."

Amanda remained silent as she mulled over that information, wondering why she hadn't thought about that herself—and then wondering if that made it more or less likely that anyone in the families could have been involved. But Michael had obviously already considered that.

"To my way of thinking, if it *was* an accidental death, it makes it even more likely that someone from the island was involved and that it happened there. Someone suddenly found a dead body on his or her hands and didn't want to have to explain why the girl was on the island to begin with."

It made a terrible sense. Jesse on the island with her drugged-out friends. Or John Verhoeven with a teenage prostitute. Death by accident. Fear of exposure. A burial place safe for all time.

Jesse, she thought. Far more likely Jesse than John. But what should she do? Jesse was emotionally fragile at the moment.

Amanda had been staring down at a half-eaten slice of pizza, and when she looked up, it was to find a very different expression on Michael's face. Even as their eyes met, his expression hardened, but still, she saw that brief empathy, or sympathy.

She had no right to expect him to understand how she felt, and yet, she knew in that moment that he *did*. What had seemed to be such a great gulf between them narrowed, though she could not bring herself to believe it had gone away completely.

MICHAEL WAS HAVING a hard time with his eyes. No matter what he tried to do with them, they kept turning back to the V of skin exposed by Amanda's open-collared lacy shirt. The contrast between the shirt and the severely tailored suit was about as sexy as it got, as far as he was concerned.

He wondered if she'd chosen it because she knew she'd be seeing him today—or was that just his good old male ego puffing itself up for no cause? For all he knew, she did just what he himself did: reach sleepily into the closet and put on the first thing that came to hand.

Yeah, right, he thought. *Tell me that you didn't pay just a little more attention to what you wore today because you knew this meeting was scheduled. And tell me that you didn't find the time to get a haircut because you knew you'd be seeing her.*

And while you're at it, why don't you convince yourself

*that you decided to let her get away with keeping what could
be vital information from you because you're already jug-
gling too many cases and a twenty-year-old skeleton isn't a
top priority?*

The two detectives he'd brought with him so they could
give Amanda and her assistant a firsthand report on the progress of a case involving the robbery and assault of a local
doctor finished their presentations, and Michael was forced
to turn his attention back to where it belonged. But it wasn't
easy. The lacy shirt reminded him of the lacy lingerie she
was probably wearing beneath that suit, and that reminded
him of—

"Could they really be naive enough to believe that a doctor carries a veritable pharmacy of drugs with him?" Amanda
asked.

"Not naive, just dumb," Michael said. "We're talking
room-temperature IQs here. The other possibility is that they
had good reason to believe that he was carrying drugs that
would interest them."

"What do you mean?" she asked, frowning.

"I want a court order to look into his prescribing habits.
We've been hearing for some time that there's a local doctor
who's got a nice business going in painkillers and steroids.
It could be him."

"It sounds to me as though you're trying to turn a victim
into a suspect," Amanda stated.

They went around and around on that for a while before
she agreed to the court order. It did not escape Michael's
attention that the others present seemed to sense some un-
dercurrents between them. They couldn't even be in the same
room without the temperature going up and a certain amount
of ionization occurring, like a thunderstorm was somewhere
in the vicinity.

The meeting ended and the others filed out. Michael hung
back, after telling his men to go on without him. When he
turned back to Amanda, her eyes had gone wary. He was

close enough to see the pulse at her throat begin to flutter rapidly.

"Do you have anything for me yet?" he asked. It had been four days since he'd caught her playing detective.

"No. I haven't found her yet." She refused to look at him as she spoke.

After casting a quick look over his shoulder to be certain they were alone, Michael hooked a finger beneath her chin and drew her face up to meet his gaze. She reacted to his touch as though it burned. And maybe it did. In fact, he hoped it did. He hoped she wanted him as badly as he wanted her.

"Give it to me, Amanda. I'll find her."

She pulled away and shook her head. "Just give me a little more time, Michael. Please let me do this *my* way."

Their gazes met and held, and he finally nodded. As he left her office, it occurred to Michael that there was a real irony here. Others might think that *she* was the one whose judgment would be swayed by their relationship. But in fact, *he* was the one who was letting his good sense take an extended vacation.

AMANDA LINGERED over coffee as most of the others left the banquet tables and moved off toward the dance floor. Fortunately, it would appear to those she was trying to avoid that she was simply being deferential to her former boss, in whose honor this gala was being held.

Lewis Brogan, her predecessor as D.A., sat next to her at the head table, regaling everyone with tales of his ten years in that office. Amanda, who had only spoken to him a few times on the phone since his hospitalization and then sudden retirement, was shocked at how much he'd aged in a few months. Some people had suggested that he'd merely seized upon his illness to retire a few years early so he could spend more time golfing, but she knew now that they'd been wrong.

She both liked and respected Lewis, but she couldn't help being troubled by the comparisons being drawn between

them by the four hundred or so people here. Even this di-
minished version of Lewis Brogan was so much closer to
what people expected of a D.A. How many of them were
thinking about that, and then comparing her to her opponent
in the upcoming election?

Neal Hadden was one of the people she was trying to
avoid. He hadn't been seated at her table, which had probably
irritated him, but he'd already managed to stage a hearty
handshaking scene with her before dinner. How on earth had
she ever considered marrying him?

The other person she was trying to avoid was Michael. He
hadn't approached her at all and had favored her with nothing
more than a brief nod when their eyes met across the room.
But she knew that his patience must be running out—in fact,
probably would have run out already if he hadn't been over-
worked at the moment.

She'd gotten nowhere with her efforts to find Tina Jacobs.
It amazed her that someone could lose him- or herself in a
city this size. Furthermore, she was learning more than she
wanted to know about the temporariness of the restaurant
business: both the restaurants themselves and their employ-
ees. She'd tracked Tina to two places where she'd once
worked, but no one there now remembered her, and when
she'd asked about personnel records, she'd gotten some very
strange looks.

So it seemed that the only thing left to her was just what
Michael himself would be doing: checking every restaurant
in the area in the hope that she hadn't made an abrupt career
change.

Lewis Brogan and the others who remained at the table
finally began to drift off toward the dance floor or the smaller
tables set up along its edge. Amanda thought about leaving,
but decided that her early departure might be commented
upon. So she reluctantly began to make her way through the
crowd toward the table in the far corner where her father was
seated with the mayor and his wife and a few others.

How she wished that she could unburden herself to her

father! The closeness they'd found in recent years made her want that even more. But John Verhoeven was his best friend and Jesse was still his darling, even though he was well aware of her faults by now.

Besides, she was certain that her father would not approve of her withholding information from the police—even if she was doing it for a reason he would surely understand. His attitude would be to let the chips fall where they may, because he would be serenely confident that they couldn't possibly fall on anyone close to him.

Amanda envied him his serenity, his complete confidence that his world held no dark secrets. She watched him relaxing with his old friend the mayor, his handsome silvered head nodding, and it suddenly occurred to her that if her suspicions were true, it might put at risk his chance to be named to the Supreme Court.

She was stunned to realize that she hadn't considered that before. Perhaps she hadn't yet begun to realize that it could happen. After all, the nation's highest court had been his goal for years, probably all his life.

By rights, a scandal involving either his oldest and best friend or even his daughter shouldn't have any effect on his chances. But in the present highly charged atmosphere, she knew it was possible.

"Amanda! How about a dance for old times' sake—or for the sake of bipartisanship?"

Lost in her reverie, Amanda started nervously at the too-loud voice and the hand on her arm. She managed a polite smile, while quickly scanning the faces of those near enough to have heard. People were smiling at them, so she smiled back, hoping that it looked more natural than it felt to her.

"Of course, Neal. I'd be delighted."

She was, in fact, anything but as he circled her waist with his arm and led her out to the dance floor, where still more faces turned in their direction. In this crowd, there wasn't anyone who didn't know that they were political opponents—

and most of them probably also knew of her past relationship with Neal.

Neal was a very good dancer, smooth and agile. She, on the other hand, had never been particulary graceful, perhaps because the awkward teenager she'd once been still lurked within her on such occasions, reminding her of all those school dances where she'd towered over her partners.

"Has Lewis told you yet that he's going to remain neutral in the race?" Neal inquired with that half smile she'd once thought sexy.

Neal knew full well Brogan wanted Amanda to succeed him. "No. I haven't sought his endorsement," she responded with a smile of her own. "I wouldn't try to back him into a corner."

"Politics isn't a game for the fainthearted," Neal said.

"I think there's a difference between being considerate and being fainthearted, Neal."

He chuckled, drawing her closer. "Just what I would have expected you to say. There *is* an advantage to knowing your opponent intimately."

She managed to push away without seeming too obvious about it. Then she raised her eyes to meet his. "I hope you aren't planning to make our past an issue, Neal, because no one else will be interested in it, I can assure you."

"Oh, I don't plan to drag in the past, but it might enter the picture anyway. Have you got Michael Quinn on a short leash?"

She just stared at him, too stunned at hearing Michael's name to guess what he meant.

"I asked him earlier what progress there'd been on that body that was discovered on the island, and he reacted by telling me that it was none of my expletive-deleted business. He seemed just a bit too touchy about it."

"Maybe that's because it *is* none of your business," she replied, hiding her relief. Once she'd recovered from hearing him utter Michael's name, she'd feared that he'd somehow found out about them.

"I'm not so sure of that—not when the acting D.A. has a serious stake in the outcome of the investigation."

"Exactly what are you trying to say, Neal?" she asked, giving up any pretense of dancing as they moved toward the edge of the floor.

"From what I've heard, Lieutenant Quinn hasn't ruled out the possibility that one of the families is involved—and let's face it, you're related to them all."

"Well, if he hasn't ruled them out, then you have no cause for concern, have you? That means that I can't possibly have him on a 'short leash.' Besides, you don't know Michael Quinn very well if you think I could interfere in his investigation."

She almost held her breath, waiting for him to ask how well *she* knew Michael. But the question never came. Instead, he swept her back onto the dance floor, then thanked her elaborately when the music ended.

Amanda made her way to the ladies' room, hoping it would be empty. It was, and she closed the door, then leaned against it briefly, willing herself to calmness.

Had she ever really believed that they could conduct a civil campaign? Surely she'd known it would come to this—or to something like this. Neal hadn't gotten over her rejection of him. She knew that now. He would use whatever weapons came to hand.

She wondered if that remark about the families being under suspicion was based on anything other than conjecture on his part. Did it mean that he had a source in the police department?

She saw now that it was quite likely that he did. After all, he'd worked in the D.A.'s office for nearly four years—more than enough time to have built up a few close relationships with the police.

And it appeared that Michael had ruffled his feathers. Did that mean that Neal might at some point begin to wonder if anything was going on between them?

She thought about meetings she'd had with Michael, when

others had been present, both from the police department and from her own office. She'd been sure that the tension between them had been noticed by others. How long would it be before someone would make a remark, perhaps in total innocence, and it would reach Neal Hadden's ears?

She used the facilities, then left the rest room, determined to spend some time with her father and his friends, then leave as soon as possible. But just as she pushed open the door and stepped into the hallway, Michael Quinn pushed himself away from the wall opposite the door.

Chapter Seven

"Talk to me," Michael said when she simply stopped and stared at him.

"About what?" She should have guessed that her little scene with Neal hadn't escaped his attention. Even in a crowd of several hundred people, Michael would have noticed if she'd so much as tugged at an errant bra strap, let alone danced with her former lover and current opponent.

"Oh, about the weather, the orchestra, the lousy food," he replied blithely. "Or maybe even about the reason for that thundercloud that followed you out of there."

Had others noticed that? She'd thought she'd been concealing her feelings quite well.

"There's a smile you wear only when you wish that looks could kill," he went on. "But don't worry. No one else there is as observant as I am."

"I hope you're right. I'm afraid you've made an enemy of him, Michael—not a good thing if he becomes the D.A."

Michael shrugged. "If he does, I've only moved up the time frame. Besides, my money, for what it's worth, is on you."

"Thanks."

"So what did he say?"

"Nothing, really. He was just trying to imply that the discovery of a body on the island could pose problems for me. Michael, does he have a source in the police department?"

"Probably," he said with an obvious lack of concern. "There's not much either one of us can do about that."

"You know, I never considered until this evening how this could affect my father's chances of getting onto the Supreme Court."

Michael nodded, giving her the impression that even if *she* hadn't thought about it, *he* had. And he'd made it clear that he didn't like her father.

"All the more reason to get it resolved quickly," he stated. "Assuming, of course, that we're both wrong."

"You mean that *you're* wrong, and *I'm* right," she corrected. "You think that either Jesse or John Verhoeven was responsible in some way, while I know that they're not."

"Have you made any headway in your search?"

"Not yet, but I'm working on it."

"Yeah, I know, and I can save you some time. I've been to most of the restaurants you haven't made it to yet."

Amanda's eyes widened. "You've been *following* me?" she asked. "But how could you know who I'm looking for?"

"That's easy. I went in and asked right after you left."

"Michael, *please* don't do this! If you find her before I do, she may not even speak to *me*." Then she glared at him. "I can't believe that you're following me around like this!"

"As a matter of fact, neither can I. You know, there's a phrase that's used to describe guys like me."

"I don't want to hear what it is."

"But you know it. And it makes me wonder about myself—and about us."

"There *is* no 'us,' Michael," she said, but the huskiness in her voice belied her words.

"There is—and you know it. We want each other just as much now as we did then—maybe more, since we both know just how good it was."

The images tumbled through her mind, sending curls of heat all the way through her. She started to turn away, but he reached out and grasped her arm.

"There's more to it than just sex, Amanda. You know that,

don't you? If that's all it was, I wouldn't be letting you get away with keeping her name from me."

"I haven't kept her name from you," she argued, but her voice was even huskier. His words had had the effect of opening up a dark pit beneath her feet. As long as she could convince herself that the only thing between them was this sexual chemistry, she felt reasonably safe. But now...

"You *want* to think it's just sex, don't you," he taunted her softly. "Because you feel safe that way."

How did he know her this well? How had it happened? But then, didn't she think she knew him that well, too? Sometimes, anyway. At other times, he could seem to be a complete stranger to her.

He let go of her arm, and she missed the connection, the heat that traveled through him and into her.

"Is Jacobs her married name?" he asked.

"No. I don't know what that would be. I gave the people I talked to her description and said that her last name could be different."

"Yeah, I got her description from them, and the voice should have triggered their memories even if the name was different. But if she's married, she didn't get married here."

She sighed. Michael was always one step ahead. It figures he'd already checked the courthouse records for a marriage license.

He chuckled. "Looks to me like you'd better get elected. You sure don't have any career prospects as a criminal or as a detective."

She ignored his taunt. "She has children—young children."

"Right. So she *must* have a husband."

"I didn't say that. I was thinking about court-ordered support."

"I checked those records, too. For all we know, each kid has a different father and they all decided they didn't want to be daddies."

"Somehow, I doubt that. The girl I remember was very responsible."

"Well, you might as well tell me the rest of what you know, while you're at it."

So she did. "But I still want to be the first to approach her—if we find her, that is."

"Like I said, there are ugly names for guys like me, but okay."

"Michael, I…" She faltered, not certain how to say what she wanted to say—or didn't want to say—but *had* to say. "I really appreciate your…sensitivity in this matter."

He grinned. "Comes as a shock, doesn't it?"

Their gazes met and locked, and those memories threatened to sweep her away. She shook her head. "No, it doesn't."

Michael took a step away from her, then ran a hand through his hair. "Are we talking about love here, do you think?"

Amanda stopped breathing. Every word he'd spoken, except that one, faded to nothing. Her throat closed painfully, cutting off any attempt she might have made to respond to that.

"It's, uh, not something I've had any experience with, you know? I mean, there've been women—but… Why am I having to do all the talking here?"

"I think you're supposed to *know* if you're really in love." she murmured huskily.

"What if we're both too busy denying it to know it?" he challenged.

She was saved from having to respond to that by two women who suddenly appeared in the hallway—one of whom was a judge's wife she knew. They exchanged greetings, and the women both cast curious glances at the two of them before going on to the ladies' room.

"I need to get back there. Others might have noticed what you noticed."

Michael nodded. "I'm leaving. I have some rounds to make."

They parted without another word in the lobby of the country club. Before she returned to the party, Amanda cast a quick glance back at him, thinking that he'd seemed just as relieved as she was.

THE PHONE WAS RINGING when Amanda returned after church and then brunch with her father and Jesse. As she walked into her condo, Amanda's thoughts were on Jesse. She'd been withdrawn and obviously uncomfortable the whole time.

"It's Michael," he said unnecessarily as soon as she answered. "Are you free for a couple of hours?"

"Yes. Why? Have you found her?" Given her thoughts about Jesse, it was easy for her to assume that he was calling for that reason.

"I'll pick you up in a half hour."

She went upstairs and changed into slacks and a sweater. Had he found Tina Jacobs? Given his eagerness to escape last night, it seemed unlikely that he had anything else on his mind today.

She brushed her hair and stared at herself in the mirror, feeling a rush of heat as his words replayed in her mind. "No!" she cried aloud. She could not let it happen to them. She had her career to think of. She'd never be happy with him even if it weren't for her career.

But could she ever be happy *without* him?

The first inkling she had that his visit might not have anything to do with Tina Jacobs came when she opened the door and found him standing there in a sweater and jeans. He wouldn't be dressed like that if this were police business.

"Where are we going?" she asked as he backed the Porsche out of a visitor's parking space.

"It's not far."

"Michael! Have you found her?"

"No."

"Then where are we going?"

He slanted her a quick glance. "Calm down, Counselor. I'm not kidnapping you."

"I'm certainly relieved to hear that," she replied, wondering if it was her imagination, or was he actually as nervous as he seemed?

They drove through the city and out into the northern suburbs. Most of the recent growth had occurred in this area, and Amanda was surprised to see just how built-up it was. She never had occasion to come out this way.

She commented on the changes to Michael, but received only grunts in response, which further convinced her that he was nervous about something. And after he had made a series of turns through residential areas and it finally dawned on her where they must be going, she was dumbfounded. But because she thought she might be wrong, she said nothing.

The land became mostly wooded and hilly and the houses were bigger and farther apart, and then Michael slowed and turned into an unmarked driveway that led uphill through the woods.

Amanda knew she must be right, but she still wasn't prepared to see the house at the top of the hill. It was big and modern, with lots of glass and evidence of continuing construction, although from the outside, at least, it looked almost finished.

"This is your house," she said finally as he rolled to a stop next to a pile of construction materials.

"Uh-huh. I didn't know if you knew about it."

"Someone mentioned it to me. It's beautiful, Michael."

He studied her carefully. "Are you just being polite, or do you really like it? I mean, I kind of thought you might prefer the kind of house you grew up in."

She did—and she didn't. But right now, liking it wasn't really the issue—or was it? A flock of butterflies took up residence in her stomach.

"I *do* like modern houses," she told him. "It's just that I've never been in many of them."

She got out of the car and stared back down the driveway. From this spot, any view was blocked by the trees, but the house sat on still higher ground.

Michael got out, too. "I bought two lots, five acres each. I guess it was kind of extravagant, but I really wanted space."

He didn't face her as he spoke, but instead jammed his hands into his pockets and stared up at the house. Amanda wasn't an impulsive person and moreover, she'd grown up in a family that wasn't inclined toward demonstrations of affection. But before she quite realized what she was doing, she had slipped an arm around his waist.

"This is a dream come true, isn't it?" she asked.

He nodded and put one arm around her. "Yeah, it is. Come on. It's not finished inside, but you'll be able to get the idea anyway."

A walkway of used brick that matched the brick on part of the house itself led up to the front door. Michael gestured to it.

"Guess where this brick came from."

When she shook her head, he gave her a crooked grin. "An old tenement down in the Bottom. Ironic, huh? You can take the kid out of the Bottom, but…" he chuckled.

Amanda joined in his laughter, wondering if there'd ever been a time in her life when she'd been able to share so intimately in someone else's pleasure. Was that what love was all about?

The question hung there in her mind, overwhelming all other thoughts as Michael unlocked the door and ushered her inside with a broad, sweeping gesture.

The house was gorgeous: big, airy rooms with huge windows and skylights and exposed beams—and certainly no expense spared. Given what she'd heard about the cost of the new homes out here, Amanda decided that Michael had indeed struck it rich with his software company.

He kept up a running commentary as they walked from room to room, making it clear to her that he'd planned this place himself right down to the smallest detail. There was much work yet to be done, but he described each room as it would look when finished. Then, at one point, he stopped and shook his head.

"I guess I'm getting carried away."

"No, you're not," she assured him. "You're just being you. I've never known anyone like you, Michael. You're pursuing this the same way you pursue criminals—giving it everything you've got."

He nodded. "Yeah, I guess I am."

Then he bounded up a short staircase. "Come on. Wait till you see the view from the master bedroom."

Amanda followed him. From the outside, she'd noticed a small balcony off the top level, and now, as she stepped into the spacious room, she saw that it was here—and the view was even more breathtaking than she'd expected.

Michael opened the sliding doors, and they both stepped outside. Far below them lay the city and the river. Even a small portion of the lake was visible, though most of it was hidden by a hill, including the island itself.

"I didn't really know for sure that the view would be this great until the house was built," he said, leaning against the railing.

Amanda followed his gaze, staring at the area known as the Bottom, which bordered the river. From this distance, it didn't look so bad.

"How did you survive it, Michael?" she asked in a tone far more plaintive than she'd intended.

He turned back to her briefly, his arms braced against the railing. "I don't know," he said simply. "If I did, then maybe I'd be able to help some of the kids I work with."

"You mean the ones you arrest?" she asked, not certain that *was* what he meant.

He shook his head and turned back to the view. "I do some volunteer work at a community center down there. I've had more time since I hired someone to run the company."

"I didn't know that—about your volunteer work, that is."

He turned around to face her, folding his arms across his chest as he leaned against the railing. "Don't you think it's kind of weird that we know each other so well in some ways—and not at all in others?"

His words so closely mirrored her own thoughts that Amanda could do no more than nod her agreement as his dark eyes bored into her.

"There's some old saying about the course of true love never running smooth," he said, shaking his head. "But this is ridiculous!"

"Are we in love, Michael?"

"You tell me."

She took a deep, ragged breath . "I think we might be."

"Gee, that's encouraging," he replied with gentle sarcasm. "A typical lawyer. Never a straight answer."

"How can I give you a straight answer, with all the... obstacles in our way?"

"I'll tell you how. Forget about the damn 'obstacles' for a minute and think about *us*."

"That's not easy to do."

"I didn't say it was, but do it anyway."

She took another, even more ragged breath. "Okay. Yes, I think we *are* in love, but..."

He reached out and pressed a finger to her lips. "Stop right there. I know we've got problems. But we'll work through them."

He dropped his finger, and Amanda shifted her gaze once again to the view beyond the railing. Perhaps it was easy for him to believe any obstacle could be surmounted; after all, he'd done it.

She kept her eyes on the view, even though she felt his gaze touch her, reach into her. Her world was spinning. How did they manage to get to this point? Was the beginning of love there even nine years ago? Or did it go back even further than that—all the way back to a teenage crush? Was it possible that that naive girl had recognized even then the true value of this man?

And what, exactly, did he love about her? *That* was the question she couldn't ask, because she feared the answer. Was she still a challenge to him? Did that matter?

"You still think it's because of where we both came from, don't you?" he asked, interrupting her thoughts as though he'd heard them.

"Is it?"

He shrugged. "Maybe partly. But I can't change that, and neither can you. It's who we are."

Then he chuckled and reached out to take both her hands in his. "We're a good team. You think and I act. Sounds fine to me."

When she said nothing, he began to draw her slowly into his arms until she was pressed against him, feeling the heat of his body and the power of his desire.

"I didn't bring you out here just to show the house, you know," he murmured against her ear. "I know there's no bed yet, but there's a big quilt in the trunk of my car."

His low voice was teasing, and she responded in kind, even though her body was growing heavy with desire. "Were you a Boy Scout?"

He laughed, and the sound vibrated through her. "Only where you're concerned. I put it there this morning. I also reserved a room at the inn that night."

She drew back within the circle of his arms. "You did? I remember when we left the restaurant, there was a couple arriving with luggage and it reminded me that there were rooms."

"And…?" He arched one dark brow.

"And I thought about it. That night was a disaster."

He nodded. "Too planned. That's why I decided to do it differently this time."

She had to laugh. He seemed so serious. "You decided to make it more like the first time."

"Uh-huh. Will it work this time, too?"

"Yes," she said, not allowing herself to think about it. "I believe it will."

He leaned forward and kissed her: a quick, light touching of lips that was over almost before it began. Then he went back inside and she heard him running down the steps, as though he feared that she might change her mind before he could get the quilt.

Amanda remained on the balcony, watching as he ran out to the car and opened the trunk. She was still stunned by the suddenness of it all, even though a few moments ago, she'd been wondering if it had been there all along.

The images of that other time floated through her mind, and suddenly, she feared that the reality couldn't possibly match those memories. But when Michael reappeared in the doorway and their eyes met, she knew that this time would not only match it, but far surpass it.

And so it did. But there was also a difference. Despite their mutual hunger, despite the flames that were licking at them as they undressed before the half-finished fireplace in the master bedroom, there was no hurry.

Even the act of removing their clothing became a part of a slow, erotic dance as their eyes feasted on each other. The air was cool, but as she stripped off her clothing, her skin was heated by his dark, intense gaze. The quilt lay spread out between them, beckoning.

Time stretched out as they came together in a tangle of arms and legs. Michael had positioned the quilt to catch the warm rays of the sun, but they were generating their own heat as their bodies flowed together, fitting perfectly, just as they had nine years ago.

But unlike that time, there was no hesitation in her now, no attempt to preserve something of herself for herself. Michael Quinn had been her fantasy lover for years now. How could she deny him—or herself?

Their mouths tasted each other, and their hands traced each other's shape and texture: smooth skin, bristly hair, sensitive places that summoned soft cries and moans. Slow, lingering kisses. Languorous movements. And beneath it all, the drumbeat of passion that built inexorably toward a climax.

When at last it came, Amanda had lost all of herself, yielded up all that was her to him even as she welcomed him into her, body and soul.

"Fire and ice," Michael murmured as he stroked her slowly cooling body. "That's part of it, too."

She opened her eyes and stared at him, seeing his disheveled hair and noting the tiny crescent marks on his shoulders where her fingernails must have dug into his flesh. She felt faintly embarrassed at that, but it faded quickly.

"That doesn't sound like me," she said uncertainly, more to herself than to him. And yet, she knew that it *was* her— or at least it was her when she was with *him*.

"Not just now," he said, once again seeming to reach right into her thoughts. "It's there when you're in court, too."

"I hope not," she replied, shocked because she was always carefully controlled during her court appearances.

Michael laughed. "It's what makes you so good," he persisted. "That cool exterior, combined with just a hint of fire underneath it."

Amanda wondered if she was only now coming to know herself, thanks to him. She moved closer to him. "I do love you, Michael."

He kissed the top of her head. "I know. But it's still kind of nice to hear you say it."

But we still have problems, she reminded herself, unable even now to let go of reality.

Chapter Eight

From a big house on the Hill to an old school in the Bottom. Amanda started to frown at the image, then stopped, remembering that at least a hundred pairs of eyes were on her at the moment.

But the image lingered: a metaphor for many things. She'd come here following a successful fund-raiser at the home of an old neighbor on the Hill, where the money spent on food and drink alone was probably more than anyone here spent in several months—not to mention the large checks that had been written on her behalf.

Taking from the rich to benefit the poor? She wanted to see it that way, but she wasn't sure. Most of the crime was down here, but so were most of the criminals. Every time she offered the victims justice, she was also creating pain for someone else: the mother or wife of the criminal she was prosecuting.

Amanda was part of a panel for drug-free schools night. Beside her was the police community-relations officer. On her other side was the school principal, and at the far end, a woman who ran a shelter program for runaways and out-of-control kids.

Her campaign manager had pronounced it one of the perks of office that gave her an advantage over Neal Hadden, but Amanda had agreed to participate not to get votes, but to learn. Following the opening remarks by all the panelists, there was to be plenty of time for questions from the audience of parents.

The police community relations officer was talking about the current drug scene in the city. Amanda tuned her out, since she already knew what the officer would be saying. Lewis Brogan had instituted regular monthly briefings from the police regarding the current drugs and crime scene in the city, and Amanda had continued that tradition.

She hadn't seen Michael for two days, though he'd called each evening. His team was in the midst of a search for a drive-by killer who'd wounded his apparent target, but had also killed a nine-year-old girl nearby in the playground of this very school.

Michael. There were more images now, but what she seemed to picture every time she thought of him were his eyes, now lit not only by passion, but also by love. Michael, with his black hair disheveled by her fingers, staring down at her with a warm, glowing love.

It seemed to her that once they had set loose those feelings, there was no stopping them. The words could not be taken back again. And yet the problems remained, despite Michael's steadfast belief that they could be overcome.

The community-relations officer had finished her summation of the drug scene, and now it was her turn. Amanda talked about the system, in particular the juvenile-justice system, making no secret of the fact that she opposed the current tendency to prosecute children as though they were adults. Her campaign manager had told her, in effect, to keep her mouth shut because it would make her seem soft, and Neal Hadden would quickly take advantage of that.

But Amanda had the statistics on her side and she used them now, arguing that while incarceration was certainly necessary for the most violent juvenile offenders, it was not the answer for the majority of offenders. As she spoke, she wondered what the officer beside her was thinking. It was possible that she agreed, but she doubted that Michael would.

Amanda was a good public speaker, and she knew to make

eye contact with her audience, but it was impossible in this setting. The panel sat on a stage, bathed in bright track lighting, while the audience was in shadow: dim figures whose faces she could barely see, and then only those in the first few rows.

When she was finished, the questions began. There was a sharp edge to them, which she'd expected, given the shooting that had taken place yesterday only a few hundred yards from where they all sat. The officer next to her fidgeted under the onslaught, then held up a hand for silence, to no avail.

"Lieutenant Quinn is heading up the investigation and he'll be here in a few minutes to update you and talk to you," the officer said, shouting above the din.

Amanda tried not to look startled, but she knew she probably hadn't succeeded. Then she heard a stirring at the rear of the auditorium, and Michael came jogging down the center aisle. Instead of using the stairs at either end of the platform, he vaulted onto it in the middle. The audience fell silent.

When she got past her astonishment at his sudden appearance, Amanda found herself intrigued. She'd never seen Michael in a situation like this and she was curious about how he would handle it. He'd acknowledged her presence with nothing more than the briefest of nods before he leaped onto the platform, but it was still enough to send little curls of heat through her and make her wonder if he'd keep his promise to sneak into her bed one night soon. She'd given him a key.

Tonight, he was the quintessential Michael. The expensive suit had given way to worn jeans, an open-necked shirt and a dark leather bomber-style jacket that was also old and cracked in places. She cast a side-long glance at her fellow panelists, all of them in suits, and wondered if Michael had deliberately chosen to blend in with the audience, instead of appearing to be part of the panel.

"Look," he said, his voice strong enough to carry without a mike, "I know you're all upset about this shooting, and you should be. But don't start dumping on the police. We're doing our best, and we're not getting any help.''

He began to pace back and forth on the stage. "Someone saw something. Someone knows something. And I'm getting pretty damn tired of getting doors slammed in my face. I know you're scared to talk, but you'd better get over it unless you want more kids to die. Maybe the next one will be *yours*.

"I'm looking for information. It doesn't have to be proof. Just give me some names and I'll lean on them—*hard*.''

Amanda winced. She could feel the eyes of the community-relations officer on her. She probably expected her to stand up and protest Michael's suggestion of police aggression. In fact, she found it rather surprising that no one in the audience had spoken up. But there was scarcely a murmur from them.

Michael reached into the pockets of his jacket and pulled out two thick packets of what looked like business cards. He held them up to the audience.

"I've got cards here with a phone number. It's for an answering machine. I'm going to pass them out. Take a couple of them and pass them along to your friends and neighbors. I don't need the names of the callers. I just want information.''

Then he jumped down off the stage and began to work his way back along the rows, handing out cards. From what Amanda could see in the poor light, everyone was taking them.

Her gaze shifted briefly to the small group of reporters in the front row. Would they report what he said about "leaning'' on any suspects? Or would they ask her to comment on his statement?

After Michael had gone, the principal, who was acting as moderator, urged the audience to cooperate with the police and then asked for questions for the panel.

Amanda could almost feel the room settling down again after Michael's dramatic appearance. His voice, urgent and harsh as his words had been, contrasted sharply with the more reasoned tones of her fellow panelists and herself.

There were a few questions for her, but most of them were for the principal, since the audience knew him best. He deflected some of the questions to the others, including her, but for the most part, Amanda remained silent as she thought about Michael's appearance and wondered just how far he would go to capture this killer. She'd been hearing occasional stories for years about his methods, about how he sometimes came very close to the line—and maybe went over it.

She was so lost in her thoughts that the voice didn't actually register until the last possible second. Then her eyes widened and she peered out into the dim light. Tina Jacobs! There couldn't be two people with that little-girl voice and that lisp!

The principal had someone down in the audience with a mike to make the questions heard. Amanda found him and then saw the slim figure retreat into a seat near the back as the principal began to answer her question: something about an after-school program.

No matter how hard she tried to see into those back rows, Amanda could make out nothing more than shadowy figures. She shifted nervously in her seat, nearly unable to keep herself from jumping up and going back there. She couldn't let her get away!

It seemed to take forever for the questions to come to an end. Amanda felt like a coiled spring, ready to launch herself into the audience the moment the principal brought the proceedings to an end.

In reality, however, she managed to get up with the other panelists, then murmur something about needing to find a rest room before taking off. She saw the reporters starting to surge toward them, so she used the stairs at the other end of the platform.

Some people were leaving, while others lingered in the aisle, talking among themselves. Amanda tried to push past them as fast as possible, scanning the throng ahead for any sign of Tina, hoping that she would recognize her if she saw her.

She had all but given up hope by the time she reached the hallway. Tina could have gone already, or she might still be back inside, invisible in the crowd. She was small, probably only about five-three or so, and she might have changed her hair color.

Amanda's eyes scanned the departing parents—then stopped as she saw two women turn the corner, heading for the front door. One of them was the right size, she thought, though her hair wasn't blond. She turned briefly and looked back into the auditorium, where the reporters now surrounded the panelists. She should be there; her absence would be noted.

Then she turned and hurried after the two women. By the time she reached the intersecting hallway, they were pushing through the outside doors. "Tina!" she called, her voice echoing crazily in the empty hallway.

The two women stopped, and the smaller one turned toward her. It was Tina: a different, more subdued Tina, but definitely her. Amanda forgot her dignity and everything else and ran toward her, fearing that Tina might disappear before she could get to her.

But she didn't. Amanda saw her say something to the other woman, who then continued on her way. A few seconds later, Amanda was standing before this new version of Tina Jacobs, who gave her a nervous smile.

"It was my·voice, wasn't it?" Tina asked. "I knew I should have kept my mouth shut in there. But I figured you probably wouldn't remember me after all this time—my name, that is."

"I've been trying to find you ever since you called," Amanda told her as they both walked through the door. "Well, not exactly since then. I had to go through my old cases from the P.D.'s office to find you—or your brother, actually. How is he, by the way?"

She knew she was babbling, but she also knew that she

couldn't just grab this woman and force her to talk. It was clear that Tina was nervous.

The quick smile that Amanda remembered transformed her face into that of a gamin. "He's doing great! He went into the army and decided to make it his career. He's an electronics specialist. Don't ask me to explain what he does. It's complicated. But he's in Germany now."

"And your mother?"

"She's in Pennsylvania, living with my aunt. She hasn't been well. I try to get to see her as often as I can."

"And you? Tell me what's going on in *your* life."

Tina rolled her eyes, then sighed. "Well, I guess it's getting better, but it's still kind of rough. I've got two kids. Their father took off a year ago. We were on welfare for a while, but then I took some courses at the community college and I've just started a job at the bank—in data processing."

Amanda laughed. "Well, I guess that explains why I couldn't find you. It sounds like a good career move."

Tina shrugged. "I made more money at a couple of my waitressing jobs than I'm making now, but the hours are a lot better—with the kids, you know."

"How old are they?"

"The boy is ten, and the girl just turned three. They're good kids, but..." She heaved a sigh. "I'm just hoping that I can get out of here soon, before he starts to get into trouble."

Amanda followed her glance and saw the playground where a little girl just about her son's age had been killed. "Can I give you a ride home? We could talk on the way. Or if you have the time, maybe we could go somewhere."

Tina shook her head. "I'd better get home. My sitter's only fourteen and she has to get back to her place. It's only a couple of blocks, but you can drive me there if you want."

As soon as they were in the car, Tina began to talk about her life and her children. Amanda could feel her nervousness, which did little to ease her own qualms. Whatever she knew, it was clear to Amanda that Tina was finding it difficult to tell her, and to Amanda, that meant that Michael must have been correct in his initial impression that Tina knew it was something that could hurt her.

Amanda was still seeking a way to ease Tina into the reason for her calls when she broke off in midsentence and pointed to a building just ahead on the left.

"I live there—the brick building with the dark trim."

Amanda pulled into the small parking lot beside the building as Tina gave her a tentative and rueful smile. "It's not much, but it's better than where I grew up, anyway."

"It looks nice," Amanda said, aware of how dumb her comment must sound—and how patronizing, coming from someone who drove a Mercedes, and had grown up on the Hill. But she'd seen the building where Tina had lived before, and this one *did* look better, at least on the outside. The neighborhood was better, too.

"There aren't any junkies in the hallways," Tina went on, "and the landlord *does* make repairs."

There were no empty spaces in the lot, so Amanda just stopped in the middle, and a tense silence filled the car. When it became apparent that Tina, whom she remembered as being outspoken, was going to remain silent, Amanda gave up trying to think of a gentle way to begin asking questions.

"Why did you call me, Tina—instead of calling the police?"

"I'm not really sure about it, you know?" Tina replied in a softly pleading voice.

"I understand. But any information you have might help the police in their investigation."

"Is Lieutenant Quinn still in charge?" Tina asked.

"Yes. Do you know him?"

Tina shook her head. "I've never met him, but I've heard people talk about him. I know he grew up down here, and I heard that he had it real tough when he was a kid."

"He did. What do people say about him?" she asked curiously.

Tina shrugged. "I guess it depends on who's talking, you

know? Everyone says he's real tough, but most people think he's fair. And he was right when he said at the meeting that there are people who know who killed that little girl."

"Do *you* know anything about it?" Amanda asked.

"No. If I did, I'd tell him."

"But Tina, you *do* know something about another murder, and you haven't told him."

"Yeah, I know. But it was so long ago."

"But if you're right about the victim, she was your friend. Don't you want to see her killer caught?"

"She wasn't really my *friend*," Tina protested mildly. "We just knew each other, that's all. You know how it is when you're a kid. Sometimes, you aren't too careful about who you hang around with."

"Tina, are you afraid that someone might hurt you if you tell what you know?"

Tina threw her a surprised look. "Oh, no. That's not it. I just don't want to see…anyone hurt, that's all."

"By 'hurt,' you don't mean physically hurt?" Then, when Tina shook her head emphatically, Amanda plunged into it. "And when you said 'anyone,' you really mean *me*, don't you?"

Tina nodded, and Amanda could see the sheen of unshed tears in her eyes. "You were really good to us, you know? I mean, I'd heard about public defenders and how they just try to get everyone to plea-bargain. But you listened to us and you helped."

"I'm going to be completely honest with you, Tina. If your brother had come to me a year or so later, instead of when I was new on the job, I might not have done the same thing. It's a terrible system and it wears all P.D.'s down, no matter how decent they are. There are so many cases—and most of them *are* guilty. That's a fact."

Tina nodded. "I understand. It's like any new job. You want to do your best, but after a while, you stop trying so hard because it doesn't seem to be getting you anywhere and you stop trying so hard because you see that no one else is."

"Exactly."

Tina sighed. "It isn't like that at my job now, though. Everyone really does try and you get lots of praise."

She was silent for a moment, and this time, Amanda let the silence go on. She could tell that Tina was trying to get her thoughts straight, and she held her breath, waiting. Her heart seemed to have moved up into her throat.

"Her name was Eve Lauden. She was really pretty, you know—and she knew it, too. She was kind of different—more sophisticated than the rest of us. She had this aunt who bought her nice things and took her to nice places. But then her aunt died. I think she was twelve when that happened.

"That's why she decided to do it, you know. She wanted the nice things again. So she went to…to this woman and said that she wanted to be one of her 'girls.'" Tina put an unpleasant emphasis on the word.

"This woman was… well, she wasn't a dealer, exactly. She was a sort of go-between. A lot of people were using coke in those days, not just people in the Bottom, you know. So this woman would give them the names of dealers she trusted.

"Then she started to supply them with girls, too. She didn't force anyone, you know, but if a girl was interested, she'd arrange it. Eve didn't take drugs, but she wanted to make money. She'd tried stealing stuff from nice stores for a while, but she got caught. See, at first, she still had some nice clothes and she could go into good stores, but then she outgrew them and so she knew she had to find another way to get them.

"She told me that the men were all nice, and they all had lots of money. So she wasn't worried about getting hurt, you know. She said that's a big problem for most hookers, but…the woman she worked for was careful about who she sent them to.

"The last time I saw her, at school, she said that she was thinking about quitting school and going down to the city. One of the others had done that, and Eve said she'd told her you could make a lot more money down there and live in a really nice place and all.

"So, when she disappeared, everyone just figured that's what she'd done. Her mother never reported her missing. She was seventeen—close to eighteen—and her mother told me that the police wouldn't look for her anyway. See, she'd told her mother the same thing she told me. Her mother was living with some guy at the time and she had two other kids to worry about, and I think the guy was abusing her.

"Anyway, I always kind of wondered about her because she didn't say goodbye. I mean, we weren't all that close, but she *was* good friends with one of the other girls—another hooker, I mean—and she didn't say goodbye to her, either.

"I'd almost forgotten about her until I read about the skeleton they found."

Tina stopped, and this time, Amanda could tell that she wasn't going to continue on her own. Fear vied with hope inside her. Was that all it was? Had the discovery of the skeleton merely revived old, unanswered questions?

"There's more, isn't there?" Amanda asked, praying that there wasn't. "Why would you think that a skeleton found on the island might be Eve's?"

Tina took a deep, quavering breath, and Amanda felt her heart leaping still higher into her throat.

"It's because of something she'd told me." She glanced at Amanda, then looked away quickly. "She liked to brag, you know? I mean, she never said the men's names, but she'd throw out hints, like she wanted us to know that they were important men.

"She told me that she'd been to the island—to one of the cottages. She said that was what they...you...called them. And then she told Lori, one of the other girls, that she'd found a way to make some *real* money, that she'd be set up for life.

"I thought she must have meant that she'd decided to go down to the city, but Lori thought she might be pregnant."

Amanda had to force her question out through a badly

constricted throat. She could feel icy sweat prickle her skin. "So you're saying that one of her customers was someone from the island?"

"Yes, at least if you believe her. I didn't want to tell you because I'd heard somewhere that you're all related out there."

"Yes, we are, more or less." Amanda was struggling to remain calm. "Did she ever say anything else about this man—anything at all?"

"Only that he'd told her that his wife was sick and she didn't want sex anymore. But she knew he wouldn't leave her. Lori thought that's why she got pregnant—to force him to leave her, you know? But maybe he killed her instead."

Her final words dropped like stones into the heavy silence. Amanda could hear her own heart pounding and hear her ragged breathing. John Verhoeven. It all fit. Uncle John—not really her uncle, though they were distantly related. He was her godfather, her own father's closest friend.

"This Lori," she began, forcing herself to think like a prosecutor. But she had to stop and clear her throat. "Do you know where I can find her?"

"No. She left long ago. She went down to the city."

"What about her family?"

"There was only her mom and she died years ago."

Amanda could see that Tina wanted to leave, so she managed to smile and thank her for the information. Tina gave her a quick smile and escaped gratefully.

Amanda drove home in a cold fog. Then she poured herself some sherry and sat in her darkened living room, thinking. It was still circumstantial. There was no proof of anything. Her prosecutor's mind ran through it and confirmed that.

But she wasn't acting as a prosecutor now. As Michael had pointed out, she was playing detective, and the standards were different. There certainly wasn't enough proof to make an arrest, but there *was* enough information now to ask John some very tough questions, and to do some more digging.

And as she reviewed the conversation with Tina, she realized that she hadn't played detective very well. She should have asked for the name of the woman—the madam, as it were. Tina had very carefully not identified her, she thought, though she'd nearly slipped that one time before catching herself.

The identity of that woman was critical, Amanda thought, because if she was arranging the "dates," then she would know the name of Eve's last customer.

Amanda got slowly to her feet and let them carry her out to the kitchen. She hadn't asked for Tina's phone number, but she *had* gotten her last name: Workman. And Amanda found her listed in the directory.

"Tina?" she said when the soft, lisping voice answered. "It's Amanda. I'm sorry to be bothering you again, but I need the name of the woman who was sending Eve and the others out."

After a long silence, Tina said, "I can't tell you that. I'm sorry."

"Are you afraid of her?"

"No, it's not that. She's a good person, you know? People really respect her. I mean, what she did was wrong and all, but she's changed. I don't want to see her hurt."

"Was she ever arrested?" Amanda asked.

"No. Or at least I'm pretty sure that she wasn't. She didn't do it for very long."

Amanda thanked her and hung up. She could check old court records but she doubted that she'd find anything. It seemed likely that the woman was the one from Parkside that Sam Hadley, the vice head, had told Michael and her about, and he'd said there were no arrests, just rumors.

Furthermore, Michael had told her that Sam had gotten in touch with some retired vice cops and none of them had a name to give him—either because there'd been nothing more than rumors, or because they didn't want to give out a name.

So where did that leave her—or them? Michael's image flashed into her mind, and she found herself hoping that he wouldn't show up tonight. Tears of frustration sprang to her eyes. She'd never before wanted so badly to lean on someone, but she couldn't lean on Michael now, no matter how broad his shoulders or how gentle his words.

There was, she knew, only one thing she could do. No, there were actually *two* things, but even as she admitted that, she knew she wasn't ready to hand it over to Michael.

She glanced at the phone, thinking briefly that she should call Tina again and ask her not to say anything about Eve's having been to the island if Michael should happen to find her. But she couldn't do it. She was walking on the very edge already—and asking that would be stepping over the line.

Instead, what she had to do was to talk to John herself. If she confronted him with what she knew, he wouldn't be able to lie to her. But she had to give him a chance to explain.

"LIEUTENANT QUINN IS waiting for you in your office."

Amanda could feel the blood draining from her face, and the expression on her secretary's face told her that she wasn't imagining it. She turned quickly and pushed open the door to her office.

How could he know? It was impossible! He *couldn't* have found Tina between the time she'd met with her last night and this morning! But he must have. What was she going to do?

She pushed the door shut behind her. Michael had his back to her as he stared out the windows into the plaza below. Fear and pain and love mixed explosively inside her. She wanted to run to him and feel the strength and warmth of his arms around her—and at the same time, she wanted to turn and run *from* him.

Instead, she stood rooted to the spot, and when Michael turned to her, she saw her worst fears confirmed by the look of triumph on his face. Anger moved in quickly, supplanting all the other emotions. He was *enjoying* this! He *wanted* to bring down John Verhoeven!

But his expression shifted quickly when he saw her. His dark brows knit together into a frown. "What's wrong? What happened?"

She couldn't speak. Had she guessed wrong? She knew she hadn't misread that initial expression, but was she wrong about the reason?

Michael closed the space between them quickly and drew her into his arms. She remained rigid, nearly paralyzed with fear and confusion. Still holding her securely with one arm, he tipped her chin up to meet his searching gaze. And then, at the last possible minute, she remembered the drive-by shooting and Michael's plea last night for information. She still couldn't relax, but at least she found her voice.

"Did you get some information about the drive-by?"

He continued to frown for a second, then relaxed and nodded as the triumph returned to his eyes. "Three calls came in last night—all of them identifying the shooter as the same guy—Weems. He was already one of our suspects, but we hadn't been able to find him. Now we've got him—and the gun. I hauled our ballistics guy out of bed at six this morning, and we've got a match.

"Then an hour ago, we picked up the driver—on another tip—and he's talking, trying to save his own butt by claiming that he didn't know Weems was going to shoot anybody. So we need to talk about how to handle him."

He paused and frowned at her again. "What was wrong with you? You looked...strange."

She shook her head. "It's nothing. I just didn't sleep well last night."

He still looked doubtful, but he let her go after planting a quick, soft kiss on her lips. "I'm sorry I didn't get over to your place last night," he murmured. "But I spent most of the night tracking Weems down."

"You were...very effective last night at the meeting."

Michael arched a dark brow. "Okay, so I came off a little too strong. But everyone understood my motive. It told them that we care about getting the guy. And I didn't lay a hand on him, if that's what you're thinking.''

She found her way to the protection of her chair. Michael took a seat across from her, and they began to talk about the driver and whether or not they should offer him a deal. Amanda called her secretary and asked her to get Annie Wetherspoon, her assistant who'd been on call last night. The case would be assigned to her, since she'd handled it initially.

"I've cleared your calendar for the afternoon," her secretary said over the speakerphone after Amanda had asked her to get Annie.

"Thank you," Amanda replied, avoiding Michael's questioning gaze.

"What was that about?" he asked.

"Nothing. I just decided to take the afternoon off, that's all."

"Ah, well, maybe I can manage some time off myself," he said, his dark eyes gleaming.

"I have some things to take care of," she said, then breathed a sigh of relief when Annie knocked and pushed open the door.

CLUTCHING HER TICKET, Amanda boarded the train to the city. John's office was only one subway ride from Grand Central. Besides, she wanted the travel time to think out her approach to him. She'd called him first thing this morning, asking to see him on an "important matter." Being the discreet person he was, he hadn't asked any questions, though she didn't doubt that he was puzzled—or perhaps even suspicious.

But as soon as she dropped into a seat, it was Michael who claimed her thoughts. Even in the midst of his elation at catching the drive-by killer, she knew he probably doubted her pathetic explanations. The only thing that had saved her from a grilling—gentle or otherwise—was the appearance of one of her other assistants just as she and Annie and Michael had been wrapping up their discussion.

Well, she thought, it didn't matter now. Regardless of the outcome of her meeting with John, she would have to tell Michael everything. She'd already compromised herself professionally—and perhaps even put her election at risk. Certainly, Neal Hadden would try to make an issue of it, regardless of what she did.

During a long and mostly sleepless night, Amanda had begun to wonder how it might have happened. Even if Eve Lauden had confronted John with a pregnancy and then tried to blackmail him, she simply could not bring herself to believe that the gentle, quiet man she'd known all her life would be capable of a murderous rage. And yet, what other explanation could there be?

She leaned back against the headrest and closed her eyes, wishing fervently that she'd missed something—or that Eve Lauden had lied about having a "customer" from the island. After all, Tina had said that she liked to brag.

She'd chosen a window seat, and the seat next to her remained empty as the train pulled out of the station. But now she felt movement next to her. She didn't open her eyes, instead praying that whoever had sat down wouldn't be the talkative kind.

But then a faint scent tickled her nose: a very familiar and pleasant men's cologne. No! It couldn't be! She kept her eyes closed. If it was Michael, he would have said something. But the coincidence of someone sitting down next to her, wearing that same cologne...

She opened her eyes very cautiously to mere slits—then widened them. All she could see was a pair of long legs stretched out and one hand that rested in his lap, but that was all she needed to see. She knew those muscled thighs, and she knew those strong hands very well. He'd followed her!

Keeping otherwise perfectly still, she swiveled her head in his direction. He was sleeping—or he appeared to be, at any rate. She remembered that he'd said he'd spent the night tracking down the killer.

She turned her head again and closed her own eyes. She

couldn't show up at John's office with Michael in tow! That
would seem to John like a terrible betrayal. She thought about
getting off at the next stop, then taking another train or rent-
ing a car. But there was no way she could get past Michael
to the aisle. He was sprawled in such a way that she couldn't
step over his legs, but couldn't step between them, either.

She had to persuade Michael to let her see John alone. But
that brought her back to her thoughts of earlier this morning,
when she'd misinterpreted that look of triumph and believed
he was glad to have before him the prospect of arresting John
Verhoeven.

They were nearing Poughkeepsie, and the train began to
slow. Amanda opened her eyes again. Michael was still
asleep. She envisioned herself making a break for it: leaping
over his legs and rushing off the train at the last possible
moment. Even if he woke up, could he move that quickly?

She thought it might be worth a shot. He'd talked to John
while he was in Port Henry, and he might not have his office
number, and even if he had that, he would still have to get
the address. If she could rent a car quickly—or even take a
taxi—she could get there before him.

The train slowed still more, then came to a stop. She was
only two rows from the door. She got up carefully, watching
Michael all the while, then hitched up her slim skirt and
started to step over his legs.

She almost made it. One foot was already planted in the
aisle and the other one was in midair when his arm suddenly
snaked out and caught her around the waist and his dark eyes
gleamed with amusement at her awkward position. The doors
hissed shut and the train lurched into motion and she fell
against him.

"Nice try," he murmured, holding her close for a moment
before helping her back to her seat. "But you might have
tried trusting me instead."

She settled back into her seat, caught somewhere between
anger and embarrassment. He shifted in his seat until he was

facing her. "I'd like to get some sleep. We can talk when we get to Grand Central."

Then, without waiting for her to respond, he leaned back against the seat and closed his eyes again. Amanda looked over at him after a few minutes and saw his chest rise and fall with slow, easy motions. He really *was* asleep. Now, in addition to being angry and embarrassed, she envied him.

The towns and cities of Westchester County passed by, and then they were in the Bronx. A short time later, the train clattered across the bridge into Manhattan, and shortly after that, they were in the long tunnel that carried them to Grand Central. And still, she didn't know what she was going to do.

Chapter Nine

Michael woke up as the train came to a halt in the bowels of Grand Central Station. He stretched and yawned, then hauled himself from the seat and stood aside to let her out. Neither of them said a word as they joined the other passengers in a long line down the ramp and up the stairs into the main concourse. Michael drew her out of the hurrying masses of people, seizing her hand and holding on to it as though he expected her to bolt at any moment, which was exactly what she considered doing.

"When is he expecting you?"

There was no point to her asking whom he meant. Even in the midst of her present emotional confusion, it occurred to Amanda that honesty was not only the best policy where Michael was concerned, but also the *only* policy.

"Two o'clock," she said, glancing at her watch. The train had been on time. She had forty-five minutes to reach John's office.

"I assume, since you're rushing down here to talk to him, that you must have found Tina Jacobs."

She nodded. "Last night. She was at the meeting."

"And?"

She told him all of it. He listened quietly, not interrupting her. Then, when she had finished, he released her hand and jammed his own hands into his pockets.

"Damn! This does not sound good."

She gave him a startled look. "What do you mean? I thought…"

"You thought wrong," he stated, cutting her off. "Or partly wrong, anyway. I'm not eager to arrest any of them, despite what you think. But it's only because of what it means to *you.*"

"John Verhoeven is my godfather—my father's oldest and closest friend."

"I know. You told me that."

"There isn't enough evidence to arrest him anyway," she told him, unable to keep a note of defensiveness from her voice.

"I know that, too. Unless he admits his involvement, the only way he can be nailed is if I find out who that madam was."

"Tina won't tell me."

"But she knows."

"Yes. Michael, I want to talk to John alone. I'd feel as though I were betraying him if I bring you with me."

"Dammit, Amanda, don't you see how you're putting yourself at risk? You're too smart to do something like that." He glared at her. "I'm coming with you. That makes it official. And if it gets out that you were there, I'll deny it. I'll explain it to Verhoeven. Regardless of what he might have done, he'll want to protect you."

She lowered her head as tears stung the backs of her eyes. He was right. She thought about how she'd wanted to run to him for protection, and how here he was, protecting her from herself.

"I still can't believe he'd…hurt someone," she murmured.

"Maybe it *was* an accident," he said soothingly. "But things will still get ugly. Come on. We'd better get going."

He took her arm and started off toward the stairs that led up to the exit. "I was planning to take the subway," she told him.

He continued to guide her toward the stairs. "I hate the subway. We'll take a cab."

They climbed the stairs and immediately got a cab. Amanda gave the driver the address. Michael leaned back in the seat and smiled at her. "You were really going to take the subway?"

"The subway is faster."

Michael stared out the window. "I hate the subways—and everything else down here. You never know what's coming at you."

"That's because you're a cop, and you always expect the worst. I love the city. In fact, I almost moved here after law school."

"Okay, so I don't mind coming down here once in a while."

She turned to him quizzically. "What's that supposed to mean?"

"It means I'll compromise. When you want to come down here, we will."

She smiled, but it drained away quickly. "You seem to be making a lot of compromises where I'm concerned, Michael."

"Yeah, well, that's what love is all about, isn't it?"

She nodded, feeling a lump begin to form in her throat. She wondered if she'd ever imagined it being like this. She didn't think so. She must have envisioned flowery declarations, like most women did.

"You'll have to make some compromises, too," he said after a brief silence. "Being married to a cop won't be easy."

He'd done it again! He'd just tossed the word out there casually, as though it were a fait accompli.

"We haven't discussed marriage," she said huskily.

"Maybe not, but exactly where did you think we were headed? Like I said, I know it's going to be rougher on you than on me. Some people will be questioning every decision you make."

"Assuming I win the election," she reminded him.

"You will," he said confidently. "And after you do, we'll get married."

"Michael, don't you think you're compromising yourself by being in charge of this investigation? If people know about our relationship…"

"Let me worry about that."

JOHN VERHOEVEN RAISED his brows in mild surprise when Michael followed her into his elegant office high above Wall Street. But if he was at all concerned about a police presence, he hid it well.

"Uncle John, you remember Michael Quinn—Lieutenant Quinn? I'm sorry I didn't tell you he was coming with me, but I didn't know it at the time."

The two men shook hands, and Michael said, "I invited myself along—for her protection."

"'For her protection?'" John echoed, clearly puzzled.

"We want to talk to you about some information that came to Amanda last night," Michael said. "We now think we know the identity of the body from the island. Her name was Eve Lauden."

Amanda had taken a seat, but both men remained standing. John was frowning as he glanced from Michael to her, then back again to Michael. "Eve Lauden? Should I know her?" He turned to Amanda again. "The name isn't familiar."

Michael took the chair beside Amanda and John sat down, as well, still clearly puzzled. She felt a surge of hope. Surely he couldn't be that good an actor. But Michael's next words put a considerable dent in those burgeoning hopes.

"She might have used a different name. Hookers often do."

John's blue eyes grew wide. "She was a *prostitute?* But what was she—?" He stopped abruptly, and his pale skin flushed. "I see. You think that *I* might have taken a prostitute out there, a *child* prostitute? Didn't you tell me that she was in her teens?"

"Eve Lauden was seventeen at the time of her death," Michael confirmed. "She probably looked older, of course."

John was quiet for a long time, his gaze turned inward.

Amanda held her breath. Her blood was turning to ice. Beside her, Michael was poised on the edge of the leather chair, his full attention on John.

Finally, John shook his gray head. "I can see how you might think that. You know that I was going out there, and you know that my marriage was in trouble." He paused and shook his head as a tiny rueful smile touched his mouth.

"This is beginning to feel like a nightmare. You know, I've always enjoyed reading crime fiction—police procedurals mostly. But I never expected to find myself in the middle of one."

"Are you saying that you never took anyone out there?" Michael asked.

John looked straight at him. "That's exactly what I'm saying, and it's what I said before. There were no other women in my life until long after Sara and I had split up. And even if there *had* been, it certainly wouldn't have been a child— or a prostitute."

Amanda believed him, and she was sure it wasn't just because she *wanted* to believe him. But what she believed wasn't important here. She cast a glance at Michael, but he was wearing his cop face and she couldn't begin to guess what he thought.

"There was a ring of them," Michael went on. "They were being run by a woman in Parkside, who also dealt drugs to middle-class types who didn't want to deal with street peddlers. We haven't found her yet, but when we do, she should be able to identify her customers."

A faint frown crossed John's lean, attractive face. "Drugs, too," he said with a sigh. "There *was* a lot of that back then—I mean, among people who'd never use them now. Cocaine, mostly. I knew some people who tried it, but I never did. I don't even drink that much. I dislike losing control— especially back then."

He glanced at Amanda for the first time in a while, then returned his attention to Michael. "As Amanda may have told you, Sara, my first wife, was mentally ill. It was a...very difficult marriage. She wouldn't seek help. I was even more afraid of losing control then.''

Amanda was listening and remembering, remembering how John had always been so gentle and careful with his sick wife—and so determined to protect Lise from everything.

''You said that you knew people who had used cocaine back then. Were any of them from the families on the island?'' Michael asked.

Once again, John's gaze flicked briefly to Amanda. She knew what he must be thinking. ''Michael knows about Jesse, Uncle John.''

There was no mistaking the relief in his eyes. He nodded. ''I don't know about anyone else, and I think I would have known.''

Then he frowned. ''Is it possible that this girl went out there with Jesse and some others—and then some sort of terrible accident happened and they panicked and just buried her? I know that sounds far-fetched, but...''

''It's possible,'' Michael said, pulling himself out of his chair. ''I haven't wanted to lean on Jesse too much, but it looks like I'll have to.''

John turned to Amanda. ''Lise tells me that she's...having problems again.''

''She is,'' Amanda acknowledged sadly. ''But at least this time, she didn't have to be pushed into getting some help.''

''I'm glad to hear that. I'd hate to see her marriage destroyed. I like Steve, and I think he's good for her.''

''Steve and Michael are friends,'' Amanda told him.

John turned to Michael. Then his gaze traveled between them, and he seemed to be about to say something. But before he could, Michael put out his hand.

''I'm sorry to have bothered you like this, Mr. Verhoeven, but I guess you understand.''

John took Michael's outstretched hand. ''Yes, I do. And if there was any way I could help you in your investigation, I would. Believe me when I say that all this has been very troubling to me. Not only has that poor child been buried in my front yard all that time, but it also brings back a very sad time in my own life—and in yours, as well, Amanda. We nearly lost you that spring—and we *did* lose Trish, of course.''

As he spoke he let go of Michael's hand and came around the desk to take both of Amanda's hands in his. ''I hope Jesse knows nothing about this, but if she does, I'm sure it couldn't have been her fault.''

Amanda merely nodded, then brushed a kiss against his cheek. But the truth was that she was already thinking just what she suspected Michael must be thinking. Jesse *had* to know something.

''YOU BELIEVE HIM, don't you?'' she asked as the elevator carried them down to the lobby.

''Yeah, I do. I don't think he could lie that well.'' He arched a brow at her. ''I also think he knows about us.''

She smiled. ''I think so, too. He's just too discreet to ask, but he'll probably be quizzing Lise.'' She let out a sigh. ''So now we *have* to talk to Jesse.''

''Yeah. I probably should have started with her. She was always higher on my list anyway, because of the crowd she was hanging with then.''

The elevator stopped and several people got on. They both remained silent until they reached the lobby. Then Michael turned to her. ''Have you ever stayed at the Plaza?''

''No. Why?'' she asked with a frown.

''I was thinking maybe we could get a room—just for the rest of the day. I have to be back by sometime tonight.''

''Michael,'' she said in exasperation, ''we can't just walk into the Plaza with no luggage.''

''Why not? Are you going to tell me that no one else does that?''

''I don't care if they do or don't. *I'm* not going to.''

''Okay. It was just a thought.''

"Why the Plaza?" she asked curiously, not quite able to banish a certain wicked pleasure his suggestion had aroused.

"I've never been there. When I was a kid, I sometimes baby-sat for the little girl next door when her Mom had to work at night. She had this ratty old book that she loved, and I'd read it to her."

"Eloise at the Plaza," Amanda said, smiling. "I had it, too."

"Yeah, that was it. It kind of stuck in my mind—probably because I must have read it a hundred times. And I figured it must be a really great place if there was a book about it."

"It *is* lovely. I've had lunch in the Palm Court." She smiled and took his arm. "We'll go there sometime."

"With luggage."

"With luggage."

"We could go buy some luggage first."

"No. I need to get back. I have a campaign meeting this evening."

"Humph! I guess it wouldn't do to call your campaign people and tell them that you've decided to shack up at the Plaza instead."

She laughed. "No, I don't think that would be politic."

Michael hailed a cab, and they returned to Grand Central, where a train was just boarding. They settled into their seats, and Michael was once again asleep within minutes and she was once again envying him.

Amanda was glad that Michael believed John, but it didn't really solve anything. In fact, in a way, it only made things even worse, if that was possible. Now his suspicions—and hers, as well—turned to Jesse.

She leaned her head back against the headrest and closed her eyes. Her thoughts were muddled, but gradually, they came into focus. And that focus was on Tina Jacobs Workman and what she'd said.

Tina had never suggested that it was John. She'd merely said that Eve Lauden had claimed to have a customer from the island. What if it wasn't John—but it *was* someone else from the island families?

In her mind, she ran through them all, but she couldn't see any of them being involved with a teenage prostitute. It just wasn't possible.

She hadn't asked Michael whether or not the forensics people would be able to identify the body as being that of Eve Lauden. But if they could, didn't that make it far less likely that Jesse was involved?

On the other hand, given her behavior at that time, it was possible that Jesse had known Eve Lauden. And if she did, *that* could be the basis for Eve's story that she had a customer from the island. Perhaps she'd been out there with Jesse, and had just made up the rest of it.

She decided that she would call Tina this evening and ask her, even though she thought that Tina would have already mentioned it.

"TINA? IT'S AMANDA Sturdevant. I'm sorry to be bothering you again, but I have another question. And by the way, Lieutenant Quinn will be contacting you to hear what you told me, and probably to ask a lot of other questions."

"He won't come to the bank, will he?" Tina asked nervously.

"No, I didn't even tell him where you work. But just to be sure, I'll call and ask him to see you at home."

"Thanks. It's just that I haven't been there long and I know banks must get pretty suspicious if the cops come to see someone."

"I'll call him tonight," Amanda promised, though that wasn't going to be necessary. Michael was likely to be on her doorstep any moment.

"What I wanted to ask you is if you knew my sister, Jesse, back then."

"I knew who she was. I guess everybody did. She was always so gorgeous."

"Is it possible that she could have been hanging out with Eve and her crowd?"

"No, at least not that I know of. Jesse's a bit older than any of them. Besides, why would she have had anything to do with them?"

"Uh, well, Jesse had some problems with drugs back around the time that Eve disappeared."

"Oh." Tina was silent for a moment. "I guess having all that money doesn't mean you can't have the same problems as everybody else, does it?"

"No, it doesn't," Amanda replied, wondering if it was her imagination, or if she'd heard a note of satisfaction in Tina's voice. And if so, why was she inclined to be more understanding of it in Tina than she was in Michael?

"I'd appreciate it if you didn't say anything about it. Jesse's fine now, and she has her business to think of." Half of that was true, anyway, she supposed.

"Yeah, don't worry. I won't say anything. She has great clothes in her shop. I've just been thinking. I remember that someone told me once—it could have been Eve—that there were some rich kids who bought their drugs through...the same woman Eve worked for. But she never mentioned any names, and she probably would have if she'd known them."

Amanda's grip on the phone tightened. Tina had said before that the woman had a middle- and upper-class clientele. So the connection *could* be there, even if Tina didn't know about it. On the other hand, Tina was right: if Eve had known Jesse, she probably would have bragged about it. Sometimes, she forgot just how prominent her family was.

"Michael—Lieutenant Quinn, that is—is going to try to get the name of that woman from you, Tina."

"I won't tell on her!" Tina said vehemently. "I'm not going to hurt her! She's a good person."

"Well, I thought I'd better warn you." She wondered just how hard Michael would push Tina.

MICHAEL SHOWED UP only moments after she'd hung up from her conversation with Tina. He looked exhausted, despite his naps on the train. She supposed that she must look the same, even though she'd had more sleep than he had.

"You know how 'sleeping together' is usually—what do you call it?—a euphemism?"

She nodded, smiling.

"Well, tonight it isn't. Plus I've got to be out of here at the crack of dawn to avoid your nosy neighbors.

"We got Weems, by the way—the drive-by shooter. He's already lawyered up and trying to cut a deal."

"No deal. But we'll make that official tomorrow when we meet with Annie. I know she'll agree."

"We might have to deal if we can't get any witnesses other than the driver. He doesn't exactly have a lot of credibility."

"Then find someone. I can't cut a deal on this one. He killed a *child,* for God's sake!"

Michael grinned. "And you're running for office."

Anger flashed from her eyes. "I wouldn't deal on this one—and you know it!"

"Yeah, but I like to see you get riled up."

"Let's not talk about business now."

"No, let's face the fact that we're *always* going to be talking business."

She sighed. "You're right. I talked to Tina a few minutes ago, by the way, and she…"

"Dammit, Amanda, I told you to stay out of it now. Let me handle it."

She ignored his outburst. "She doesn't want you coming to see her at work."

"Okay. I'd planned to see her tonight, but I didn't get around to it, so I'll wait till tomorrow night."

"I called her to find out if she knew Jesse—or rather, if Eve Lauden did."

"Thank you, Ms. Detective. That was on my list of questions."

"She doesn't think Jesse knew her, and she says she won't give you the name of that woman." She paused, glaring at him. "And I don't want you harassing her about it."

Michael rolled his eyes. "Heaven forbid that I should try to get information about a murder."

"You don't even know that it *was* a murder, let alone that the body is Eve Lauden."

"Let's go to bed," he said, taking her hand and pulling her toward the stairs.

She resisted. "Now that you have a name, will you be able to find out if it *is* Eve?"

"How should I know? That's up to the forensics people."

"But you can guess," she persisted, backing off as he reached for her again.

"My guess is probably," he replied as he scooped her up in his arms and started up the stairs.

"I thought you were too tired to do anything but sleep."

"I was wrong," he said, his breath fanning softly against her bare skin. "But it would have been better if we'd gone to the Plaza. You're a prude."

"Not here I'm not," she said, laughing.

They were both tired, but their hunger for each other overcame that. Lovemaking in slow motion, bodies moving languorously, voluptuously. Smooth skin against bristly hairs, gentle curves entwined with hard muscles. Their tiredness took the sharp edge off their passion, revealing a tenderness that both knew was there, but that had mostly lay hidden before.

And before the last shudder had passed through them, they were both asleep. But their dreams were dark. Michael hadn't quite told her the truth, and Amanda wasn't as certain as she wanted to be that Jesse couldn't have been involved.

'JESSE, WE NEED TO TALK about that spring, when you were home from school and Amanda had her accident."

Amanda didn't want to see the sudden surge of fear in her sister's eyes at Michael's words. From the moment Jesse had opened the door to them, she'd been wary. It was clear that she'd have preferred not to open it at all. But now that wariness had turned to fear.

"What about it?" Jesse demanded, her voice rising as it always did when she was upset. Steve, who was sitting beside her on the sofa, shot her a look intended to calm her and took her hand. Amanda thought Steve was fearful, too, worried about Jesse's fragile state right now.

"We think that the girl whose body we found died that spring, too," Michael said, and Amanda noted silently that he didn't use the word *murdered*. Michael, she realized, was capable of subtlety, for all his reputation as a hard-nosed interrogator.

"Her name was Eve Lauden. Did you know her?"

Amanda knew that wasn't, strictly speaking, true. They hadn't yet made an identification. Michael's team was trying to track down her family.

She watched Jesse carefully. Michael had told her on the way over that he would handle the questions, and that she should try to determine if Jesse was telling the truth. At the moment, Jesse was frowning, her gaze turned inward. Amanda was surprised that she hadn't immediately denied any knowledge.

"Eve Lauden?" Jesse echoed softly. "I...what did she look like?"

Michael opened his attaché case and produced the photo that Amanda had already seen. It was a candid shot from her high-school yearbook, taken not long before her disappearance. She'd been rather surprised, given what she knew about Eve, to learn that she'd still been in school.

Eve Lauden *had* been attractive, and she'd certainly looked older than her years or, as Tina had said, more sophisticated. Amanda watched Jesse carefully as she took the photo from Michael and studied it in silence for a long time. Her face was lowered, so Amanda couldn't see her expression, but tension was evident in her posture and in the way she gripped the photo in both hands. Finally, she handed it back to Michael.

"I didn't know her, but she looks vaguely familiar. I might have seen her a few times."

"Where?" Michael asked as he put the photo back in his attaché case.

Jesse affected a casual shrug that didn't quite work. "Just around, that's all."

Michael's dark eyes regarded her solemnly. "Look, Jesse, all of us here know you were doing drugs back then and hanging around with a bad crowd. I need some names—people she might have hung out with, and especially the name of the madam she was working for."

Amanda had to hand it to Michael. He'd managed to slip that last in very casually. Prior to this, he hadn't said anything about Eve's being a prostitute, and there was no reason why Jesse should have assumed that, either.

She felt pricks of ice along her spine as she stared at Jesse. Her sister gave no indication that she found this information to be shocking.

"I don't know anything like that," Jesse stated, instantly becoming defensive.

"This madam was also supposed to be a supplier of drugs to middle-class types—the kind of person a kid from a good home would go to if she wanted something. We know she lived in Parkside, but we don't have her name yet."

"I don't know anything about her," Jesse said stubbornly.

"So where were *you* getting the stuff, Jesse?" Michael demanded, his attitude changing along with hers.

"From a friend, and I don't know where *he* got it. I never asked."

Michael stared at her in silence for a moment, then nodded. "Let me tell you what *I'm* thinking," Michael went on, his tone dropping back to neutral again. "I'm thinking that there's a connection between Eve Lauden's death and Amanda's accident. I'm thinking that maybe Amanda and your cousin saw something that night and were maybe even chased by the killer. That means that not only did he kill

Eve, but he also is responsible for the death of your cousin—
and for nearly killing Amanda."

"You're crazy!" Jesse said, but her tone was less certain
than her words. Her gaze swiveled from Michael to Amanda,
then back again. "You're out of your mind, Michael!"

Jesse turned to Amanda, who was still recovering from her
shock at hearing Michael say that. He'd said it before, but
since he hadn't brought it up again, she thought he'd dismissed the notion.

"Do *you* believe that?" Jesse demanded.

"I don't know," Amanda admitted honestly. Then, with a
brief glance at Michael, she went on. "There *is* one reason
I could believe it, Jess. You know as well as I do that Trish
wasn't reckless, and she knew the lake well—including the
location of the ski jump. But if we *did* see something, that
could explain why she was running the boat so fast and why
she hit the ski jump."

"And then there's the question of the anonymous call to
the police about the accident," Michael added. "Why
wouldn't the caller identify himself? Why not rescue
Amanda? Trish was almost certainly dead, but if the witness
saw it happen, he must have guessed that Amanda could still
be alive."

Jesse said nothing. Her gaze was faraway. Then, finally,
just as the silence was becoming unbearable, she turned to
Michael. "You came here because you thought I might have
had something to do with this Eve's death, didn't you?"

Amanda expected Michael to demur, but he didn't. "I had
to consider the possibility that you might have gone out to
the island with some of your friends—and something happened."

"I never went out there with anyone other than family,"
Jesse stated. "But if I need an alibi for that night, I've got
one—that is, for the night of Amanda's accident."

"You do?" Amanda blurted out, realizing that of course
Jesse would remember where she was that night.

Jesse glanced at her briefly and nodded, then turned her

attention back to Michael. "I was over at the Verhoevens, with Mother. Aunt Sara was alone because Uncle John was in Europe on business. I remember where he was because he'd wanted her to go with him and she wouldn't. But by the time we got there, she was claiming that he hadn't wanted to take her, which was probably true, but I know that he *did* ask her to go. Mother said so.

"Sara Verhoeven was mentally ill. I don't know if you knew that. Uncle John stuck with her longer than he should have, since she wouldn't get help. She only did that after he left." She shrugged.

"Anyway, I was planning to go out, but Mother caught me at the door and practically begged me to go with her to Sara's. Sara had just called, and Mother thought she really sounded off the wall, which she was. Mother had to call the doctor, who came and gave her something.

"We were still there when Father called to tell us about the accident. The police had just called him."

Amanda belatedly became aware that her mouth was actually hanging open. She'd never wondered where anyone else was that night. It was too painful for her to think about that night. She felt Michael's eyes on her and turned to him.

"Then John couldn't have..."

"Apparently not," Michael said.

"John?" Jesse echoed. "What does John have to do with this?"

"We already knew that John was going out to the island that winter and spring, and..."

Jesse cut her off. "And you thought that Uncle John could have killed that girl?" she asked incredulously. "Uncle John? He was going out there to escape from Sara!"

"Amanda never believed it," Michael said. "But I had to consider him as a suspect."

"Well, you can just forget about it—that is, if you think it happened the night of the accident. Or even if it didn't. John was in Europe—Paris, I think—for some big conference."

Amanda frowned, trying to remember the parade of visitors to her hospital room. And all the flowers, and...

"Yes!" she cried. "I remember that now. Uncle John sent me flowers and he called me from Paris, and he brought me a box of French chocolates when he came back. I was home by then."

Jesse nodded. "We both pigged out on them. I get them from the same shop every time I go over there."

Amanda smiled, remembering. The box had been huge—at least two or three pounds—and they'd both made themselves sick over them. Jesse had scarcely left her bedside during those weeks of recovery. Whatever else might have been going on in her life then, she'd been a good sister.

"SO NOW WE KNOW that neither John nor Jesse could have been involved—that is, if you still believe that it happened the night of my accident."

Michael glanced at her briefly as he started the car. "I don't know that it did—and I'm not convinced that Jesse doesn't know something she isn't telling us."

"You're wrong, Michael! I'd swear that she didn't recognize Eve's name—and she admitted that she might have seen her around."

"Yeah, probably at our missing madam's house while she was getting drugs."

Amanda sighed. "Yes, that's possible. But why would she lie about it? She knows that we know she was doing drugs then."

"Maybe she wants to protect the woman, too," Michael said after a few moments. "Whoever she is, people seem to want to keep me from finding her."

Amanda thought about that. "Tina said that she's done good things—or something like that, anyway."

"Yeah. That's what she told me, too. Has Jesse been involved in any civic things?"

"She's on a committee of business people who help support the youth center in the Bottom. Or she was, at any rate. I'm not sure how active she's been. Why?''

''Nothing. It's just that I wonder why Jesse would still be trying to protect the woman's identity. But if she's run into her recently—if she knows that woman is doing good things…''

Amanda stared at him. ''You mean that you think this woman could be involved in community affairs?''

''That's doing good things, isn't it? But it could be any one of a number of people. There's a lot of community activism down there now.''

Amanda nodded. She'd served on various committees and panels with many of them. Even before Lewis Brogan retired, he'd often sent her to such meetings and panels in his place. He'd made no secret of the fact that he wanted her to be his successor and had wanted her to get the exposure.

''Michael, if it *is* someone who's active in the community, you'll have to be very careful. Those are groups that are trying hard to gain credibility at city hall, and accusing one of them of having been involved in prostitution or drugs— even years ago—could be devastating.''

''Spoken like a true politician,'' he said with a smile.

She bristled. ''If you think you can stay completely out of politics, even in your position, you're mistaken.''

''I'm aware of that.''

''No, I don't think you are—or if you are, then you don't care. The city's finances are finally in good shape again, and those groups are trying to get funding for a number of projects. Neal Hadden and his allies are already saying that it would be throwing good money after bad.''

''He's just put out a position paper stating that any surplus funds in the city treasury should be spent on law enforcement, not on what he calls 'feel-good' programs.''

''Good for him. We could use some more cops and new computers.''

''Have you managed to forget where you came from?''

she demanded angrily. "The city has ignored the Bottom for far too long as it is."

"If I were you, I wouldn't say something like that in public. Some people might get the idea that you're not tough enough for the job."

"I'm already working on a response, saying that studies have proved that the kind of programs the activists want can keep kids out of trouble. I'm really tired of all this emphasis on dealing with them after the fact—when it's too late."

Michael chuckled and reached over to grasp her hand, holding on when she tried to pull it away. "Okay, okay. I was just yanking your chain. I happen to agree with you."

"Do you?" she asked suspiciously.

"Yeah. I'm not overly fond of seeing little kids get killed in drive-by shootings. It wouldn't bother me at all to see my caseload lighten up a bit.

"Police work is changing, you know, and cops' attitudes are, too. We know the value of prevention. In fact, I don't think anyone knows that better than a cop, because we're the ones who are left to clean up the mess—along with you, of course."

He squeezed her hand, then let it go to downshift as they turned into the parking lot of her condo complex. "Just be careful that you don't come off sounding *too* squishy. Hadden'll jump on that."

"Let him. If I can't get elected as the person I am, then I don't want the job."

"Yes, you do. And you know you'll do it better than he could."

"Are you coming in?" she asked.

Michael shook his head. "Not tonight, love. I've got some thinking to do—and I don't do that very well when I'm with you."

They both looked around the dark, deserted lot, then moved together, embracing awkwardly in the confines of the Porsche. Michael kissed her very thoroughly, then reached past her and opened the door.

"Out. You're still messing with my head."

HER BED ALWAYS FELT lonely now when Michael wasn't there. It amazed her to think that she could have changed so much so quickly. What were they going to do? Was it really fair to those who had to decide if she should keep her job to conceal their relationship? But if they were open about it, Neal Hadden would destroy her chance of being elected. Even if people didn't really care, he would convince them that they should.

She tossed and turned, her thoughts veering from Michael to the question of Eve Lauden's killer. The key now seemed to be the woman that Tina and possibly Jesse wanted to protect. If Michael started to ask too many questions, he could cause problems for the activists in the Bottom. But *she* might be able to make some discreet inquiries. There was one woman she'd gotten to know quite well from various committees. She'd grown up in the Bottom and still lived there, and she was old enough to know what had been going on twenty years ago.

Amanda drifted off to sleep, thinking that Michael would not be happy if she continued to involve herself in this investigation. But then, he didn't have to know, did he?

Chapter Ten

Mary Walters was a remarkable woman. She was in her fifties—perhaps even her sixties—but she seemed to Amanda to vibrate with energy. It was she who had organized the community activists. Amanda both liked and admired her.

She knew something of Mary's background: born into dire poverty, abandoned by a husband when she had three small children, whom she then struggled to support by working for various families on the Hill, one of whom had been Amanda's neighbor, the longtime mayor.

Then, once her children were grown and educated, she'd turned her attention to community activism, and somewhere along the line had managed to get a college degree, as well.

When Amanda entered the restaurant, Mary waved to her from a corner table, and for just a moment, Amanda wondered if she might be presuming upon her relationship with this woman. She trusted Mary to keep confidences, but would Mary be willing to help her—especially if she actually knew the woman Amanda was seeking?

As soon as they had ordered, Mary plunged into a discussion about the arrest of the drive-by killer, and how proud she was that two witnesses had now come forward to confirm what the driver of the car had already told the police.

"Did you have anything to do with their coming forward?" Amanda asked, suspecting that she might have.

Mary chuckled. "Let's just say that sometimes people need a little push to do their civic duty."

"Are they worried about reprisals?" Amanda asked.

"They'd be fools if they aren't, but I think they'll be okay. I understand that a certain police lieutenant paid Kevin Weems's friends a visit and told them that if anything happened to the witnesses, he was going to take it *very* personally."

"I don't think I want to hear about it," Amanda said with a smile.

"Did I give you a name? There must be lots of lieutenants on the police force." She paused and narrowed her eyes. "Now don't get on your high horse, Amanda. The man I'm talking about knows just how far he can go."

"I hope so. And speaking of this unnamed lieutenant, has he approached you recently about that body that was discovered out on the island?"

"No." Mary frowned. "Why would he?"

"She's been tentatively identified—this is confidential, by the way. It's police business, of course, and I shouldn't be involved at this point. But from the moment they found her out there, this has felt...personal to me, because of the island."

Mary nodded. "I can understand that. I know how you love that place. So who do they think she is?"

"A girl named Eve Lauden. If the forensics people are right, she died about twenty years ago—in the early spring. She would have been seventeen at the time."

"Eve Lauden?" Mary frowned. "You know, I think I remember her. At least I remember a family of Laudens, and there was a girl who would have been about that age. What did she look like—do you know?"

Amanda took the photo from her purse and handed it over. She'd gotten it the same way Michael had: from a yearbook at the high school Eve had attended.

"Yes, that's her," Mary said, nodding. "I seem to remember that she quit school and took off for the city. Or at least that was the story at the time. And I doubt if her mother did much to find her.''

"Why not?"

Mary sighed heavily. "Eve was a bad one—not that her mother was much better. And anyway, the police never paid much attention to teenage runaways from the Bottom. That's why I fought so hard to open the center and the shelter.''

Mary operated a teen center and shelter at the Bottom. Both she and her assistant, Elaine Barker, had served as surrogate mothers to a lot of troubled kids.

"Why do you say she was a bad one?" Amanda asked, though she already knew the answer.

"If I remember correctly, she was into drugs and she was probably also hooking. Most of the druggies did—the girls, anyway. Thanks to Elaine's outreach, there are fewer of them now.''

Amanda nodded. "That's what I'd heard, but I wanted to confirm it. What I was also told was that there was this woman operating in Parkside, acting as a madam and also selling drugs to middle-class types. I was told that Eve worked for her." Amanda paused. "And what I need is her name.''

"I can't help you there. There *were* some stories, but I never knew who it was.''

"Do you know anyone who might know?" Amanda asked, disappointed. "What about Elaine? Would she know?''

"I doubt it, but I'll ask her if you like.''

"I'd appreciate it—or any other help you can give me.''

"Is Michael Quinn working this case?" Mary asked.

"Yes. He'll probably be coming to see you himself.''

IT WAS ONLY LATER, when Amanda was on her way back to her office, that she began to wonder if Mary had told her the truth. Was it only her imagination, or had Mary seemed distracted after she'd asked for the name of the woman?

Amanda was certainly no conspiracy theorist, but she

couldn't help wondering if there was, in fact, a conspiracy to keep the identity of the woman secret. And if so, what did that mean? Didn't it seem to confirm what Tina had told her: that the woman could be someone who'd since earned the respect of the community?

Then she began to ask herself why she was pursuing this. As she'd told Mary, Michael would soon be asking her the same questions. Could she actually be engaged in some sort of competition with Michael?

That thought unsettled her, to say the least. But it also raised still more questions about her tangled relationship with him. She loved him, but did she completely trust him? Surely if she did, she'd be content to let him handle the investigation.

Or maybe she was being driven simply by her own curiosity—a curiosity that stemmed not only from the fact that Eve Lauden had died on the island, but also from the possibility that her own accident, and Trish's death, was somehow caught up in this.

AMANDA FELT ILL PREPARED for this important case. Her chief assistant had been handling it, and when it had suddenly mushroomed into something even bigger, she'd been reluctant to take it away from Ted. Her relationship with him had been prickly ever since she'd been named acting D.A. Ted felt, and with some justification, that he should have gotten the top position.

Most trial work was done by the assistant D.A.'s, acting in consultation with Amanda. Historically, the D.A. himself or herself handled only the big cases. But since this one hadn't seemed to fit that category at the time, Ted had gotten it. Then, thanks to the work done by Michael's unit, it had suddenly ballooned into the biggest armed-robbery case in years: a ring of clever crooks who had operated with inside information to rob various warehouses in the city.

Two days ago, after the first day of trial, Ted had been involved in an auto accident that left him hospitalized with serious, though thankfully not life-threatening, injuries. The trial judge, who was politically aligned with Neal Hadden, had granted only a one-day delay. When Amanda had protested, the judge had said that he assumed she was on top of the work being done by her office and should certainly be able to step in.

It was politics, pure and simple. Even the defense attorney, who'd argued strenuously for the trial to continue, was a political ally of Neal's. There was considerable media interest in the trial, and she knew that both the judge and the defense attorney—and Neal himself—were hoping that she'd make some mistakes that would prove her lack of fitness for the job.

The truth was, unfortunately, that she had no one but herself to blame for the fact that she *wasn't* prepared. She hadn't wanted to further strain her relationship with Ted by looking over his shoulder as he prepared his case. She might have done that anyway if she hadn't respected Ted's abilities. But as it was, she'd been forced to spend most of the past day and night trying to prepare herself, all without Ted's help, since he was too heavily sedated to discuss it with her.

The judge was too concerned with his own reputation to be blatant about his antagonism toward her, but judges have a lot of leeway, and he was denying all her objections that he possibly could, while sustaining those of her opponent, who himself was taking every opportunity to try to make her look incompetent.

If she could just get through this day without any glaring or irrevocable errors, she told herself, Ted would surely be able to give her some assistance from his hospital bed. The nurse had told her that they would be cutting back on the painkillers that had rendered him useless to her.

But as she stood before the bench, arguing yet another point, Amanda was very much aware of the representatives of the media who had claimed the front row of seats directly behind her desk. Still, when she turned away from the bench, trying to contain her irritation, it wasn't the media she saw, but the man who was now leaning casually against the rear wall of the courtroom.

She hadn't seen or talked to Michael for three days. He'd called and left messages, and she'd left some for him, but that was all. Her first thought, upon seeing him there, was that she wanted him to be anywhere else but here. Or at least that was what her brain was telling her; her body told her something very different.

The trial dragged on through a series of minor witnesses. Amanda was walking a very fine line—delaying the course of her case to the extent she dared, so that she could have the benefit of Ted's help by the time she got to the important witnesses.

"Those are all the questions I have for now. Your turn, Counselor," she said with a polite nod toward her opponent.

Then, when she turned to go back to the prosecution's table, she saw that not only was Michael still there, but he'd been joined by Steve. The two men had their heads bent to each other as they talked, and as she watched, they both left the courtroom.

It hadn't occurred to her to question why Michael was there. She assumed it was because his unit had handled the case. But now, with Steve's appearance and their joint departure, her mind went, for the first time in several days, to the Eve Lauden case.

Steve's unusual appearance forced her to focus on Jesse. Had something happened to her? She hadn't spoken to her sister since five nights ago, when she and Michael had talked to her together.

Amanda had to struggle hard to keep her attention focused on the trial. Her fears for Jesse escalated. What if she'd gone out drinking—and hadn't returned? Amanda knew that even if Jesse hadn't been involved in any way in Eve Lauden's death, she could still be beset by memories of her own behavior at that time: memories that were surely difficult for her to deal with in her present fragile state.

She glanced discreetly at her watch, hoping that the judge

would call an early noon recess at the end of her opponent's cross-examination. She'd intended to return to her office and study the statements of the afternoon's witnesses, but now she wanted only to satisfy herself that nothing had happened to Jesse.

After she declined an opportunity for redirect, the judge looked at her, clearly expecting her to proceed. Cursing silently, Amanda called her next witness: one she'd hoped not to have to deal with until after the lunch recess.

By the time she got through that, and through the defense counsel's lengthy cross-examination, Amanda was sure that something had happened to Jesse. When the judge finally called for an hour's recess, she knew better than to request some additional time. Instead, she dug her cellular phone out of her briefcase and began to dial the number for Jesse's store.

When her sister's assistant answered, Amanda asked for Jesse and held her breath.

"I'm sorry. She's not here right now. May I help you?"

"Vicki, it's Amanda. Has Jesse been in today?"

"Oh. I didn't recognize your voice." There was a brief pause. "No. She didn't come in. She was supposed to open because I had a doctor's appointment. But when I came in at ten-thirty, the place was still locked up. We're having a sale, too. It was advertised in the paper."

"Did you call Steve?"

"Yes. I called him right after I called Jesse at home and didn't get an answer. He…seemed really upset."

Amanda thanked her, then put the phone away and hurried to her office, three floors up. Her secretary told her that Steve had called at 10:45 a.m., but there was no call from Jesse. She then called Steve's office, but he hadn't returned there. So she tried him at home, but got only the machine. Finally, she called police dispatch and asked them to page Michael. Then she paced around her office, the case completely forgotten as she worried about her sister.

She pounced on the phone the second it rang. "Lieutenant Quinn is on line one," her secretary informed her.

"Michael," she said without preamble. "Where is she?"

"We don't know. Steve and I are checking the bars right now. The shop was open late last night, and she didn't come home after it closed, so Steve hasn't seen her since yesterday morning. But we know she was at work all day yesterday.

"Steve says she'd been having nightmares ever since we talked to her." Michael paused briefly. "He thinks she *does* know something. But whatever it is, she won't tell him."

"Michael, you've *got* to find her."

"I'm doing my best. Steve and I have divided up the most-likely places."

"I should be helping you."

"No, you should be trying your case. They're trying to hang you out to dry, honey. Don't let them do that."

His voice had dropped to an intimate tone that, even in her present frame of mind, sent little curls of heat through her. "I'm not prepared," she told him.

"You're doing fine. Just keep at it and let Steve and I handle this. Page me when you recess."

She managed to force down some yogurt that her secretary pressed on her as she studied the witness statements. And somehow, she got through the afternoon. When they took a short recess, she had Michael paged, but he hadn't answered by the time she had to return to court.

After court recessed for the day, Amanda had to endure a lecture from the judge about her "foot-dragging" before she could get back to her office. There were no messages from Michael, but she hadn't really expected any. He'd know that she wouldn't want to have her secretary know what was going on. She had him paged again, and this time he got back to her quickly.

"She was at the River House for a while last night, but she left early," he reported. "I got hold of the bartender, and he said that she just suddenly walked out halfway through her second drink. He's pretty sure that she left alone. He hadn't seen her talking to anyone while she was there.

"Steve called your father's house, but the housekeeper said that she wasn't there, and as far as she could tell, hadn't stayed there. She said that your father's in Boston."

"Yes," Amanda confirmed. "Court's in session."

"Steve was wondering if we should call him. Maybe he's heard from her."

"I'll try to reach him now. What are you going to do?"

"I'm going back to the office to take care of a few things. Then I'm going over to Steve's. Why don't you meet us there, and we can try to figure out what to do next."

Amanda managed to catch her father just as he was leaving his chambers. He hadn't heard from Jesse. She told him that Michael had talked to her recently about the case of the dead girl on the island, and that necessitated telling him the rest of it: that they were fairly certain they knew who she was, and they suspected that Jesse might have some information she was unwilling to divulge.

"Amanda, you should have stopped him from harassing her!" her father stated angrily when she had finished.

Taken aback by his outburst, Amanda protested that she couldn't interfere in a police investigation—even though, of course, she'd been doing just that.

"Jesse can't be expected to handle this. She doesn't need to be reminded of her past problems."

Angry now, both at his unreasonable attitude and at his defense of Jesse, Amanda reminded him that Michael was investigating a possible homicide.

"A 'possible' homicide that happened twenty years ago isn't a good enough reason to destroy my daughter!"

"She's my sister, too!" Amanda protested. "And…"

"I don't want Jesse harmed just to find the killer of a little slut!"

Amanda was shocked into silence. It wasn't as though she didn't already know what a snob her father was, but hearing it now was still a shock. And in the same moment, she knew that if the situation were reversed and it was *she* who might have such information, his attitude would be very different. Jesse was still his darling. Nothing had changed.

"I'm sorry, Mandy. I shouldn't have said that. It's the pressure right now. I've just gotten word that Justice Robson is going to be announcing his retirement any time—maybe even this week. And I *am* worried about Jesse. She's not strong, and she never will be. We both have to face up to that—and so does Steve."

They hung up after Amanda promised to keep him informed. She gathered up her papers and stuffed them into her briefcase, signed some other papers that her secretary brought to her, then left the office.

Partway to Steve's, it occurred to her that someone should check with Jesse's therapist. It was certainly possible that Jesse had contacted her. She knew that confidentiality would preclude the therapist from telling them where Jesse was, but perhaps she would at least tell them if she'd spoken to her in the past day.

But when she arrived, Steve told her that he'd already talked to the therapist and she hadn't heard from Jesse for a week. He then asked if she'd contacted her father.

Amanda nodded. "He hasn't heard from her."

Steve stared at her, obviously hearing the pain and anger she couldn't quite suppress. "What did he say?"

"He's angry with Michael for having questioned her, and angry with both of us for not protecting her."

"That doesn't surprise me—maybe he's right."

"What were we supposed do to—ignore a possible source of information just because we don't want to upset her?" Amanda demanded, her voice rising.

They were still standing in the foyer, and at that moment, the doorbell rang. Steve opened the door, and Michael joined them. After glancing quickly from Steve to her, he asked what had happened.

"Nothing," Steve said quickly.

"Your father?" Michael asked, ignoring him and turning instead to her.

Amanda was surprised that he'd guessed, and nodded before she could stop herself. Perhaps he'd overheard her. She'd been all but shouting.

"He's angry because we questioned Jesse, but he hasn't heard from her."

She turned away, moving toward the living room, but Michael put a restraining hand on her arm. He said nothing, but when she turned to him, there was no mistaking the love and understanding in his eyes.

But how *could* he understand? How could he possibly know how it felt to discover that nothing had changed, that Jesse was still the favored daughter, despite Amanda's accomplishments?

"For what it's worth," Steve said, breaking the silence as they all sat down, "I think Jesse *does* know something."

Then, seeing that he had their full attention, he went on. "She's been having nightmares ever since we talked to her about it. But she won't tell me what they're about. In fact, she hasn't said more than a few words to me since then. It's like she's lost in some world of her own.

"But she hasn't been drinking—at least not that I know of. I tried to get her to go see her therapist, but she refused. She said it wouldn't help, that she had to deal with it herself."

"'It'?" Michael echoed.

Steve shook his head. "She wouldn't say what it was."

"Did you check the bank and her credit cards?" Michael asked.

Steve nodded. "No withdrawals and no charges. The store account is in her name only, but I persuaded the bank to check it for me and she didn't touch it, either. So she couldn't have gone far."

"When can you begin an official search?" Amanda asked, not certain just what the law was in such matters, since she didn't generally deal with missing persons.

"Not for another two days—unless I want to put out an APB and call her a material witness to a crime. But I don't think that's a good idea, under the circumstances."

Then Michael stared solemnly at both of them. "Look, I don't like having to bring this up, but is it possible that she could have committed suicide?"

"No!" Amanda said quickly. "She's never been suicidal!"

"I'm not so sure," Steve said reluctantly. "You haven't seen her these past few days. She didn't say anything, and I don't think she would, but…"

His voice trailed off into a silence that grew heavy as they all contemplated that terrible possibility. But Amanda continued to shake her head.

"Whatever it is that she knows, it can't be *that* bad," she stated. "*She* couldn't have killed Eve Lauden."

"But if she knows who did and failed to report it, she'd know that she's in trouble," Michael argued. "Or even if Eve's death was accidental and she failed to report it, she's still in trouble."

Amanda was still shaking her head. "Neither thing makes any sense. Whether she knew that Eve was murdered or she knew that it was an accident, she would have known where Eve was buried—right?"

Steve and Michael both nodded, and Amanda hurried on. "But she was probably the only one who didn't protest at all about Jan and Stacey building their cottage. In fact, she said more than once that the rest of us were being ridiculous about it."

She turned to Michael. "Remember when you first told me about Eve's body being discovered? You asked me then who had protested about the cottage. All of us did, to one extent or another, though we eventually accepted it. But Jesse said from the beginning that we were all being ridiculous. And she knew, just as the rest of us did, exactly where the cottage would be built. So she *couldn't* have had any knowledge that a body was buried there."

Amanda finished on a triumphant note and saw Steve nodding. "You're right," he said. "I'd forgotten about it, but Jesse *did* say that she thought everyone was being ridiculous about it."

Michael frowned thoughtfully, but said nothing, then abruptly changed the subject, asking Steve if Jesse had any friends she might have gone to stay with temporarily.

"I've called everyone I can think of," Steve replied, "And no one's heard from her."

They seemed to be at a dead end. Michael finally said that it would be best for Steve to stay home, in case Jesse contacted him. Then he got up to leave, his eyes sending a silent message to Amanda to come with him.

"Do you think we should check the bars again?" Amanda asked as they paused next to her car.

Michael shook his head. "I've left word at the places she tends to frequent for them to contact me if she shows up." He paused, then went on.

"You know, it occurred to me in there that there's one place we haven't checked—the island."

Amanda shook her head. "Jesse wouldn't go out there. She *never* goes there."

"I'll follow you home so we can drop off your car. Then we'll go check it."

Amanda opened her mouth to protest again, then closed it. She couldn't see Jesse going out there, but...

"I HAD SOMEONE GO OVER to the high school Eve attended and check her attendance records," Michael said as they set off to the marina. "It took some time because they were buried in a storage place the school uses, but it might have been worth it."

He paused and slanted a quick glance her way before returning his attention to the road. "Believe it or not, she wasn't absent all that much—even toward the end."

"That's surprising, given what we've been told about her," Amanda commented.

"Yeah, it is. Her last day of school was April 8."

Amanda stared at him as a chill went through her. Michael nodded. "Your accident happened April 8."

"No! I mean it did, but..." She simply ran out of words as her mind slipped back to that terrible night.

Michael took his hand from the gearshift and covered hers. Warmth seeped into her icy flesh. "It could be just a coincidence," he said gently, "but my gut is telling me it isn't."

"Cops always hate coincidences," she stated angrily. "But they *do* happen."

He said nothing. Amanda stared out the window. It was April again, and the weather was much as it had been that night: a sudden spell of unnaturally warm weather, a hint of spring in the air. She wished they were going anywhere but to the island.

But we won't *be going to the island,* she reminded herself. *If* Jesse is out there, her car would have to be at the marina— and it *won't* be.

The marina was mostly deserted. A few boats were missing from their slips, and she could see one sailboat out on the lake, tacking toward the dock.

"Our boathouse is down there, at the far end," she told him.

"I know," he replied as he drove along the docks.

The land-side doors to the boathouse were closed. Michael heaved a sigh. "I guess you were right. Her car's not here."

"We have a garage. It's that building up there." She pointed to a metal building that squatted near the fuel station.

"I didn't know *that*," Michael said as he turned in that direction.

"It's because we're usually out there for the weekend, not just for the day, like most boat owners. Father decided we should have one built after someone broke into his car one time."

Michael rolled to a stop in front of the row of doors, and Amanda took her keys from her purse, silently praying that the garage would be empty.

But it wasn't. Michael took the key from her and unlocked the door, then rolled it up. Jesse's dark green BMW sat inside. Amanda turned away, her gaze going to the dark bulk of the island across the water. It was dusk, but no lights were on at the house, which was plainly visible from here because it sat on the highest point of the island.

"Do you want to wait here?" Michael asked quietly.

She shook her head, even though that was *exactly* what she wanted.

He reached for her, drawing her gently into his arms. "It's okay for you to be scared, honey. What's *not* okay is for you to let your father pile a load of guilt on you."

She shook her head and moved away. "Let's just check the boathouse first."

The old launch was gone. Now there could be no doubt that Jesse was on the island. Michael drove back to his own boat, and she waited while he pulled the cover off it. It was growing steadily darker, but still there were no lights at the house. The evening breeze was warm, but it did little to chase away the iciness that encased her.

And it got worse as they left the dock behind and sped over the water. Michael's boat was very similar to the one they'd borrowed that awful night. The memories inundated her, but there was nothing new.

Halfway across, they could finally make out the outline of the old launch at the dock, half-hidden by a large, flat-bottomed boat piled with building materials. Amanda kept her eyes on the cottage, until they were too close to the island to see it through the trees. Still no lights, even though by now it was full dark.

Michael managed to find berthing space between the launch and the construction company's boat. He cut the motor, then turned to her.

"Give me your keys. You're going to wait here."

She shook her head. "I'm coming with you. If she's... I'd have to identify her anyway—officially, I mean."

"No, you won't. Steve can..."

He stopped and they both stared at each other, realizing that they were both certain what they would find.

"I'm coming with you," Amanda said again, and climbed out of the boat.

Michael brought his flashlight, and they walked along the path that led up the hill and through the woods—past the new cottage that was in the process of being framed. Neither of them said a word, but Michael held her hand in a firm grip.

Amanda's thoughts had moved beyond the moment, beyond what she was certain must be awaiting them. What could be so terrible that Jesse would choose to end her life rather than tell them? It made no sense to her, and she desperately needed for it to make sense.

She walked on through the darkness with Michael's hand the only anchor she had to the terrible present. Her mind had now turned away from the unanswerable questions to the past: both the dim, distant past and the more recent past. She acknowledged to herself now that she'd *hated* her beautiful older sister—hated her because their father had loved her more. And she'd envied her, too, of course, with all the jealousy of a gawky, metal-mouthed kid toward a girl who'd been everything she wasn't.

And recently—very recently—she'd been annoyed by Jesse's problems intruding into her hectic life, making demands she didn't want to meet.

And none of it, of course, had been Jesse's fault. She hadn't set out to deny Amanda their father's love, and neither had she deliberately chosen the mental illness that had plagued her. Even the drinking and the drugs had been nothing more than manifestations of that illness: "self-medicating," Jesse's therapist had called it—a way of trying to deal with her pain.

They had reached the edge of the woods and the still dark house loomed up ahead of them, a dark bulk in the light of a nearly full moon. They walked up onto the porch, and Michael rapped loudly on the door, shouting Jesse's name and announcing their presence.

Amanda was numb by now, her mind's way of preparing her for what she was sure they'd find. Michael called out again, then reached for the doorknob. Amanda started to dig into her purse for her keys, then saw Michael pull them from his pocket. He'd taken them from her to unlock the garage back at the marina.

He inserted the key and turned it, then frowned and turned it again. She heard herself telling him that sometimes the lock was stiff.

"It must have been unlocked," was his reply as he pushed the door open.

They both stopped in the foyer, listening. The only sound was the faint creaking of the big old porch swing as it moved in the breeze. Her hand went automatically to the light switch on the wall near the door. Then she blinked at the sudden wash of light. Michael glanced into the living room and dining room, then headed back toward the kitchen. Her feet felt leaden, but she followed him.

In the kitchen, they found a half-empty coffee mug on the table and some dirty dishes in the sink. She remained just inside the kitchen door while Michael went over to the sink, picked out two glasses and sniffed at them before putting them back.

"No booze," he said, his voice seeming very loud in the silence. "Where do you keep it?"

"In a cupboard in the dining room." She started in that direction, and he trailed along behind her.

Amanda opened the cupboard, then turned back to Michael with a frown. "Jesse drinks Scotch, but the bottle hasn't been opened." She knew that there hadn't been an open bottle because she'd checked the supplies the last time she'd been out here.

"Maybe she brought it with her," she said, as much to herself as to Michael.

"She wouldn't be likely to do that if she knew there'd be some here," he suggested.

They returned to the foyer and both of them stared up at the darkened staircase. Amanda flipped the switch that turned on the upstairs-hallway light. Michael turned to her and gripped both her arms.

"Why don't you wait here while I go upstairs? Which room is hers?"

She wanted to do as he asked, but she shook her head and started up the stairs, her brain tormenting her with the images. She told herself that she'd already imagined the worst.

Jesse's room was directly across from hers, a large, pleasant room that had seen almost no use in recent years. The door stood open, but so did the others. Michael was behind her now, and a part of her was glad, finally, for his presence. All the resentment she'd felt of his intrusion into her family was gone, as though it had never existed.

I really do *love him*, she thought, wondering why it had taken something like this to make her understand that.

Jesse's room was empty. Some clothes had been tossed onto a chair, and the bed was unmade. A faint aroma of Private Collection, Jesse's favorite scent, lingered in the room.

Michael had moved on to the small adjoining bathroom. He returned before she could follow him, shaking his head in response to her unasked question.

They checked the other bedrooms, and Michael even went down to the basement. Jesse was nowhere to be found. Amanda was beginning to pull back from her darkest fears. But where could she be?

"Could she have gone to one of the other cottages?" Michael asked. "You said you have keys to all of them."

"I can't imagine why she'd do that," Amanda replied, but she was already heading toward her father's small study. The keys were kept in a desk drawer. Michael had checked the study before they went upstairs.

She opened the drawer and held up the keys, then put them

back. Michael was frowning in thought. "What about the tree house? Would she go there?"

Amanda shook her head slowly. "I'm sure she hasn't been up there since we were kids. She wasn't even all that interested in it then."

"I thought you told me that your father had it rebuilt after Jesse fell and broke her ankle."

She was startled for a moment, unable to recall having told him about that. Had she also told him that *she'd* played regularly in it, but that their father had had it rebuilt only after his precious Jesse had been injured?

"That's true, but she never used it much after that."

"I think we'd better check it," Michael said.

He began to shout her name again as they made their way up to the tree house, which sat on slightly higher ground than the house itself. But by the time they reached it, there was still no response.

Michael went first, moving quickly up the wooden steps nailed into the thick trunk. By the time Amanda reached the platform, he had set down his flashlight and was crouching next to the shadowy figure in one corner.

"Jesse, it's Michael," he said softly. "And Amanda's here, too."

When she'd first seen her sister there, Amanda was certain that she must be dead. She was pressed against the railing in one corner, her knees drawn up and her face turned away. But Michael's voice told her that Jesse must be alive. She crossed the platform and knelt beside Michael as he continued to speak softly to her, then reached out and turned her face toward them.

Jesse's eyes were open, but she seemed not to see them. Her hair was disheveled and there were dried tears streaking her makeup. Amanda's first thought, after her relief at finding Jesse alive, was that her sister looked old.

Michael bent close to her, still talking quietly, and sniffed. "No smell of alcohol," he said, turning briefly to her. Then he picked up the flashlight and shone it directly into her face.

Jesse tried to turn away—the first voluntary movement she'd made.

"I don't see any overt signs of drugs," Michael said as he began to shake her gently, grasping her shoulders.

Jesse murmured something, but Amanda didn't catch it. Michael began to try to get her onto her feet, but she sagged against him and he let her slide to the platform again.

"It's too risky for us to try to get her down the steps," he said, moving away from her. "We'll have to get some help. I'll go back to the house and call Steve and get the EMU out here. They can bring a stretcher and get her down that way."

Amanda nodded and watched him start down the steps. Then she turned to Jesse and tried to move her into a more comfortable position. Jesse mumbled something that sounded like a protest, but she didn't resist.

"See if you can get her to talk," Michael shouted from below. "Try to find out what she took."

Confronted with this unresponsive stranger who was her sister, Amanda wasn't sure what to say. She tried to do as Michael had suggested, but got no response. So she began to talk about the times they'd played up here before Jesse's accident. At one point, Jesse mumbled something, but even when she leaned close, Amanda couldn't make out the words.

Finally, in total frustration, Amanda demanded to know why she'd done whatever she'd done. "I *know* you couldn't have killed Eve Lauden! Why won't you tell us the truth?"

Jesse's body began to twitch, and then she drew up her knees again and hugged herself. "Can't. Can't tell."

By now appalled at her outburst, Amanda still could not resist asking, "Why?"

But Jesse merely buried her head in her arms and shook it.

MICHAEL RETURNED. Both Steve and the EMU were on their way. If Steve arrived in time, he would come out with them on the boat the police and emergency services kept at the marina. Otherwise, he would have to wait at the marina until they brought Jesse there.

"Did she say anything?" he asked.

Amanda shook her head, too ashamed to admit that she'd tried to badger her sister.

"It's possible that she didn't take anything," Michael said. "I checked the bathroom and her room and I didn't find any pill bottles." He knelt beside Jesse and checked her pockets, then played the beam of the flashlight over the platform and on the ground beneath them.

After staring at her for a moment, he knelt beside her again. "Jesse, if you took something—even something illegal—I want you to tell me. If you don't, they'll probably pump your stomach, and that's not pleasant."

Unlike his earlier tone, his voice was now all business, all cop. Jesse didn't move, but after a moment, she said, in a low but distinct voice, "Nothing."

"Jesse, listen to me. The emergency medical people will be here soon. If they ask you if you took something, be honest with them. But if they ask you anything else, just keep quiet. Steve is calling your therapist. She'll meet you at the hospital. You can talk to her, but don't talk to anyone else. Do you understand?"

Jesse nodded. "Won't talk to anyone."

"Why did you tell her that?" Amanda whispered when they had moved off to the far corner of the platform.

"For her own protection. Steve is right—she *must* know something. But I don't want her to start babbling to the EMTs or to anyone else. If she confesses to someone, it could be used against her, though I'm sure a good lawyer could get it thrown out."

He saw her shocked expression and went on. "Look, I'm doing the best I can to protect her. If I can get her to talk later, then it can be a voluntary statement and that would be in her favor."

"Michael, I…" Amanda stopped, then stretched up to kiss him. "Thank you."

"Don't thank me yet. If I can't get her to volunteer a statement, then we're still in trouble."

LATER, WHEN JESSE WAS on her way to the hospital and Michael was following, she turned to him, stared at his strong profile in the dim light from the dashboard and thought about his use of the phrase, "*we're* still in trouble." And she knew that nothing Michael might have said could more clearly show his love for her.

But they *were* still in trouble, and it was getting worse.

Chapter Eleven

The bedside clock read 5:03 a.m. when Michael opened his eyes. He was one of those rare people who had no need of an alarm to awaken him. He would simply fix in his mind the time he had to get up, then fall asleep secure in the knowledge that he would awaken at that time.

Most people would have found such a trait to be remarkable, but Michael simply accepted it, much as he accepted everything else that made him what he was. He understood—in a somewhat vague manner—that it was probably the result of his chaotic childhood, when he'd been responsible for getting himself up in the morning for school, then fixing his own breakfast and his lunch, as well. He'd done his own laundry, and even such ironing as was required, from the day he started school.

Michael Quinn was a highly disciplined man, but it was a self-discipline that had come at a very high price.

He slid carefully out of bed, then paused to let his gaze rove over its other occupant. She had pulled the covers up to her neck, and her golden hair spilled over the pillow, catching the dim light that poured in from the hallway.

After gathering up his clothing, Michael padded quietly out of the room, then went into her home office across the hallway and dressed. A few minutes later, he was out into the night, where the sky was just beginning to lighten a bit.

The low rumble of the Porsche's engine seemed very loud

in the predawn silence. He left the parking lot and turned toward his condo, only a short distance away. When he saw the sign at the entrance to the parking lot, he began to downshift, then took his hand off the gearshift and instead continued past it.

After a quick stop at an all-night convenience store for a big container of coffee and some doughnuts, he drove through the still sleeping city, his eyes automatically seeking out the shadows, already the cop again.

Then he'd left the city behind and was climbing into the hills, finally turning into the unmarked driveway that led to his house. Ever since construction had begun, he'd made it a habit to come out at least a couple of times a week to check on things. Before he'd hired the architect and the builder, Michael had devoured every book he could find on the subject of home construction and the pitfalls of building your own home. He knew it was important to keep tabs on even the best builder.

But it had been more than a week since he'd come up here, and now, when his headlights swept across the structure, he was surprised to see that the exterior was completely finished, and the piles of materials that had littered the yard were gone.

He rolled to a stop in front of the double-garage doors and climbed out, then reached back into the car for his breakfast. A minute or so later, he was out on the deck off the master bedroom, having paused only briefly to survey the work inside.

Some time ago, he'd brought out a cheap folding chair and he dropped into it now, then pulled the lid off the coffee container and stared at the slowly awakening city spread out below him. A mist was rising from the river, nearly obscuring the Bottom. He remembered that mist well. He'd walked to school in it many times, a stolen knife in his pocket to protect him from the older boys who liked to prey on little kids. He wouldn't be able to do that now; his old school had metal detectors in the doorways because kids like him often carried guns now.

His gaze shifted to the small corner of the lake that was visible from here, and with it, his thoughts shifted, as well: away from his childhood to the present and the immediate future. And to the past as well, really.

Like all good detectives, Michael trusted his instincts, but this was a time when he wished that he didn't trust them quite so much because he didn't like what they were telling him.

The suspicion had been there all along, even though he'd tried to ignore it. But now, with the near certainty that Jesse knew something, he couldn't afford to ignore it any longer. The only question in his mind was how to proceed—and what price he would have to pay to see that justice was served.

"OBJECTION, YOUR HONOR. Counsel is leading the witness." Amanda kept her eyes on the judge and ignored the outraged expression the defense counsel had contrived to fix on his face.

"Sustained. Reframe your question, Counselor."

Amanda sank back into her seat, grateful for even this small victory. Behind her, she could feel the eyes of the media on her. She knew it wasn't likely that they'd heard about Jesse or that they'd consider it to be newsworthy if they did, but she couldn't quell the fear that they were going to pounce on her the moment court recessed, demanding to know what her sister knew about Eve Lauden's death. Even though she hadn't yet been positively identified, Michael had released her name in the hope that someone who remembered her or knew the whereabouts of her family would contact him.

Fortunately, the drive-by shooting and the case she was now trying had kept a twenty-year-old murder from receiving the coverage it might otherwise have garnered, especially given the fact that the body had been found on the island. But with the arrest of the little girl's killer and with this trial winding its way toward conclusion, she didn't doubt that the media would be seeking something new to titillate viewers, listeners and readers.

Worst of all, Amanda was really winging it today. After she'd gotten to the hospital last night and had assured herself that Jesse was doing as well as could be expected, she'd tried to see Ted, her chief assistant. But he'd already gone to sleep and the nurse had told her that waking him would do her little good because he'd been given a sleeping pill.

This morning, she'd gotten up early with the intention of seeing Ted before court began, but any possibility of that had ended when her father called her.

She had, of course, called him last night, and while he'd had little to say then, he'd obviously spent the night worrying, and by this morning was back to blaming her and Michael for having driven Jesse to her present state.

Most of his criticism this time, however, had fallen on Michael, and at one point, Amanda had nearly told him that the man he was so obnoxiously condemning was his future son-in-law. But she'd stopped herself, realizing that that would only serve to convince him that Michael was influencing *her*.

After that conversation, she'd just barely had time to call the hospital. The private-duty nurse they'd hired to stay with Jesse reported that she'd had a quiet night and was still sleeping under the influence of the drug they'd given her.

During the brief morning recess, Amanda called Jesse's therapist, but was unable to speak with her because she was in session. Then she called the hospital again and learned that Michael had been there only moments before, but had left quickly when Jesse became agitated and refused to speak to him. Steve was with her now, and he said that Jesse was awake and aware of her surroundings, but incommunicative otherwise.

Over the lunch recess, Amanda went to the hospital. Jesse was awake and sitting up in bed, but the moment she saw Amanda, she slid down in the bed and pulled the covers over her head. Fighting her frustration, Amanda managed to murmur some soothing words, then went to the floor below to see Ted.

They spent a half hour going over the case, and Amanda returned to court feeling much more comfortable about how to proceed. Ted told her that some of the other staff, who'd managed to pop into the courtroom from time to time, had told him she was doing a great job. She could only hope that it wasn't just empty praise for the boss, because she had no sense herself of how it was going. She'd been operating mostly on autopilot.

During the afternoon recess, she finally managed to speak to Jesse's therapist, who'd just returned from visiting her at the hospital.

"I'm afraid that what's happened with Jesse doesn't really fit neatly into any category," the therapist said. "We do know now that she didn't take anything—including alcohol—and she swears that she had no intention to kill herself. For what it's worth, I believe her.

"What's happening with Jesse is part denial, I think, and partly an internal struggle. There's something she's trying to come to terms with, and that's about all I can tell you."

"But can you at least tell me if she's talking to *you* about it?" Amanda asked, both understanding and at the same time hating the rules of confidentiality by which the therapist was bound.

"A little, but not in any great detail," was the maddeningly vague response.

When court recessed for the day, Amanda returned to her office, where she spent a half hour attending to other business, then turned her attention to Jesse once again. Among the messages on her desk was one from Michael, asking that she have him paged. But she ignored it for the time being and considered her sister's situation.

The best way to help Jesse at this point would be to take the burden off her, to find another way to get the information that was tearing her apart.

She was more and more convinced that the mysterious woman who had once been a madam and a conduit for drugs to kids like Jesse held the key. If Jesse knew something about Eve's death, it was almost certainly through her contacts with that woman.

Amanda had heard nothing more from Tina or from Mary Walters, who'd promised to ask her assistant, Elaine Barker, if she knew the woman's name.

Her lawyer's mind went to work. Maybe she could now use her sister's condition as a wedge to pry that information out of Tina. She thought it was possible that Mary knew who she was—or that Elaine knew—but Tina seemed to be her best bet. She supposed that she should feel guilty about using Jesse's illness so crassly, but it was for her own good.

She reached for the phone, then pulled back. It would be better to go see Tina in person, and she should be home by now. She glanced briefly at the pink message slip with Michael's name on it, and a little warmth seeped into her as she remembered his kindness and gentleness with Jesse last night—not to mention with *her*.

Sometime, when all this was over, perhaps she'd have time to reflect on just how remarkable it all was: that the dangerous boy from the Bottom who'd been the object of a young girl's fantasies had now become the man with whom she intended to spend the rest of her life.

But she didn't call him. Instead, she left the office and drove to Tina's, where she found her preparing dinner for her kids, including a little girl who looked remarkably like her mother.

Tina somewhat hesitantly asked her to join them, and then, when Amanda explained that she'd only gotten around to eating lunch a half hour ago, she said that perhaps they could have some wine while the children ate. Amanda accepted, and they moved to the tiny living room while the children ate in the kitchen and watched cartoons on a small TV mounted under the cabinets.

Amanda told her about Jesse, sparing no details when she

described her sister's condition. "I'm certain that she knows something about Eve's death—and so is her husband. But whatever it is, she can't bring herself to talk about it. Her therapist says that's why she's in this state. The only way I can think of to help her is to find another way to get the information she has. That would take the burden off her."

"You want her name," Tina said softly when she had finished.

"Yes. My guess is that Jesse was getting drugs through her, and that she somehow found out something about Eve that way." She paused.

"Look, this woman—whoever she is—can't be in any legal trouble now, unless *she* killed Eve herself."

"Oh, no, I'm sure she didn't." Tina protested.

"Then the only thing she could be charged with is being an accessory, having knowledge of a crime. But if she helps by coming forth, she won't be charged."

"I don't think she knew *anything*," Tina said. "I'm sure she just thought what *I* did—that Eve had gone down to the city."

But she knows differently now, Amanda thought, but didn't say. "Please tell me who she is, Tina. I'll do my best to protect her."

"Do you think that your sister will talk about it at some point?" Tina asked.

Amanda nodded. "I think she'll *have* to, if she's going to get over it. But right now, she's...going through hell."

"If what she knows is what I'm thinking, she's been going through hell for a long time," Tina said quietly, her eyes filling up with tears.

"What do you mean?" Amanda asked, barely getting the words out as a chill gripped her.

Tina shook her head and wiped away the tears. "It's Elaine Barker."

"Elaine Barker?" Amanda stared at her in disbelief, then nodded slowly. Yes. Now she understood why everyone, including Jesse, had wanted to protect her. The only person more revered in this struggling community than Elaine was her boss, Mary Walters. And Mary probably knew, too.

Tina nodded. "Not many people know. I only knew because Eve told me. Elaine didn't live in the Bottom then, like she does now. She grew up down there, but she was living in Parkside then. Her husband just disappeared and left her with three kids to feed.

"I know what she did was really wrong, but I can understand how desperate she must have been. No one could live on what welfare gave you, and she didn't want to have to move back to the Bottom because of her kids, you know? Her cousin was a big dealer, and that's how she got into it. The other thing just sort of happened—the girls, I mean. They were all on the street before they started to work for her—including Eve.

"In a way, she made it safer for them, you know?" Tina paused to consider what she'd said. "Except for Eve, I guess."

Amanda struggled to find something to say that wouldn't sound condescending. Michael would have understood, she knew. But this was far beyond her ability to comprehend. The biggest choices she'd had to face were where to go to college and law school, then how to structure her career. She'd never had to choose between a life of crime and the well-being of her children.

"She's made up for it," Tina insisted, perhaps seeing something on Amanda's face. "She understands these kids better than their parents do—and she helps them. Isn't that better than going to prison?"

"Yes, it is," Amanda said—and meant it. She got rather shakily to her feet.

"I'm going to talk to her, but I won't tell her who gave me her name. I really appreciate it, Tina."

She left the apartment as Tina bade her a tearful goodbye. She knew where Elaine lived because she'd driven her home once after a meeting. It wasn't far. She drove slowly through the busy streets, where everyone was out to take advantage of the pleasant evening. But she saw none of it; instead, she felt as though she were about to be swallowed by an unimaginable darkness.

Elaine's house was dark. Amanda was certain she had the right house. It was on a short street filled with tiny wood-frame houses that had been built in the twenties or thirties and were now in the process of being rehabilitated. Elaine's was the most attractive house on the street: freshly painted white, with black trim and window boxes that were filled with pansies at the moment.

She parked at the curb and walked up onto the small porch. Three newspapers lay on the painted wood porch floor, and the top of her mailbox was slightly open because of the quantity of mail inside.

Amanda pressed the doorbell and heard it ring inside, but she was certain that Elaine wasn't there, and nearly certain that she'd fled because she feared just such a visit.

When there was no response, Amanda returned to her car and made a U-turn in the quiet street, then headed toward the community center. It was possible that Elaine might be there, or at the teen shelter next door, but she doubted it. And if she wasn't there, then Mary probably was.

Amanda was impelled by a need to know the truth. What the cost to her of learning that truth might be didn't enter into the picture. There was her desire as an officer of the court to see that justice was served, and there was her need to help Jesse by bringing the truth to her as a fait accompli.

All the parking spaces near the community center were taken, but when Amanda arrived, an old station wagon loaded with kids pulled out and she was able to park directly in front of the unattractive yellow brick building that had once been a factory of some type.

Inside, she was greeted by squeals and screams and loud rock music. No one was at the small reception desk, but a tall young man in gym shorts and a T-shirt, wearing a whistle on a chain around his neck, greeted her and asked if he could help her. When she asked if Elaine was there, he shook his head.

"Mary Walters, the director, is here, though. Her office is back there—last door on the left," He grinned. "As far from the noise as she can get."

Amanda thanked him, although she already knew where Mary's office was. In fact, she recalled that Mary had once jokingly threatened to move her office out to the Dumpster in the parking lot to get away from the noise.

The noise faded gradually as she walked back the long hallway to the rear of the building. But before she had quite reached Mary's office, the door opened and Michael walked out.

Even in her present state of mind, his sudden appearance overwhelmed her, sending a frisson through her body and filling her mind with sensual images. She was faintly embarrassed to realize that he could still affect her that powerfully.

He waited for her, his dark eyes burning into her as she walked toward him. She started to apologize for her failure to return his call, but by then Mary had come to the door, as well, and was greeting her—somewhat warily, she thought.

For all that his presence had aroused her, Amanda didn't want Michael to be there now. There was a lingering trace of reluctance to involve him in this—even though he clearly *was* involved—but there were also practical considerations. Amanda felt that she stood a better chance of getting the truth out of Mary if Michael wasn't present.

But Michael made no move to leave, and she couldn't think of any excuse to get rid of him. After a moment's awkwardness, she said that she had come to see Mary because she couldn't find Elaine.

The look that passed briefly over Mary's face told her that Mary knew exactly why she was seeking Elaine, and she was sure that Michael had caught that expression, as well.

"She's on vacation," Mary said. "I finally persuaded her to get away for a while."

"Do you have a number where I can reach her?" Amanda asked. "It's really important that I speak with her."

Mary shook her head. "She's traveling—visiting family in several places. She'll be gone for a month. She had four weeks of vacation accumulated."

Amanda could have accepted that and walked out—and a part of her wanted to do just that. But she thought about Jesse, drugged in a hospital, struggling with herself. She cast a quick look at Michael, who was watching both of them closely.

"Then maybe you can help me. I need to confirm some information I've received."

Mary Walters was not good at dissembling. Her face drained of color and her body stiffened. She shot a quick look at Michael.

"Lieutenant Quinn needs to hear this, as well," Amanda said. "It concerns a possible murder investigation."

Mary said nothing, but she stepped back into her office and they both followed her. Michael closed the door behind them. Amanda began as soon as they had all been seated.

"You remember when we talked before that I asked you for the name of a woman who'd been involved with providing drugs to middle-class kids and also with a teenage prostitute ring back in the seventies? We thought she might be able to help us in the Eve Lauden investigation."

Mary nodded, but still said nothing. If anything, she'd grown even paler and was fidgeting in her chair.

"We also believe that my sister might know something about it. She was involved in drugs herself back then. She's in the hospital now. We thought that she'd tried to commit suicide. Her therapist says that she's trying to deal with some terrible secret. She's in bad shape, Mary."

"I'm sorry to hear that. Jesse's been a great help to us with the business community."

Amanda knew that Mary was sincere in her concern for Jesse and she pushed it further. "The only way I can think of to help her is to get at the truth myself. Then she won't have to carry that burden any longer.

"Today, I received some information—the name of the woman I asked you about. I wanted to see Elaine to confirm it, but since she's not here, I'm asking you."

Michael sat in a chair beside her, so she couldn't see his face. But in her peripheral vision, she could see him turn to her. She kept her gaze fixed on Mary. For a long moment, Mary said nothing. Then, suddenly, she leaned back in her chair and sighed heavily.

"I thought it was only a matter of time until Michael found out. But I hadn't counted on *you* being the one to get the information."

She sighed again. "Yes, it was Elaine. I persuaded her to get away for a while, to think things over. She knew she should go to Michael and tell him what she knew, but she's terrified of losing everything she's worked so hard for since then.

"We even talked about sending an anonymous letter to the police, but Elaine said that probably wouldn't do any good, that you'd need her testimony."

Mary paused and stared hard at both of them. "She knew nothing about Eve's death until the body was found. And even then, she wasn't sure until I spoke to her after we talked. Apparently, she thought just what everyone else did at the time—that Eve had taken off to the city.

"She *did* say, though, that she was surprised at the time, because Eve was determined to finish school, despite everything else she was doing. She'd even talked about going to college, and apparently she was smart enough to do that. Elaine had real hopes for her, and was disappointed when she disappeared like that."

"Does Elaine know how Eve could have ended up on the island?" Amanda asked, unaware of the intensity behind her words.

Mary stared at her, then flicked her eyes quickly toward Michael. "She didn't tell me."

"But you think she *does* know?" Amanda asked.

"Yes, I think so." Mary turned her full attention to Michael. "Do you know how many…innocent people could be hurt by this? It won't bring Eve back, and it could destroy other lives. Besides, you just told me that you aren't certain she was murdered, that she could have died as the result of an accident."

Amanda turned to Michael and saw a muscle twitch along his jaw as he stared at Mary. When he remained silent, she spoke instead.

"We're both committed to serving justice, Mary. If Eve's death was an accident, we need to know that. Besides, there's Jesse to think of."

"Yes, Jesse," Mary said with another sigh. "Elaine told me that she *did* know Jesse briefly back then. She bought her drugs from Elaine's cousin, through Elaine."

"So Jesse knows who could have taken Eve to the island," Amanda said, nearly choking on the words. Jesse's drug problems had begun before Eve's murder, but Amanda was now wondering if her knowledge of Eve's death could be responsible for all that had happened to her since then.

But no, that couldn't be right. She *couldn't* have known that Eve was buried out there, or she would have protested over the cottage. Confusion swarmed over her as Michael stood up.

"Thanks for your help, Mary. I'll be in touch."

He reached down to take her arm and help her to her feet, as well, and as Amanda stood up, she saw Mary's gaze veer from her to Michael and back again, a question in her eyes.

Michael's arm slid around her waist as they left the office, but Amanda was too lost in her bleak thoughts to notice his confirmation of Mary's suspicions.

"Tina told you?" Michael asked as they walked out of the center. "I'd planned to go see her next."

"Yes, she told me. I guess I should feel ashamed of using Jesse like this, but what I said is true. The only way Jesse can heal is if it all comes out in the open."

She stopped beside her car. "So you were right from the beginning. It *was* someone from the island."

"It looks that way," Michael said, watching her closely. Only someone who knew her as well as he did would have detected the struggle being waged within her. He wondered what she was thinking, but decided now was not the time to pursue it.

"Have you had dinner? There's a great little Italian place only a couple of blocks from here that I'll bet you've never been to."

Rather to his surprise, she managed a smile. "Then you'd be wrong. I've been there—with Mary and Elaine."

They took her car. Michael had left his Porsche in the lot at the restaurant, after being unable to find parking near the center. He watched her as she drove with the intense concentration of someone who knew they probably shouldn't be driving at all. In fact, he'd fully expected her to refuse his invitation to dinner.

The restaurant was old and more than slightly seedy, but what it lacked in ambience, it more than made up with the quality and the quantity of its food. Michael was greeted with the effusiveness reserved for old friends, which he was. Beginning when he was twelve, the owners had hired him off the books to help out in the kitchen. They'd also fed him, which had mattered even more to a growing and always hungry boy.

They were led to a secluded booth in the rear that was reserved for family, and after recommending to Amanda that she try the chicken *piccata,* he told her about his connection to the owners.

"I went to school with one of their sons, and when they found out I'd been picked up for shoplifting, Nick decided to do his bit to decrease crime by hiring me—off the books, of course, since I was only twelve.

"But the best thing was the food. It sure beat tuna casserole, which was about the extent of my mother's cooking—when she cooked at all, that is." He grinned and shook his head. "I still can't look at a can of tuna without wanting to gag."

Amanda laughed, but he could see that she was just being polite. He was searching for another safe topic of conversation when a large, heavy hand laid itself on his shoulder.

"I saw that fine machine of yours out there earlier," said the beefy, dark-haired man as he looked with interest at Amanda.

"Amanda, this is Tony Gambelli, the son of the owners. Tony, this is—"

"Amanda Sturdevant, our esteemed district attorney," Tony said, his big paw engulfing the hand that Amanda extended. "If you're a friend of Michael's, you've got my vote."

Amanda thanked him, and Tony joined them, launching quickly into a discussion of politics. His uncle sat on the city council. Michael relaxed and let them do most of the talking.

He was grateful for Tony's appearance because it seemed to take Amanda's mind away from the issue at hand—for a while, anyway. He wondered how far she'd gotten with her thinking and whether those thoughts would eventually veer in the same direction as his. Somehow, he doubted it.

Tony left when their food arrived, and Michael tried to keep the conservation going along the same lines. But it didn't work. Amanda soon subsided into a brooding silence.

"Do you think Mary knows how to reach Elaine?" she asked after a while.

"No," Michael lied. "I think she would have told us."

"But she'll be gone for a *month*."

"Then we'll just have to wait—unless Jesse decides to talk."

"Michael, you can't push her. She's…"

"Come on, give me some credit. I'm not even going to go see her again. But maybe her therapist will persuade her to open up—or maybe she'll come to that conclusion herself."

He didn't think for one minute that would happen, but she

seemed to accept it. "Besides," he went on, "from what you were telling Tony, you've got a heavy campaign schedule, so maybe it's time to just back off from this. Like Mary said, nothing is going to bring Eve back, and justice can wait a while longer."

She frowned at him, but he kept his expression neutral. He knew what she was thinking: that this didn't sound like him. Sometimes, he forgot that she knew him about as well as he knew her.

"I'm still having a hard time accepting that Elaine could have done things like that," she said after a moment. "She's such a good person. I've never met anyone so dedicated to helping kids."

"You've heard that old expression about not judging someone till you've walked a mile in their shoes? I think maybe that applies here."

She stared hard at him. "Do you mean that you can condone what she did?"

"No. I didn't mean that, but I *can* understand it, maybe. You have to have lived close to the edge to understand what it means to fall over it. I don't know all the details, but I do know that Elaine's husband left her with a couple of kids and no way to support them."

Amanda told him the rest of what Tina had said about Elaine, and he nodded. "So her cousin probably set her up in that house in Parkside. She had a choice—go on welfare and try to keep her kids out of trouble in the Bottom, or do what he wanted and raise them in a safer neighborhood.

"Can you really say that she made the wrong choice? I know for a fact that all her kids have done well—and that might not have happened if they'd grown up in the Bottom."

"*You* grew up in the Bottom, and so did Tina. And both of you have done well."

"So we were lucky. Anyway, Elaine has served her time, and in a better way than going to prison."

"Yes, I suppose you're right," she said, but in a doubtful tone.

Michael talked her into having some dessert: warm, fresh cannoli, and then they left the restaurant. As they were walking toward their cars, another car pulled into the lot and several men got out. One of them was Neal Hadden.

"Amanda! Michael! Well, this is a surprise!" Hadden said in his best courtroom voice.

Michael managed to nod a greeting, but his hands were itching. He'd like nothing better than to bust a few of Hadden's big white teeth. What had Amanda ever seen in him?

Amanda greeted him pleasantly, then turned toward her car. But Hadden apparently hadn't finished. "I hear you've positively identified that girl from the island. My sources tell me that she was a hooker and a drug addict. Have you got any theories about how she ended up out there?"

He addressed himself to Michael, who was now clenching his fists to keep them quiet. Out of the corner of his eye, he could see Amanda staring at him. He'd forgotten to tell her about the positive ID on Eve.

Michael smiled at him—the kind of smile he used on uncooperative suspects. It pleased him to see fear spark briefly in Hadden's eyes. "If I had any theories, Hadden, you'd be the last to know."

Hadden stared at Michael for a moment, then turned to Amanda. "I assume you'll be bringing in an outside prosecutor on this one, Amanda."

"I know my job, Neal," she replied in a frosty tone.

"Some people might say that it doesn't look so good— you getting so cozy with the police," Hadden said with a smirk.

Michael was ready to explode, but at that moment, Amanda put out her hand. "Thanks for dinner, Lieutenant. I'm sorry that things have been so busy we couldn't get together during office hours to discuss the case."

Michael shook her hand, his anger dissolving into amusement over her act. "No problem. Good luck in court tomorrow."

They both conspicuously ignored Hadden, who finally rejoined the man he was with and went into the restaurant.

"Were you really going to hit him?" she asked, her tone somewhere between amusement and shock.

"It's probably a good thing that we didn't have to find out," Michael said. "What did you ever see in him?"

"I don't know. I've been asking myself that same question. But I think he's guessed that something's going on between us."

"Yeah, I think so, too," Michael admitted, then shrugged. "We couldn't have hoped to keep it secret forever. I'll follow you back to your place, and we can talk about it."

But she shook her head. "I have to prepare my closing argument for tomorrow. Is it true that you've got a positive ID on Eve? How is it that Neal knew, and I didn't?"

"That's why I called you earlier. Her mother called. Someone she still kept in touch with from here had called her. She's living in some little burg near Schenectady.

"It turns out that there were some dental records, and we got them. She also said that Eve had broken a bone in her right arm, and the forensics people confirmed that from their examination. It's her.

"We released the information in time for the evening news. That's probably how Hadden knew about it."

"What else did her mother say?" Amanda asked, and he could see her tense up.

"Nothing of importance," he replied honestly. "She claims she didn't know what Eve was into, and she'd always thought that she ran away to the city.

"How about if I come over later, then, after you've finished your work?"

"No. I'm sorry, Michael, but I'd really prefer to be alone tonight. There's just too much on my mind."

He didn't like what he was hearing. It sounded to him like she was trying to cut him out of her life. He started to protest, to tell her that he wouldn't let her do that, that she needed him. But he stopped himself. This wasn't the time to push.

Instead, he waited until she was in her car, then surveyed the parking lot before bending down through the window to kiss her.

"I love you, you know. That's why I'm being a nice guy and letting you go tonight."

He was rewarded by a tentative smile. "I love you, too, Michael."

He watched her drive out of the lot, then started toward his own car. He had a phone call to make, but given the nature of that call, he didn't want to use his car phone.

AMANDA DIDN'T SEE her father until she had finished her closing statement, which, she decided, was probably a good thing. He'd come to court to hear her a few times before, and it never failed to make her nervous. As a teenager, she'd watched her father in court when he'd held the position she now held, and she was sure that she could never be as good as he was.

She sat through the defense attorney's closing statement, wondering why her father was here. Was it possible that he'd come to apologize for his behavior toward her? It wasn't likely to have anything to do with Jesse because she'd spoken to Steve over the lunch recess, and there was no change. Jesse was still being kept heavily medicated, though Steve said they would begin tomorrow to wean her off the powerful drugs.

When the defense attorney finished, the judge called a recess for the day, saying that he would instruct the jury in the morning. Amanda immediately got up, but by the time she reached her father, he was surrounded by the media. They were asking him about his prospects for the Supreme Court, and it was only through their questions that Amanda learned that one of the current justices had indeed announced his retirement.

"All I can tell you," Judge Thomas Sturdevant said, "is what the White House has already stated. I'm on the shortlist, and I consider that to be a great honor."

"What about that body they found on the island, Judge?" One of the more obnoxious reporters shouted from the back of the crowd. "Is that going to cause any problems for you?"

Amanda saw her father frown. "I don't see how it could. I spoke some time ago with Lieutenant Quinn, but I don't know anything that could help him in his investigation."

Then he gestured toward her. "Folks, if you don't mind, I really came here to see my daughter."

Some of them turned to her and began to ask her questions, but not with any great enthusiasm. Amanda guessed that their interest in her case had peaked—at least until the verdict came in—and they were ready to move on. It was unfortunate that the justice's retirement announcement had coincided with the positive ID on Eve, thereby forging a link between her father and the dead girl that she knew they would continue to exploit for a time.

"You were very good," her father said, taking her arm and propelling her down the hallway to the elevators.

"Thank you, but I really wasn't well prepared for this one." As they got onto the elevator, she told him about Ted's accident and how she came to be trying the case herself.

"You'll get a favorable verdict," he said as they rode up to her office—his old office.

"I hope you're right," she replied with a smile, recalling how he had always seemed to know how the jury would go—something very few attornies could do.

She led the way into her office suite, where he paused to greet several of her assistants and her secretary before following her into her office.

"Do you know anything more than you told the press down there?" she asked. "I hadn't heard about the announcement. I've been too busy to follow the news."

"I've been told privately that I'm their man. They're running my nomination by some key members of the judiciary committee before announcing it."

Amanda smiled and stretched up to kiss his cheek. "Oh, Father, I'm so happy for you."

He returned the smile. "I'm trying not to count my chickens just yet."

"Are you worried about the Eve Lauden thing?" she asked, wondering if she should tell him about the latest development.

"Not really," he replied. "The local press might try to make something out of it, but that's all."

"Have you seen Jesse?"

He shook his head. "I went by the hospital, but they told me that her therapist was with her. Has she talked at all to you?"

"No. And Michael—Lieutenant Quinn—has promised to stay away from her, too."

"I don't understand why he thinks she knows anything in the first place," he said angrily.

Once again, Amanda wondered if she should tell him. But she decided against it. He had enough on his mind right now. Instead, she said that Michael was a very good and very thorough investigator.

Her father frowned, then shrugged. "Yes, of course. I guess that it's been so long since I've worked with the police that I'd nearly forgotten how they can be."

Amanda also decided that this was definitely not the time to tell him about Michael and her. In fact, her father seemed more agitated than she had ever before seen him. Instead of taking a seat, he was pacing around the office with a nervous energy that was most unlike him.

And why shouldn't he be nervous? she asked herself rhetorically. He's on the very threshold of achieving his life's goal. For as long as she could remember, that goal had been the Supreme Court.

She wondered if his casual dismissal of the importance of the Eve Lauden case was sincere. It now seemed inevitable that someone from the island had been involved, and every one of them was a close friend. Most were distant relatives.

But who could it be? That was the question that continued to haunt her. She *knew* these people, knew them well. None of them could possibly be a murderer, but she was beginning to understand that one of them might have been capable of covering up an accidental death in order to protect his reputation. After all, every one of them had positions that could have been severely damaged by the revelation that he'd been involved with a prostitute.

Or was it still possible that none of them *was* involved, that Eve had gone out there with friends and something had happened? Tina had said that Eve wasn't always honest and that she craved status. Didn't that make it likely that she'd lied?

And if she had gone out there with friends, then died or been killed by one of them, wouldn't they have been very careful to eliminate any trace of their presence after they buried her?

"I'm going to try to reach Jesse's therapist," Amanda told her father as she picked up the phone. "We'll see what she says about whether or not this would be a good time for us to visit her."

"I don't like having to ask a therapist if I can see my daughter," he stated coldly.

"Father, we have to accept that Jesse has problems. You said that yourself. And if we, as attorneys, expect people to take *our* advice, then we should be prepared to take the advice of other professionals."

His frown dissolved into a grudging smile. "You're right. Call her."

The therapist answered her office phone herself, and after Amanda identified herself, she informed her that she'd just returned from the hospital.

"Jesse is being weaned from the drugs now, but she's still rather incoherent. And she's still refusing to talk about whatever it is that's troubling her. I asked her if she wished to have visits from her family, and she said that Steve could come. I've already spoken with him."

"My father is here," Amanda told her. "And we'd both like to see her."

"I don't think that would be wise just yet," the therapist responded. "She specifically stated that she didn't want to see anyone but Steve. I think that's a very good sign, though, that she's wanting to see Steve."

Amanda agreed. It seemed to suggest that their marriage was stronger than Amanda had believed.

She hung up and informed her father that they couldn't see Jesse just yet, but that Steve would be visiting her.

"She needs her *family*," the judge stated angrily.

"Father, Steve *is* her family. He's her husband!"

"Her third mistake," he replied in disgust. He'd never cared for Steve or for her first two husbands, either.

AMANDA SAT at the small table and listened to her father talk about the politics of a Supreme Court nomination, between interruptions, that is. People kept stopping by their table to congratulate him. The evening network news had identified him as the most likely nominee, though the White House had refused to comment.

She felt proud to be there with him, proud to be his daughter. He had told her that the Senate confirmation hearings would most likely be held before summer recess, and he would like her to be there with him. She was thrilled.

But even in the midst of her happiness for him, it seemed to her that a darkness hovered. Her life had become so…compartmentalized. There was her father. There was Michael. There was Jesse. And there was the ghost of Eve Lauden. And, of course, her campaign. All of them separate, and yet intertwined. Too many boxes—and too many secrets.

Chapter Twelve

"You're sure it was him?"

"Yes, I'm sure."

"Did you actually see them together that night?"

"Yes. He picked her up at my place. He didn't get out of his car, but I knew the car. It was an old station wagon they kept for the housekeeper's use. Besides, I saw his face when she opened the door to get in."

"How can you be sure it was that night—the night she disappeared?"

"Well, I can't be sure of that, of course, but..."

Michael listened to her explanation, asked a few more questions, then thanked her and hung up. After that, he sat at his desk for a very long time.

"Michael, where are you?"

"On my way over. Sorry I'm late, but..."

"Don't come here! I think someone's watching us."

"What makes you think that?"

"I went out to empty the trash a few minutes ago. The trash house is at the rear of the parking lot, and I went out the back door. I only checked the visitors' lot because I was expecting you, and that's when I saw him. I don't know his name, but I know he's a private detective. I think he's a former cop."

"Describe him."

She did, and Michael swore. "Fred Carruthers. Hadden's law firm has used him."

"I assumed it must be Neal. What are we going to do?"

"Can you get out the back way and come over to Westview?"

Amanda agreed to meet him in fifteen minutes. She'd left her briefcase in her car because she'd had bags of groceries to carry in earlier. She'd intended to spend the evening catching up on some work, but when Michael called, she'd very willingly put that notion aside.

Now she went out the front door, forcing herself to ignore the visitors' parking area even though she could see that the detective's car was still there. She retrieved her briefcase from her car and carried it back inside. That should convince him that she was planning to spend the evening alone.

She was seething. If Neal Hadden had been here right now, she could have cheerfully strangled him. She wondered how much of this was personal, and how much could be attributed to the results of a newspaper poll announced just yesterday that showed her with a wide lead in their race.

Probably both, she decided. But as Neal had pointed out in the accompanying article, her position gave her much greater name recognition at this point. No, she was convinced that it was more personal than political. Neal had seen them together at the restaurant that night, and he'd probably been stewing over it ever since.

The very qualities that had made her end their relationship were the same ones that were now going to get her into trouble. Neal was too possessive. At first, she'd found his attention flattering, even charming, but fortunately, she'd soon seen it for what it was: an ugly possessiveness that would rob her of herself.

She carried her briefcase inside, then up to her home office. Then she turned on the desk lamp. The room faced the front, where the detective could see it. She even let him see her before she closed the miniblinds. He probably wouldn't stay long. He'd assume that she was going to stay home and work all evening.

After that, she changed quickly into dark clothing and slipped out the back door. She made her way past the other condos, then through the narrow strip of woods that separated the complex from Westview Avenue, the street that ran behind it.

Michael was already there, waiting. He reached across and pushed the door open, and she slid into the leather seat. He saw the look on her face and grinned.

"Good thing Hadden wasn't out there himself, or I'd be bringing you in on a murder charge right now."

"Or aggravated assault, at the very least," she replied, relaxing somewhat in the face of his humor.

"We'll go out to the house," Michael said as he pulled away from the curb. "I don't think he'd have anyone watching my place, too, but the house will be safer."

"I can't believe that we have to sneak around like this!"

"That's what you have to decide. It's your call because you're the one who has something to lose."

"You could, too, you know. He might accuse you of dragging your heels on the investigation."

"It's still your call."

Neither of them said anything else as they passed through the downtown and then headed out to the North Hills area. She saw Michael checking the rearview mirror a few times, and then he began to make a series of unnecessary turns through an older residential neighborhood.

"Do you think we're being followed?" she asked, barely resisting the urge to turn and look behind them.

"No, I'm just being careful. The problem with this car is that it's too damn conspicuous."

Finally, he made his way back to the road that led to his new house, and a few minutes later, they came to a halt before the garage.

"It looks like it's almost finished," she commented in surprise.

"It will be in about another month. I'm planning to put the condo up for sale next week."

As they got out of the car, Amanda stared at the house. For the first time, she realized that she was staring at their future. The thought both thrilled her, and frightened her. Everything seemed to be moving too quickly. Where was her usual caution? Had it just gotten lost in the midst of everything else that was making demands upon her at the moment? Or was her future with Michael the one sure thing in her life right now?

She turned to him and their eyes met, and suddenly none of those questions mattered. Michael got the quilt from the trunk, and they went inside. The evening was amazingly warm for April, more like a midsummer night. He spread the quilt on the floor of the balcony off the master bedroom. Amanda stared at the distant lights of the city. Their problems seemed just as far away.

Their lovemaking began in an unhurried fashion: slow strokings and lingering kisses and soft words. Their bodies became erotic playgrounds: familiar to each of them by now, but still exciting. Michael was patient, considerate, and very thorough. He was the dream lover she could not have imagined years ago in the midst of her innocent longings.

But even as they meandered along love's byways, hunger coursed through them both, building the rhythm, urging them on. Michael lifted her atop him, and she welcomed him into her and they both shuddered and cried out, simultaneously welcoming the moment and protesting its passing. Their cries momentarily rose above the chittering of the spring peepers, then subsided into soft moans and gasps as the rhythmical sounds from the darkness swelled once more.

Wrapped close together in the quilt, they listened to the sounds. An owl called from quite close by, startling them both with its eternal question.

"That's a great horned owl," Michael said.

"How do you know that? Have you seen it?"

"No, I bought a bird book. Every time I come up here, I

keep seeing birds I'd never seen before. The best was a pileated woodpecker. Have you ever seen one of them?''

"I've seen woodpeckers, but I'm not sure which kind they were."

"If you'd seen a pileated, you'd remember it. You probably saw downies or hairies. They're pretty common. Pileated woodpeckers are huge—as big as crows. They're gray and white with this big red comb on their heads. The book says they're mostly a deep-woods bird. You should see the size of the holes they drill in trees."

She smiled. "Give a man a house in the woods, and he turns into a bird-watcher. That could be bad for your tough-guy image, Michael."

"So we're both a little schizophrenic. What about your ice-queen image, Ms. District Attorney?"

She laughed, but the laughter died away quickly as she thought about why they were out here, instead of at her condo. "What are we going to do?"

"We have two choices," he said firmly. "Either we stay away from each other until after the election, or we go public now."

"But there's a third choice," she protested. "We can continue as we are."

Michael shook his head. "Sooner or later, Hadden will catch us."

She remained silent, thinking. He was probably right. It was surprising that they hadn't been caught yet. And then there was the ethical question. Didn't the public have a right to know about them before they chose a district attorney? She doubted that it would make any difference to the public's mind, but if Neal Hadden told them why it should...

"I need to think about it for a few days," she told him. "I really want the job."

"I know you do, but will you feel as though you've really won if you win by lying?"

"It's not really lying," she protested. "I know that my decisions about cases will never be influenced by you, and if there's a case where I think it could, I can always bounce it off the rest of the staff. They wouldn't be afraid to speak up."

"I know that and you know that, but there could be those in the media who would claim otherwise."

She clenched her fists. "Do you know what I want? I want just one thing to be settled. I'm tired of questions."

Michael chuckled and planted a kiss on the top of her head. "One thing *is* settled, and that's *us*. We both know what we want."

Or at least *he* did. And she did right now. It took all of Michael's willpower not to ask for her promise that nothing could change the way they felt about each other.

AMANDA WAS STILL SAVORING her victory in court when she pulled into Jesse's driveway. Before coming here, she'd stopped at Ted's apartment to share the victory with her chief assistant. The jury had been out only three hours before convicting on all counts.

Unfortunately, Ted's medication had prevented him from enjoying the expensive single-malt Scotch she knew he liked, so they'd had to content themselves with some toasts with orange juice. Still, the victory had been just as sweet, and the evening news reports had been very flattering to her.

She got out of her car slowly, her thoughts turning to Jesse, who'd been released from the hospital the day before. Steve had called her yesterday evening. He had to go to Virginia on business—an appointment he couldn't get out of. He'd be back tomorrow, but he didn't want Jesse to be alone, and Jesse, somewhat grudgingly, had agreed to let Amanda spend the night.

Amanda was frankly surprised that she'd agreed at all. She would have thought that Jesse would prefer their father's company to hers, and he was still in town, and still disgruntled over her refusal to see him.

It was enough to make Amanda wonder, for the first time,

if Jesse had suffered too from being the favorite. She'd never given that any thought before.

Amanda had decided to tell Jesse about Michael and her. Steve already knew, but he hadn't told her, and he'd agreed that telling Jesse now might serve to take her mind off whatever was troubling her—for a time, at least. It was a way to get through what could otherwise be a difficult night, and besides, Amanda really did want to tell someone, even though she hadn't yet decided what to do.

Jesse must have heard her car because she opened the door as Amanda was coming up the walkway. Amanda was relieved to see that her sister looked well. If she hadn't yet regained her usual vivaciousness, neither did she look as haggard as she'd looked in the hospital.

Impulsively, Amanda hugged her. Jesse appeared startled, as well she might, since the two of them rarely displayed any affection. But she hugged Amanda back and thanked her for coming.

"Steve insists on babying me," Jesse said with a grimace. "I think he still believes that I was planning to kill myself."

She stepped back and stared intently at Amanda. "Did *you* think that?"

"No, I didn't," Amanda lied, then decided to be completely honest. "Okay, the thought *did* cross my mind at one point, but I didn't really believe it. You're just not the type."

Jesse nodded. "You're right, but I feel better knowing that you know that, too. Have you eaten yet? I made Mother's chicken casserole."

Amanda smiled. "No, I haven't. I haven't made that for ages."

"Neither had I," Jesse said as they walked through the dining room into the kitchen. "But I've been thinking about her a lot lately, so I decided to make it."

Amanda slanted her a glance, wondering why she'd been thinking about their mother now. But she decided not to ask. In any event, Jesse had launched into a monologue about some new items that had come into the store that she thought

Amanda might like. She'd apparently gone to the shop, which Amanda thought was a very good sign.

They ate dinner over small talk of the kind they'd always engaged in. Jesse seemed almost herself, and Amanda wondered what that meant. Had she talked it out with her therapist and made some sort of decision? But did she understand that if she had information that was relevant to the Eve Lauden case, she would have to talk to Michael?

Or would she? There wasn't much Michael—or anyone—could do if Jesse continued to insist that she knew nothing. And maybe she really didn't.

After dinner, they moved to the living room with their cups of latte, and Amanda decided that it was time to tell Jesse her own secret. She was already very curious to see what her reaction would be.

"I have something to tell you—something that I know is going to surprise you," she began.

Jesse frowned slightly, but said nothing.

"Michael and I are lovers. We're going to be married, although…"

Jesse smiled, then laughed aloud. "I *knew* it. I told Steve a while ago that something was going on between you two—the night of our party, as a matter of fact. You were hiding it pretty well, but Michael wasn't."

"Actually, we've *both* been hiding it, but I don't think we'll be able to much longer." She told Jesse about the private detective.

"Neal Hadden is a scumbag!" Jesse cried. "I never understood what you saw in him. I just couldn't imagine having him as a brother-in-law."

"You never said anything at the time."

"Of course not. I was confident that you'd come to your senses." She smiled. "I like Michael. The two of you make a great couple."

"We do? Why do you say that?"

"Because you do. I can't explain it. I remember seeing the two of you out on the terrace together at Mayor Teddy's party years ago, and thinking then that something was going to happen. Then, when it didn't, I kind of forgot about it until you were both here that night of the party.''

"Something *did* happen that night—after Mayor Teddy's party, I mean.''

Jesse's eyes widened in surprise. "And then you waited, what, nine or ten years?'' She shook her head. "You've always been so careful, but this is ridiculous!''

"We weren't seeing each other all that time. It didn't start until…recently.'' She'd been about to say *until Eve's body was found,* but now she hurried on to explain that their positions had brought them together again.

Amanda then told her about the problem: his job and hers. It took some explaining, because Jesse claimed that she couldn't see the conflict. But even when she did, she came down solidly on the side of telling the world.

"I think you should get married as soon as possible,'' Jesse stated, rather startling Amanda with her firmness. "Don't wait any longer.''

"Um, well, I was thinking about getting engaged, and then having the wedding after the election.''

But Jesse was insistent that they should do it now. Amanda felt slightly uneasy at her forcefulness. She protested that she hadn't even told their father.

"Don't tell him! Just do it! Then he'll have no choice but to accept it.''

"But, Jesse, that isn't being fair to him!''

"We both know he isn't going to approve, so what's the point in telling him beforehand? Besides, all he cares about now is being confirmed.''

"He really *is* a snob, isn't he?'' Amanda said quietly, thinking back to her father's comments about Michael—and about Eve Lauden.

"Yes, and I don't want to talk any more about him.''

AMANDA WAS DISORIENTED. It took her several panicky moments to remember that she was at Jesse's. She'd never stayed in her sister's guest room before. Then, when she remembered where she was and why she was there, she wondered what could have awakened her. Was it Jesse?

She listened carefully, but heard nothing. After seeming to be fine most of the evening, Jesse had slowly become quieter, withdrawing almost imperceptibly. As the silences between them had grown heavier and more fraught with tension, Amanda had expected that, at any moment, Jesse was going to reveal her secret. But in the end, nothing had been said, and Amanda had gone off to bed both frustrated and relieved.

The truth was that she didn't know what she would do if Jesse talked and if the information she had pointed to someone from the island being Eve Lauden's murderer. Being torn between old family loyalties and her belief in justice was, to her way of thinking, the worst possible dilemma—a dilemma that might well be tearing her sister apart right now. Jesse might not work in the legal system, but both of them had been raised in it by a father who had an unshakable faith in that system, despite its many flaws.

She continued to listen for any sounds that might indicate that Jesse was awake, but the house remained silent. Finally, knowing that she couldn't get back to sleep until she'd assured herself that Jesse was also asleep, she got out of bed, opened her door and peered down the dimly lit hallway toward Jesse's room.

Her door was open! Amanda hurried down there, only to find the bed empty and the covers askew. Fear clutched at her as she ran back along the hallway, then down the stairs. The living room was dark, but even before Amanda reached the bottom of the stairs, she could see a dim light spilling into the dining room from the kitchen.

Jesse turned away from the stove and saw her as Amanda came to an abrupt halt in the kitchen doorway. She was cradling a mug in both hands. Tears glistened in her eyes. She set the mug onto the table, and Amanda rushed to her.

The two sisters clung to each other silently for a long time, with Jesse's tears wetting Amanda's cheeks, as well as her own.

"Jesse, please don't let this destroy you!" Amanda cried, then stepped back to stare into her sister's face. "It isn't worth it."

Jesse swiped at her tears, then sank into a chair and wrapped trembling fingers around the mug. The kettle was still boiling, and Amanda prepared a mug of tea for herself, noting that her own fingers were trembling, as well.

As she sat down across from her sister, Jesse fixed her with an intent stare. "Promise me that you'll marry Michael!" she said in an oddly demanding tone.

Amanda was confused, but she managed to nod. "Of course I will. I told you that I love him."

"Don't let him change that!" Jesse said in the same intent tone.

"Let who change that?" Amanda asked in confusion.

"Father."

Amanda frowned, still not quite comprehending. Did Jesse believe that their father could somehow prohibit her from marrying Michael?

"He can't stop me," she said patiently. "Of course I'd be happier if he accepts Michael, but…"

"That's not what I meant," Jesse interrupted, then paused, her gaze fixed on Amanda unwaveringly. "What I meant was that you can't hate Michael because he has to arrest Father."

Amanda had lifted the mug to her lips, but now she set it back down again with exaggerated care. "Wh-what are you talking about?"

"He killed her," Jesse said softly, then repeated it much more loudly, nearly shouting. "He killed her!"

"Jesse, you can't mean that! I don't know what you think you know, but…"

"Don't tell me what I don't know!" Jesse cried. "I've had to live with this for years now. Sometimes, I'd almost forget about it, but then it would come back again.

"I wasn't really sure, you see. I thought that she'd gone

to the city, too. I thought he'd paid her off and sent her away. That was bad enough, but then, when they found her body..." Jesse lapsed into silence as the tears once again spilled over, running down her cheeks and trickling off her chin.

Amanda was lost in an icy fog, her mind unable to comprehend what Jesse was saying, let alone accept it. And yet, perhaps a part of her *was* hearing and accepting it, because there was a hollow space inside her that seemed to be growing with each beat of her heart.

Finally, when Jesse said nothing else, Amanda groped her way through the fog and fixed her gaze on her sister, who was watching her with eyes that mirrored her own horror.

"Are you saying that Father was...was having an affair with Eve Lauden?"

"If that's what you want to call it," Jesse replied, then made a motion as if to brush away any comment Amanda might make. "That's what I called it to myself, too. It was easier than admitting that your own father was...was seeing a prostitute who was even younger than you were."

Amanda stared at her sister, seeing the pain still in her eyes, but now seeing a rising anger, as well. She was about to try to ask a question when Jesse spoke again.

"Do you know how it made me feel, how I hated the way he always treated me? I was sure it was just because he was afraid that I knew about them."

Amanda found her voice. "But he *always* favored you, Jesse, long before that...happened."

"I knew that rationally, but it didn't matter."

"Did you see them together?" Amanda asked, knowing that a part of her was still seeking a way out of this.

"Yes. He tried to be discreet, you know. He was driving that old green station wagon we kept for Mrs. Moser to use. I saw her come out of the house and get into it with him. But he didn't see me. I was in a car with some friends."

"Was this when Eve disappeared?"

Jesse shook her head. "No, it was a month or so before

that. But I'd met Eve before that, and then I knew why she'd acted like she had toward me.

"Then, right before she disappeared, someone told me that she was pregnant and she was bragging that she'd be set up for life."

Amanda was beginning to feel sick, but she pressed on, knowing now that there was nothing to do but hear all of it. "So you don't know for sure what happened on the island?"

"I wasn't there, if that's what you mean. Like I said, when she disappeared, I thought she'd gone to the city, that he'd paid her off. For years, I kept expecting her to show up with…with our half sister or half brother.

"And then they found her on the island. I even tried to tell myself that maybe it was an accident, and he'd just buried her because he didn't know what else to do."

Amanda the prosecutor was seeking evidence even as the woman remained locked in a fog. "You don't have any proof that he really killed her or even that he was the one who buried her."

Jesse gave her a pitying look. But before she could speak again, Amanda said, "That doesn't make sense, Jess. If he buried her out there, he would have tried to stop the construction—or he would have gone back out there and…dug her up before it started."

Jesse frowned. "I thought about that, too. I can't explain it."

They were both silent for a time, considering that, both of them clearly hanging on to a slim thread of hope.

"We know about Elaine Barker," Amanda said after a few moments. "Mary sent her away, so we couldn't talk to her."

"You and Michael, you mean?"

Amanda nodded.

"I think Elaine will know if she was with him right before she disappeared. Eve and the others always met the men at her house."

After another silence, Jesse got up to reheat the kettle.

"Michael said that he thought there might be a connection between your accident and Eve's death."

Amanda stiffened. "That's only speculation on his part. We'll never know exactly when Eve was killed." She was thinking about the school-attendance records Michael's team had uncovered, but she said nothing.

"But what if it *was* that same night?" Jesse demanded, her voice edging close to hysteria. "What if the *real* reason you can't remember anything is that you *saw* it?"

"The doctors said that a loss of memory like I had isn't uncommon in a situation like mine. I mean because I was in the water for so long."

"But don't you see?" Jesse cried in that same near hysterical voice. "It would explain what we could never understand—why Trish would have been so reckless. If you both saw something and then maybe he chased you..."

"No!" Amanda found herself shouting, as well. "No! It couldn't have happened that way!"

"Father might not have recognized the boat," Jesse continued. "Rob had just gotten it a few days before that."

But Amanda was still shaking her head. "No! I can't believe that."

Instead of sitting down again, Jesse came over and put her arms around Amanda's shoulders. "It's all going to come out now. If Michael knows about Elaine, it will come out."

AMANDA DROVE slowly up the hill. When she reached the street at the top, she very nearly didn't turn. Then she was driving down the beautiful, familiar street, overhung with giant oaks and sycamores that were already showing the pale, tentative green of spring.

She was still lost in that cold fog, despite the warm spring morning, and so she didn't notice the black Porsche parked in front of the garage doors until she was nearly upon it.

Michael! So Jesse was right. She'd said that Michael would persuade Mary to tell him how to reach Elaine. And if he was here, then Jesse must also have been right that

Elaine would have known if Eve had gone with her father that night.

She cut off the engine and sat there, staring at his car, still clinging to the hope that Michael had no proof of anything and was only here to ask questions.

But why was she here? Had she come to get the truth or to warn her father and give him a chance to come up with something that would exonerate him?

The fog prevented her from thinking clearly as she got out of her car and started to the front door, her hand automatically grasping the key.

She heard the low murmur of male voices coming from her father's study at the back of the house. And as she walked unsteadily in that direction, the murmurs became more distinct.

"...no proof! Don't try to treat me like a common criminal who doesn't know the law!"

"I have all the proof I need," Michael said in a steely tone that made her shiver as she hesitated just outside the open door. "But a prosecutor will have to decide if it's enough to charge you."

"Naturally, you'd believe a woman like Elaine Barker over *me*. She's more your kind! But a prosecutor isn't going to see it that way."

"What I want to know," Michael said quietly, "is how someone like you could have a daughter like Amanda."

"You leave her out of this!"

"I'm afraid that's not possible, Judge. This is going to destroy her. She was upset enough when she thought it was Verhoeven. And when she finds out that it was *you* who killed her cousin and nearly killed *her*..."

"Get out of here, Quinn! I'm ordering you out of this house right now! Get back down there with the scum where you belong!"

"*Did* you try to kill Trish and me, Father?"

Michael, whose back was to the open door, turned at the

sound of her voice, but Amanda's eyes were locked on to her father's. Then his eyes slid to Michael.

"How dare you bring her into this?" he shouted, his face flushed with rage.

"Michael didn't bring me into it," Amanda said in a voice she heard as if from a very great distance. "I came on my own because last night, Jesse told me about you and Eve Lauden."

"Jesse's sick! You know that! You can't believe anything she says!"

"She was sick because of what she knew," Amanda replied, still in that distant voice. "Or what she feared—until Eve's body was found. Then she knew."

Michael started to move toward her, but she waved him off and walked unsteadily to her father's desk. There she stopped, now only the width of the desk away from him.

"You killed Eve because she told you she was pregnant, and then you chased Trish and me because we'd seen something. But maybe you didn't know it was us. The boat was brand-new."

Amanda could hear the plea in her voice at the end, the hope that he hadn't known who was in the boat. But all the while, she was staring at her father. And she saw the truth in his eyes. He *had* killed Eve, but he hadn't known it was Trish and Amanda in the boat.

She backed away from the desk, then turned and fled. Behind her, she heard her father shout, "I didn't know! I didn't know!"

There was more, but Amanda didn't hear it. Instead, she ran out the door. Then, realizing that she'd left her purse and her keys on the table in the foyer, she turned away from the driveway and ran around the side of the house, to the pretty little gazebo at the back of the property.

She didn't think about her father. Rather, she thought about her mother, and now she understood what had prompted those same thoughts in Jesse. Had she known anything? Had she lived—and then died—with the knowledge that her husband had betrayed their marriage? Didn't wives always know things like that?

She thought that she should get back to Jesse and prepare her for the fact that their father was about to be arrested. But she didn't move. There was time yet. Michael wouldn't take him in now. Instead, he'd have to go before a judge and request that another prosecutor be brought in to make the decision. And either Elaine would have to come back or she'd have to make a statement wherever she was and have it sent.

The D.A.'s mind took over, running through the process, guessing how long it would take. A few days at least. Michael couldn't make the case that her father might flee. Or could he?

The sound didn't register at first. From back at the edge of the woods, several hundred yards from the house, it was muffled. But then she knew what it was.

Horror propelled her out of the gazebo and across the lawn to the terrace door. It was locked! Stumbling and awkward in her terror, Amanda ran around to the front of the house. Only much later would she remember that it was *Michael's* name she was shouting—Michael for whom she feared.

She fumbled with the ornate brass handle of the front door, then finally succeeded in pulling it open. A figure hurtled toward her from the dimly lit hallway that led to the rear of the house.

"Michael," she murmured as he first grasped her hands, then pulled her into his arms.

Her relief was followed quickly by renewed horror as she felt the hardness of his gun in its shoulder holster pressing against her. "Father!" she gasped, backing away from him.

"He's dead," Michael said in a strange, hollow tone, his dark eyes pleading for understanding—an understanding she wasn't capable of as she stared at him through a dark mist.

"You killed him!" she shouted, stumbling backwards until she bumped into the foyer table.

She could barely see him now as a wave of dizziness washed over her. Her father dead? Michael? Why?

He reached for her, but she evaded him and started back down the hallway toward her father's study. Michael caught her before she could reach the open doorway. She fought him, cursed at him, made sounds that she didn't recognize as coming from her own lips.

But he held her in an iron vise, then dragged her back to the living room and pushed her unceremoniously into a chair. In the awful silence, she could hear the wail of sirens in the distance, slowly growing louder. Michael knelt before her, one hand on the carved wooden arm of the chair; close, but not touching.

"It's my fault he's dead, but I didn't kill him. I should have guessed that he might have a gun. I shouldn't have left him there."

The dark mist retreated a bit, though she still had difficulty focusing on him. "He always kept a gun in a locked drawer of his desk—here and at the island."

"He asked me if he could be alone for a few minutes— 'to collect his thoughts', he said. So I went to look for you. I knew you had to be here somewhere because I saw your keys on the table with your purse.

"I searched the house and was just about to go outside when I heard the shot." Michael stopped, the plea still in his eyes. "He left a confession. It's on his computer."

They both turned toward the door as the sirens grew louder still, then stopped abruptly. Doors slammed. Michael got to his feet.

"Are...are you sure he's dead?" she asked, knowing he must be, but not yet accepting it.

Michael nodded. "Stay here. I'll get you out as soon as possible."

A seemingly endless parade of uniforms poured into the house and vanished down the hallway, led by Michael. She heard his voice, and then it was lost in the general noise of other voices and squawking radios.

She struggled to her feet, swaying a bit at first, then walked through the dining room to the terrace door. Then she stopped. Jesse! She had to call Jesse. She stumbled toward the kitchen, fumbled the cordless phone from its base and punched out her sister's number. Steve's recorded voice came on. She spoke her sister's name and waited to see if she'd pick up, but she didn't. Then she tried the shop, but Jesse's assistant hadn't heard from her, though she was expecting her in. Amanda hung up without leaving a message.

She went back to the terrace doors, pushed them open and walked across the wide expanse of flagstone, across the soft green carpet of grass and came at last to the gazebo once again. Birds called in the trees, but otherwise, all was quiet. Her old home looked as it always had: stately, dignified, a place where nothing terrible could ever happen.

She sank into one of the Adirondack chairs and tried to gather the peacefulness to her. She had to be strong for Jesse. As soon as she could find that strength, she'd go look for her sister. Jesse would need her. Steve wouldn't be back until evening.

She couldn't see any of the vehicles from here, but now she heard the sound of engines and then more doors slamming. Could it be Jesse? Could Michael have reached her?

Amanda struggled to her feet and started back across the lawn. Several figures burst into view, cutting across the lawn in front of the house. As soon as they saw her, they began to shout her name. Video cameras were aimed at her, but only for a moment. In the next instant, two uniformed police officers appeared and herded them back to the front of the house, out of view.

She didn't know what to do. She wanted to find Jesse, but she knew her car would be blocked by all the other vehicles. Her brain seemed to be whirring at a very high speed, but no solution was presenting itself.

And then Michael was there, his hand touching her arm tentatively. "Come on. I'll get you out of here. We'll go through the woods to Mayor Teddy's. I sent a car to meet us over there.''

She let him lead her through the woods—the same stretch of woods they'd crossed all those years ago. The memories of that night, so clear for so long, now seemed lost—or nearly lost.

"I called Jesse's therapist," he said. "She's going to meet us at Jesse's house.''

"Jesse wasn't home. I tried to reach her.''

Michael's hand squeezed hers briefly. "We'll find her.''

"I WANT TO SEE his confession.'' Amanda wasn't as certain about that as she sounded, but she was struggling to fit herself into the mold of the prosecutor, a role that seemed safe right now.

"I do, too," Jesse said, sounding even less certain.

Steve reached for the attaché case at his feet. "Michael said you'd probably want to see it, so he made a copy. He also said to tell you that the Duchess County D.A. has been called in to handle it.''

He gave her the copy, and she and Jesse huddled together on the sofa to read it. Amanda had to read it twice before she could get the words to make sense.

He gave no explanation for his involvement with Eve Lauden. The statement was brief and obviously rushed. He'd known that Michael wouldn't be likely to give him much time.

He'd used the Verhoeven house for their assignations. That was the term he'd used for them. He'd chosen it because he knew that John was going out there often and that anyone who saw the lights would assume it was him. He simply made sure to go only when John was down in the city or otherwise out of town.

Eve told him she was pregnant and that he was the father. They argued about it, with him claiming that she couldn't possibly know who the father was. He'd had too much to drink. When she told him that it didn't matter who the father was, that she intended to claim it was his, he slapped her.

She staggered backwards and said she'd tell the world. He slapped her again, and this time, she fell hard against the big stone fireplace, striking her head on the mantel. The impact had killed her instantly.

He couldn't remember anything clearly after that, but at some point, he'd decided he would have to bury her on the island. She was heavy and it seemed that he'd carried her quite a distance in the darkness before he started to dig her grave. He knew that she'd been talking about running away to the city and figured everyone would think she'd done it.

A boat pulled into the dock just as he was returning to the Verhoeven house with the shovel. Its lights swept over him. He hid the shovel quickly and ran to John's boat. The other boat was already backing away, turning toward the mainland.

He followed it. He was in a state of shock and didn't know what he'd intended to do. Then the other boat slammed into the ski jump and exploded. He circled around it and saw two bodies in the water. He hadn't recognized the boat. So he went to the marina and made an anonymous call to the police, then went home only to learn within the hour that Trish was dead and Amanda was barely alive.

The statement ended there, with no expressions of regret for either Eve's death or Trish's death. Just the facts. Amanda wanted to think that he had suffered twenty years of guilt, but she'd never know. If she had to guess, she'd say that he probably didn't, that he'd managed to build a wall between the man who'd committed those acts and the man he believed himself to be.

"Where *is* Michael?" Jesse asked, breaking the silence and addressing her question to Steve. "Why isn't he here?"

Steve's gaze shifted to Amanda. "I think he's waiting for you to call. He's blaming himself for your father's death, and he's afraid you blame him, too."

"He shouldn't blame himself," Jesse stated firmly. "It was...better this way. Father could never have..." Her voice broke, and she began to sob. Steve moved to the sofa and drew her into his arms.

Amanda got to her feet. "Jesse's right. It *was* better this way. I'm going home."

"It would be better if you stayed here," Steve told her. "Michael arranged for a police officer to stay outside, to keep the media away."

Amanda nodded slowly. She hadn't considered that, although she knew she should have. The phone here had hardly stopped ringing, though the callers had gotten only the recording. She'd somehow forgotten just how big this story must be, because of her father's nomination.

The prosecutor surfaced again briefly, feeling a certain satisfaction. He'd gotten so close to his dream, close enough to know what he'd lost. Justice had been served. The prosecutor was satisfied, but the daughter mourned.

Amanda started up the stairs, wanting only to lose the warring sides of her in sleep. Jesse's voice called out to her, demanding that she call Michael. She would, but not now.

"MICHAEL?"

"Where are you—at Jesse's?"

"Yes."

"I'll be there in a half hour."

Amanda put down the phone and looked out the kitchen window into the big yard. The sky was just starting to lighten, and as she watched, the first birds were coming to the big feeder that hung from a tree in the far corner. It was one of those clear cylindrical feeders, and Amanda could see that it was empty. She could hear her mother's voice, telling her and Jesse that it was very important to feed them at this time of year because they were busy building nests and mating.

She found the big bag of sunflower seeds in the garage and filled the scoop, then carried it out across the yard to the feeder. Two chickadees twittered and flew off to a safe distance, then returned quickly when she had filled the feeder and backed away.

The sky was slowly turning gold and pink. The tulips and daffodils in a nearby bed were drooping, glistening with a heavy dew that had soaked her feet, as well. She stood in the middle of the yard, watching the daylight come, until she heard the distinctive sound of the Porsche's engine. Then she ran around to the front of the house, holding up the wet hem of the robe she'd borrowed from Jesse.

Michael was just getting out of the car when she saw him. His dark hair was still tousled from sleep—or perhaps a lack of it—and his face was shadowed by a day's growth.

She walked toward him, taking her time now. And when she got closer, she could see the wariness in his eyes, the vulnerability he was unlikely to show to anyone else.

She flung herself at him, molding herself to him, wanting to get closer than was possible. And as she did, she felt and heard his sigh of relief.

Epilogue

"I guess I'm glad I'll never have to put my theory to the test," Michael said, leaning close to her in order to be heard above the din.

"What theory?" Amanda asked.

"The way I figured it, if anyone could get away with murder, it would be an experienced homicide detective. But since you won, I won't have to find out."

"I'm sure Neal would be happy to hear *that*," she responded dryly. "It might cheer him up a bit."

Amanda smiled as she looked around the big living room, overflowing with happy people. Everyone but her had been so certain she would win. One poll had them dead even, but another had shown Neal to be slightly ahead. And now it appeared that she had not only won, but had in fact won by a fairly substantial margin.

Then the crowd grew quiet for a few seconds, as numbers flashed on the screens of the TVs they'd set up in various locations. Amanda drew in a sharp breath as she saw some of the numbers, then she understood just how she had won.

Wild cheering erupted in one corner, just as her roving gaze found them. Mary Walters, Elaine Barker and Tina Jacobs Workman. They were hugging each other and, at the same time, receiving the congratulations of others in the crowd. They'd done just what they said they would do: register the large number of unregistered voters in the Bottom, and then get them to vote for her. And those votes, it now appeared, had made all the difference.

Beside her, Michael chuckled. "Not exactly the constituency you expected, is it?"

She laughed and began to wade through the crowd. Her campaign manager was there before she was, finally ready to believe in the work done by Mary and Elaine and Tina. And equally important, he and the party would never again write off the Bottom.

She hugged each of them in turn: even Elaine, though she still hadn't come to terms with what Elaine had once done. "You three won this for me, you know," she told them sincerely.

Their proud smiles told her they *did* know, and that they also knew the political power they'd achieved in the process. Even Mayor Teddy, the party's senior leader, was bestowing his bear hugs on them.

She wasn't certain that she believed it yet. The past months still felt like both a nightmare and a dream. If it weren't for Michael and Uncle John, she doubted that she could have survived it. John had become her anchor when the past threatened to overwhelm her, and Michael had always been there to lead her to their future. And yet, her father's ghost continued to haunt her at times. Jesse had proved to be better at accepting both the bad and the good in him than she herself had been.

Michael had startled her at one point by quoting a line from *Macbeth*, stating with some pride that he'd actually played the Scottish king in a school play. "Nothing in his life became him like the leaving it." To Michael—and to Jesse—her father's suicide had been the best way out of a horrible situation.

And Mayor Teddy, acting on a plea for help from his old housekeeper, Mary Walters, had somehow managed to pull some strings to keep Elaine out of the inquest that had followed her father's death and his confession.

Neal Hadden had wasted very little time before trying to

suggest that her father's crime somehow made her unfit for office. And then, when that didn't seem to work, he tried to defeat her by insinuating that she couldn't be objective because of Michael. It was at that point that Amanda had finally agreed to marry Michael right away, in a small ceremony attended only by family and close friends.

She stayed along the fringes of the crowd now pressing against Mary and Elaine and Tina. These were party activists, and to them, the women who'd pulled off such a coup were of more interest at the moment than she herself was.

Only when it was all over had Amanda learned from Michael that Tina had known about her father and Eve. Her gratitude for Amanda's help with her brother was the reason she'd tried to keep her secret. And Mary had known, as well, because Elaine had told her long ago. She, too, had hoped to protect both Amanda and Jesse from the truth.

But the biggest shock to Amanda had been John. Only a short time ago, he'd confessed to her that he'd suspected her father had been using his house to carry on an affair. Michael had been right—as he usually was. John *had* withheld some information.

She started back across the room, seeing Michael and John deep in conversation. It pleased her to know how much John liked Michael, accepting him as her own father would never have done.

Then Jesse appeared before she could reach the two men, grabbing Amanda's arm and dragging her off to a quiet corner while Steve went to join the men.

"We've decided to do it," Jesse stated.

"Are you sure?"

Jesse nodded firmly. "We called a Realtor today, to put our house on the market. I feel like I'm doing it for Mother. You know how much she loved that house."

Amanda hugged her, breathing a quiet sigh of relief. The subject of the family home had been the one dark cloud on her personal horizon—besides, of course, the possibility that she might be out of a job.

She couldn't live there herself, because Michael was too happy in this house. And until now, Jesse had resisted the idea of moving into the house where their father had died, even though both she and Steve loved the place. It had seemed that after more than a hundred years, the wonderful old house might have to pass out of the family.

Jesse's decision was, Amanda thought, yet another indication of how far she'd come in these past months.

The two women made their way to the men. Michael slid an arm around her waist and kissed her. "Talk about perfect timing. John was just telling me that the first snowstorm is predicted for later this week."

They were leaving tomorrow for their delayed honeymoon. Michael had chartered a yacht for a leisurely cruise through the Caribbean.

Jesse told John and Michael about their decision to move into the family home, and Michael hugged Amanda. "Well, that does it, then. It's smooth sailing all the way for you, lady."

For a while, anyway, Amanda thought, but didn't say. The bumps in their future would become apparent soon enough, when they both returned to their jobs. But she knew now that they could handle it.

HARLEQUIN®

I N T R I G U E®

BROTHERS OF ROCK RIDGE

by award-winning author Aimée Thurlo

The dark, sexy and mysterious Redhawk brothers
become a family once again to track down their foster
parents' killer and their missing foster sister. But Ashe and
Travis have no idea what dark danger—and steamy
passion—awaits in their hometown of Rock Ridge....

REDHAWK'S HEART
#506, March '99

REDHAWK'S RETURN
#510, April '99

THE BROTHERS OF ROCK RIDGE—
As different as night from day...
but bound by a vow to protect
those they love.

*Available at your favorite
retail outlet.*

HARLEQUIN®
Makes any time special ™

Look us up on-line at: http://www.romance.net   HIBRR

Looking For More Romance?

Visit Romance.net

Look us up on-line at: http://www.romance.net

Check in daily for these and other exciting features:

Hot off the press

View all current titles, and purchase them on-line.

What do the stars have in store for you?

Horoscope

Hot deals

Exclusive offers available only at Romance.net

Plus, don't miss our interactive quizzes, contests and bonus gifts.

PWEB

Amnesia...
an unknown danger...
a burning desire.
With

HARLEQUIN®

―――――――――――――――――

I N T R I G U E®

you're just

A MEMORY AWAY

from passion, danger...
and love!

Look for all the books in this exciting new miniseries:

Missing: One temporary wife
#507 THE MAN SHE MARRIED
by Dani Sinclair in March 1999

Mission: Find a lost identity
#511 LOVER, STRANGER
by Amanda Stevens in April 1999

Seeking: An amnesiac's daughter
#515 A WOMAN OF MYSTERY
by Charlotte Douglas in May 1999

A MEMORY AWAY—where remembering the truth becomes a matter of life, death...and love!

Available wherever Harlequin books are sold.

HARLEQUIN®
Makes any time special ™

Look us up on-line at: http://www.romance.net   HIAMA

HARLEQUIN®

I N T R I G U E®

COMING NEXT MONTH

#505 LONE STAR LAWMAN by Joanna Wayne
The Cowboy Code

Texas lawman Matt McQuaid had his hands full with Heather Lombardi. Her search for her past incited trouble in his sleepy town, while the woman herself excited the man behind the badge. He'd do anything to wipe away her fears and keep her safe from a killer. But would he have to blur the lines between honor and duty to protect the woman he loved?

#506 REDHAWK'S HEART by Aimée Thurlo
The Brothers of Rock Ridge

Forced to work together to catch a killer, lawman Ashe Redhawk and beautiful FBI agent Casey Feist struck sparks off each other. But when the sparks became a consuming fire of passion, Ashe was compelled to choose between his heritage, and the woman who stirred his soul.

#507 THE MAN SHE MARRIED by Dani Sinclair
A Memory Away...

She'd fallen down a mountain and barely survived. Eighteen months later, Adam Ryser came to claim amnesiac Josy Hayes, saying he was her husband and that he'd searched for her ever since she'd mysteriously vanished. She'd be safe on his ranch, caring for his three daughters—if only she could remember why she'd disappeared....

#508 A STRANGER'S WIFE by Paige Phillips

Jake Chastain was a woman's wildest dream—rich, handsome, sinfully sexy. But someone was trying to kill him—while Meg Lindley pretended to be his wife. Once Meg revealed her deception, could she ever win his trust—and his heart?

Look us up on-line at: http://www.romance.net

HARLEQUIN CELEBRATES

FIVE DECADES OF ROMANCE

In March 1999, Harlequin
Historicals introduce you to the sexy,
heroic men of medieval England and
the Wild West as we celebrate
Harlequin's 50th anniversary.

JOE'S WIFE
by Cheryl St.John

**MY LORD
PROTECTOR**
by Deborah Hale

**THE BRIDE OF
WINDERMERE**
by Margo Maguire

SILVER HEARTS
by Jackie Manning

*Look for these fabulous Historical
romances at your favorite retail store!*

Look us up on-line at: http://www.romance.net

H50HH/L